Anthony Gilbert an

Anthony Gilbert (1899–1973)

Anthony Gilbert was the pen name of Lucy Beatrice Malleson. Born in London, she spent all her life there, and her affection for the city is clear from the strong sense of character and place in evidence in her work. She published 69 crime novels, 51 of which featured her best known character, Arthur Crook, a vulgar London lawyer totally (and deliberately) unlike the aristocratic detectives, such as Lord Peter Wimsey, who dominated the mystery field at the time. She also wrote more than 25 radio plays, which were broadcast in Great Britain and overseas. Her thriller *The Woman in Red* (1941) was broadcast in the United States by CBS and made into a film in 1945 under the title *My Name is Julia Ross*. She was an early member of the British Detection Club, which, along with Dorothy L. Sayers, she prevented from disintegrating during World War II. Malleson published her autobiography, *Three-a-Penny*, in 1940, and wrote numerous short stories, which were published in several anthologies and in such periodicals as *Ellery Queen's Mystery Magazine* and *The Saint*. The short story 'You Can't Hang Twice' received a Queens award in 1946. She never married, and evidence of her feminism is elegantly expressed in much of her work.

By Anthony Gilbert

Scott Egerton series
Tragedy at Freyne (1927)
The Murder of Mrs
  Davenport (1928)
Death at Four Corners (1929)
The Mystery of the Open
  Window (1929)
The Night of the Fog (1930)
The Body on the Beam (1932)
The Long Shadow (1932)
The Musical Comedy
  Crime (1933)
An Old Lady Dies (1934)
The Man Who Was Too
  Clever (1935)

**Mr Crook Murder
  Mystery series**
Murder by Experts (1936)
The Man Who Wasn't
  There (1937)
Murder Has No Tongue (1937)
Treason in My Breast (1938)
The Bell of Death (1939)
Dear Dead Woman (1940)
  aka *Death Takes a Redhead*
The Vanishing Corpse (1941)
  aka *She Vanished in the Dawn*
The Woman in Red (1941)
  aka *The Mystery of the
  Woman in Red*

Death in the Blackout (1942)
  aka *The Case of the Tea-
  Cosy's Aunt*
Something Nasty in the
  Woodshed (1942)
  aka *Mystery in the Woodshed*
The Mouse Who Wouldn't
  Play Ball (1943)
  aka *30 Days to Live*
He Came by Night (1944)
  aka *Death at the Door*
The Scarlet Button (1944)
  aka *Murder Is Cheap*
A Spy for Mr Crook (1944)
The Black Stage (1945)
  aka *Murder Cheats the Bride*
Don't Open the Door (1945)
  aka *Death Lifts the Latch*
Lift Up the Lid (1945)
  aka *The Innocent Bottle*
The Spinster's Secret (1946)
  aka *By Hook or by Crook*
Death in the Wrong Room
  (1947)
Die in the Dark (1947)
  aka *The Missing Widow*
Death Knocks Three Times
  (1949)
Murder Comes Home (1950)
A Nice Cup of Tea (1950)
  aka *The Wrong Body*

Lady-Killer (1951)

Miss Pinnegar Disappears (1952)
 aka *A Case for Mr Crook*

Footsteps Behind Me (1953)
 aka *Black Death*

Snake in the Grass (1954)
 aka *Death Won't Wait*

Is She Dead Too? (1955)
 aka *A Question of Murder*

And Death Came Too (1956)

Riddle of a Lady (1956)

Give Death a Name (1957)

Death Against the Clock (1958)

Death Takes a Wife (1959)
 aka *Death Casts a Long Shadow*

Third Crime Lucky (1959)
 aka *Prelude to Murder*

Out for the Kill (1960)

She Shall Die (1961)
 aka *After the Verdict*

Uncertain Death (1961)

No Dust in the Attic (1962)

Ring for a Noose (1963)

The Fingerprint (1964)

The Voice (1964)
 aka *Knock, Knock! Who's There?*

Passenger to Nowhere (1965)

The Looking Glass Murder (1966)

The Visitor (1967)

Night Encounter (1968)
 aka *Murder Anonymous*

Missing from Her Home (1969)

Death Wears a Mask (1970)
 aka *Mr Crook Lifts the Mask*

Murder is a Waiting Game (1972)

Tenant for the Tomb (1971)

A Nice Little Killing (1974)

Standalone Novels

The Case Against Andrew Fane (1931)

Death in Fancy Dress (1933)

The Man in the Button Boots (1934)

Courtier to Death (1936)
 aka *The Dover Train Mystery*

The Clock in the Hatbox (1939)

Footsteps Behind Me

Anthony Gilbert

This edition published by
The Orion Publishing Group Ltd
Orion House
5 Upper St Martin's Lane
London WC2H 9EA

An Hachette UK company
A CIP catalogue record for this book is available from the British Library

ISBN 978 1 4719 1000 5

www.orionbooks.co.uk

To Georgina, with my love.

CONTENTS

CONTENTS

CHAPTER ONE

INVITATIONS TO A PARTY

TEDDY LANE was pulling a flower to pieces, a rose that, characteristically, he had neither bought nor grown, but had picked up on the pavement where someone had dropped it.

" She loves me, she loves me not," he murmured. " Shall I ? Shan't I ? " Shall I send those letters, he meant. Or, say I do send them, shall I send them all to-night ? Or shall I spread them out, one at a time ? Aren't four people four times as dangerous as one, considering who the four are ? And not forgetting, of course, the link that bound them together, probably the only thing they had in common, the fact of being in Teddy Lane's power. But—and here he flung down the dismembered and ruined rose—if that's the case, wouldn't one by himself be more dangerous still ?

There's safety in numbers, declares the old saw. Teddy Lane made a sound that really was a hollow groan, and not because he was feeling theatrical but because he was horribly afraid, and with more cause than even he knew. Safety was something he never expected to meet again, probably wouldn't even recognise it if he did, it was such a stranger to his experience. He hadn't been safe when, as Captain Edward Lane, aged nineteen, he had been recommended for a Military Cross—though, characteristically, thought the embittered man that young hero had become, he had never got it, but there had been nobility in that kind of danger. There was no nobility at all about the peril that encompasses the path of the practised blackmailer. Because, shorn of frills, that was his profession. Battening on other men's misfortune a judge had recently described it ; collecting dues from society, retorted Teddy Lane.

The last rose-petal fell. Teddy picked up the four letters, saw he'd run things precious fine, and bolted for the post before he had time for more consideration. The fellow was just locking the box as Teddy came panting up, but he took the letters none too graciously and dropped them into his bag. Teddy walked slowly back to the shoddy little flat where, provided you didn't actually leave a body on the

1

doorstep or get embroiled with the police, no one asked uncomfortable questions. He took the lift to the sixth floor,
went into what he called the hall of his flat, a minute black
hole with a telephone and a couple of coat-hooks, and thence
to the living-room, furnished by the management with due
consideration for their pockets.

All the flats in this block—gentlemen's chambers they
were called in the prospectus and gentleman covered practically anything—were alike. Living-room looking across the
street leading to bedroom looking into a well, minute bathroom, no kitchen. Tenants went out to their meals or ate from
paper bags. Some, like Teddy, relied mainly on bottles.
Take them by and large, cheerless surroundings for existences
more at home in the dark than the light.

Teddy was so used to it he scarcely noticed the meanness,
the sordidness of it all, any more than he noticed the porter's
bad service and innuendoes. Chaps have to live somewhere,
he'd tell you, and when you're fifty-six and haven't a job or
any prospect of one, no influential relations, no money, no
pull of any kind, you can't expect Buckingham Palace. He
shut the door, switched on the light and routed out the
whisky-bottle. Presently he went into the other room and
took something more potent to pull him together. He administered this second pick-me-up with a syringe. But it didn't
cheer him much, because it reminded him of another source
of trouble. People who tell you money isn't important are
people who've never felt the pinch. Money, or rather the lack
of it, shaped all Teddy's wretched existence. It was because
he needed money that he had ever entered into his vicious
partnership with Morell. Morell was a chemist who, as the
police well knew, didn't make his living out of selling tubes
of tooth-paste and bottles of aspirin. He had a shady little
shop in a shady neighbourhood, and Teddy acted as his contact
man. Because, though there was a yawning gulf between
young Captain Lane who had even thought it might be a
privilege to die for your country, and the creature he had
become, he still retained a veneer that Morell would never
have, something called tradition that he'd inherited from a
long line of simple country gentlemen, and that could still
buy him the entry into company that wouldn't even acknowledge Morell's existence. And, no doubt about it, the demand
for drugs was on the increase. The police were worried, the
Church was worried, the Government was worried. Doctors

were warned and a sharp look-out was kept, but the leakage went on. Young people got hold of the stuff and started ruining their lives ; older habitués infected newcomers with the craving, and for all their efforts the police couldn't stop up all the holes. The big men weren't so difficult to trace, though it was often pretty difficult to pull them in ; but the men on the fringe, the Morells and the Teddy Lanes, slipped in and out of the net, doing a little job for a little profit.

Still, it was all grist to the mill—Teddy never gave a thought to the possible consequences of his activities—and if ever a mill needed grist Teddy's did. He passed the stuff and handed the price to Morell, who gave him his share on a commission basis. Recently he'd been more than usually hard-pressed and had been compelled to use some of these payments for his own needs. He had been stalling Morell for some weeks, but a show-down was imminent. Somehow he had got to raise the money in the course of a few days ; hence his desperate action in posting the letters to his four would-be victims.

Julia Silk's letter was brought to her by her husband, Sir Charles Silk, Member of Parliament for a country Division, who sat on the foot of her bed, drinking her coffee and opening his own post, while she glanced through the bundle of envelopes he had brought her. Teddy's was at the bottom of the pile, a neatly typewritten envelope with a London postmark. She didn't think it looked very interesting, probably an advertisement or an appeal.

Charles threw his last envelope on the floor and stood up. He was a handsome, tough ex-Commando, passionately in love with his wife, and devoted to their eight-year-old son, Johnny.

" Snow coming," he remarked from his stance by the window. " And by the same token who's coming to dinner to-night ? "

He didn't say, Is anyone coming ? because the house was always full of people. He complained sometimes it was like living in a hotel, but he couldn't blame the visitors. The old axiom about bees and honeypots was applicable one hundred per cent where Julia was concerned. It was the same when he took her out. Heads turned, voices whispered. The charming thing about Julia was that she took her beauty for granted, expecting no special favours because of it. Charles never stopped wondering why she had chosen him, she who could, as they say, have had practically anyone.

" Because I love you, darling," returned Julia, sensibly.

It had been true more than a dozen years ago, when she was Julia Gray, the brilliant young actress for whom a magnificent future was prophesied, and it was equally true more than a dozen years later, when she had set aside all hopes of personal ambition and was content to be Charles's wife and Johnny Silk's mother. For no one else, probably, would she have abandoned her career, but Charles said that being married to an actress was like being married to a night-watchman, and because he was her whole world she outraged the critics and retired into private life on her marriage. Not that there had been much time for personal happiness. War had broken out twelve months later, Charles had been whirled overseas on secret duties, and Julia found herself driving an ambulance at a First Aid Post.

It was there that she met Teddy Lane. He had drifted into Civil Defence uniform via a number of rum activities, disillusioned about war and its rewards, disillusioned about peace, too, but still retaining some of that surface charm that had made him so successful in the mad twenties as a squire of dames, a paid dancing-partner and escort, a gigolo Charles would have said with immense scorn. But chaps have to live and you can't afford to quarrel with your bread and butter, if it does take the shape of the elderly wives and widows of well-to-do men who want to recapture the illusion of youth. Anyhow, that was what life had handed Teddy Lane on a plate and he wolfed it down.

On this Monday morning, receiving no reply to his question, Who's coming to-night ? Charles Silk turned to repeat it, but was stayed by the reflection of his wife's face in the oval Sheraton mirror on the dressing-table.

" Trick mirror you've got there," he exclaimed. " You look—or rather it makes you look—like one of your famous old-time heroines, stricken with a mortal wound."

He said the words with a half-laugh, but his face was troubled. He was perfectly well aware it wasn't only the mirror. And still Julia did not reply. She was staring at the sheet of paper in her hand as though she could not believe what she beheld. When her husband came up to take it from her she lifted eyes incredulous and anguished to his questioning face. She was beyond speech. It's like that sometimes ; when the thing too dreadful to contemplate suddenly becomes reality, then you're stricken and dumb. Charles drew a shocked breath. For the first time he realised how his beloved would look in the hour of her death. All youth, all happiness, even the beauty he had thought imperishable, were extinguished.

At first sight there seemed nothing in the letter to account for Julia's alarming change of expression. It read :

DEAR JULIA,

Are you surprised to hear from me after all this time ? The fact is I've managed to find a flat at last, and am planning a small reunion party on Friday next about six o'clock. I'm counting on you to be there (I mean that literally) so break your other engagements—believe me, it will be worth while. It's a long time since we met, and there's so much to talk about.

It was signed Teddy and there was a postscript.

How is that splendid son of yours ? I often think of him.

" He's a pretty cool card," observed Charles, tossing the letter on to the blue silk eiderdown. " Expecting you to crash all your engagements to please him. Who is he, anyway ? "

Julia came slowly back to life. " Teddy Lane ? Oh, someone I met in the war."

Charles frowned. " I don't seem to recall the name. Do I know him ? "

" I shouldn't think so. I've only met him once since the war and that was by chance. I'd taken Johnny to the Zoo and he suddenly appeared . . ."

" Like a bad fairy," suggested Charles grimly, and she started. Because that was just how it had seemed, one minute as happy as any woman alive with her eager handsome son, and the next knowing all that happiness menaced by a shadow she could not dispel.

" I expect he's lonely," she said, speaking at random.

" So lonely he expects you to come at the lift of a finger ? Tell him to take a running jump at himself."

" I don't think I can do that. I do owe him something,

Charles. I really think I should have gone out of my mind
if it hadn't been for Teddy when you were reported missing.
I couldn't forget you were on special duties, and nobody let
us forget what the Nazis did to their prisoners, particularly
if they were obstinate and wouldn't talk. Even now I can't
bear to think of it."

" Then don't think of it and don't pick up with this chap,"
urged Charles, sensibly. " It's ten years ago."

" It seems like yesterday." Julia's voice was muted. " Do
you know what happened ? I—I developed a yellow streak,
lost my nerve completely, couldn't stand any more of the
bombing and the burning and the bodies. Teddy did my duty
for three nights as well as his own. You don't forget that very
easily."

" I suppose not." Charles spoke grudgingly. " All the
same . . ." All the same, why suddenly pop up again after
all this time he meant. He glanced at the address on the
plain notepaper. " I know chaps can't afford to be fussy
about where they live these days," he acknowledged, " but
Ellison Mansions isn't the sort of neighbourhood one cares
for one's wife to visit." When Charles became stilted Julia
knew he wasn't liking the situation. Come to that, she
wasn't liking it herself. It wasn't only bombs and fires you
didn't forget ; there were other things that in a way were
worse, and she knew Teddy Lane hadn't forgotten them
either.

" Isn't it ? " she murmured vaguely. " I suppose it's all
he could find."

" Hasn't the chap got a wife ? "

" He hadn't when I knew him. Oh, I shouldn't think so.
In a sense, Charles, you could say he was a casualty from
World War One. He went straight out from school and
afterwards he couldn't settle down. He was abroad for several
years, doing various jobs. (Yes, she reflected grimly, as
gigolo, escort, paid companion to rich, dissatisfied women
whose husbands had to buy the thrills they themselves could
no longer provide for their wives. And when the good times
came to an end at the close of the disastrous twenties he'd
fiddled and played the Black Market and picked up any sort
of living any way he could, until World War Two brought him
back into uniform and, most unhappily, into Julia Silk's
life.)

" Look here," said Charles, " I never heard anything so

6

ridiculous. Let him give his piffling party without you. I'm
indebted to him for past favours, if any, but bills can't be
collected after seven years, and I don't see the sense of
resurrecting memories that are much better buried. It's not
as if you were ever particularly friendly, because if you had
been you'd have kept up with him all this time. So . . ."

But Julia was shaking her head. " I think I will go,
Charles. It's your week-end for visiting your constituency,
so I shan't be neglecting you, and if I refuse I shall feel I ought
to ask him here, and you wouldn't have much in common . . ."

She broke off there, repressing an appalling thought. Not
much in common. If Charles knew . . . if Charles knew !
But he must never know.

" I suppose you do realise what he's after ? " said Charles
rather brutally. " Chaps who pop up after ten years only want
one thing, and that's to make a touch." Julia was a sweetie,
but she had no sense where money was concerned. Anyone
could empty her purse. It troubled him that she did not
immediately deny his suggestion, Julia, the generous, the
impulsive. Because, she told herself, that's just what he does
mean. The letter spoke of a reunion, a small party, but she
wasn't deceived. Oh, it would be small enough, just the two
of them, and it wasn't affection or kindly memory on his
part that prompted the invitation. Invitation ? It was
virtually a command and he knew she would not dare disobey.

After Charles had gone, with a shrug for the folly of women
and no notion that a black mamba couldn't work more havoc
in his household than Teddy Lane, Julia lay back and thought
about the past. Her choice now was simple, either to dance
to Teddy's piping or to tell Charles the truth, and even now
she dared not risk that. How would he understand the
shattering effect the news of his presumed death had had
upon her ? It had come after months of endless bombing,
dirt, danger, terror and death. And Teddy had been kind.
You had to give him that. To no one else had she confessed
the actual physical fear that rent her, and Teddy had said
comfortingly, " That's all right, Julia. It's the same with
me. Honestly it is. But it doesn't really matter, so long as
no one else knows."

And he had done double duty for the best part of a week,
while she officially had influenza. Then, when she had a
week's sick leave, he had offered her the use of a cottage someone had loaned him—and how typical of Teddy to have

had kept the letter. Teddy wasn't the kind that would give a crumb to a sparrow ; he'd keep it to brown Friday's fish.

So—" I shall have to go," said Julia, pushing back the blue silk eiderdown. " But Teddy Lane shall die before Charles knows the truth."

Harmsworth Ames was known to the whole country as the man who broke the Leaminster Case, thereby laying the foundations of a considerable fortune. He had come to success the hard way, starting on the lowest rung, and on the morning that he opened Teddy Lane's letter he was a man of about fifty, big, dark-skinned (born on the Nile, said his enemies), ruthless as Teddy himself, equally unscrupulous and a great deal more efficient.

" Get Harmsworth Ames," solicitors told their clients when the situation seemed hopeless. " If anyone can save you, he's the man."

The Leaminster Case had attracted attention because of eleventh-hour evidence that had made the court gasp. Joseph Leaminster had been accused of murdering his wife, and he hadn't a hope in hell, said the critics. But Ames had set his magnificent teeth (he was a young silk then and the figure on his brief would scarcely buy him a pair of the hand-made shoes he wore nowadays) and sworn to best Skewbald, the terror of the bench. And so he had, by producing a witness called Sykes, whose evidence turned the tables. And if traducers had whispered that it was a put-up job and Sykes had been well paid and well briefed, and the mad hundred-to-one chance had come off, well, there was no proof and Joseph Leaminster was acquitted (and passed into oblivion) while Harmsworth Ames's reputation was made.

He had walked warily for a time, but the nine-days-wonder passed and he had hardly thought of Leaminster in twenty years. And now here from the blue was evidence that someone not only suspected the truth but was in a fair way to be able to prove it, and meant to do that very thing unless he got his price.

" He's waited a hell of a time," reflected Ames. That might mean that Teddy Lane (and what an echo of a dead and dusty period *that* name awoke !) had only just discovered Sykes in some dump or lodging-house, or he might have held his hand for a considerable time, knowing that every year the information would increase in value. A scandal now, reflected Ames grimly, would break him at the height of his success.

He pulled out this diary and made a note. *Lane, Friday.* **6.15** *p.m.*

" Zero hour," he said aloud, as he put the little book away. But zero hour for whom ? For himself ? Or the challenging Teddy Lane ? Only time would show, but Ames already had precious little doubt. The most gallant Quixote can tilt at a windmill, but when it comes to a crash it isn't the windmill that falters into dust.

The third victim did not open her letter till Tuesday, when she returned from a long week-end with her doctor son. Alice Tempest was the oldest of all Teddy's victims, a woman past sixty, whose whole life centred on her son. For Henry she had worked, schemed, lain awake, gone short of food and worn old clothes, forgotten what the word holiday means, in order to make up to him for what could never be his, a father of whom he might be proud as his young sons were now proud of him.

A father ! Just to remember George Tempest made his wife shrink. She had not set eyes on him for years, and when she thought of him it was to remember the heavy cunning lowering face in the dock—George Tempest standing trial for his life on a charge so horrible even the press shrank from too much detail. The victim had been a girl of seventeen, and the condition of the body had really saved George from the rope. Only a madman could be responsible, urged Counsel. Mrs. Tempest, twenty years her husband's junior, with a child of three, had mortgaged everything to get that verdict. Some-times in the decades that followed she wondered if she'd done right, because George Tempest was still alive almost forty years later, alive and hopelessly insane now, whatever he had been at the time he was sentenced. And all that long while she had prevented Henry knowing of his existence. Drowned in a boating accident when you were three, she told him steadfastly ; and if he noticed there were no photographs of his father in the flat, and no intimate stories to tell a little boy about the man he couldn't remember—well, Henry was no fool either. But he was a thousand miles from guessing the truth ; the story had died away before he was in long trousers, and hardly anyone now remembered it. Only sometimes, when she couldn't sleep or, sleeping, had bad dreams, Alice

Tempest still saw that menacing face and recalled with a shock, that was still vital and horrible, the few years of her married life.

And now, when she had thought the affair virtually forgotten, someone had appeared who knew the truth, someone who, though he was too wise to put it into so many words, intended to cash in on his knowledge. Pay up or your precious son shall learn the truth, that was what the letter meant. She read it again. The signature meant nothing to her ; quite probably, she thought, it wasn't even the writer's real name. She couldn't guess if it had been chance or a deliberate search for a victim that had taken him down to George's part of the world. Most likely he had learned George Tempest's story and wondered, in his crafty, crooked mind, if there were any relatives who could be soaked, and so he had bided his time and sifted the facts, and at last had come to her.

It might, of course, have been worse. He might have gone to Henry direct, and it does a doctor no good to have it known that his father is a criminal lunatic, even if they did use some softer expression in these enlightened times. That wouldn't prevent his patients eyeing one another, remembering something called heredity, and, after all, they'd tell themselves, there are plenty of doctors, and in matters like these it's best to play safe. There was Angela, too, Henry's wife, and Henry's two boys. Alice had no intention of offering them a monstrous lunatic grandfather. She had not been defeated in over thirty years, and at any cost, at any cost, she repeated, she did not propose to break that record now. Her own life didn't matter a straw ; nor, for that matter, did Teddy Lane's, and she was perfectly prepared to destroy them both, if necessary, so long as no hair of Henry's head was damaged.

The fourth victim was a young man called Gerald Ross. The public might not know much about him, but the security authorities had him noted on their files as one of the most promising of the younger experimental chemists in Government employ. Papers and plans of extreme secrecy passed through his hands, and obviously a man in his position could not afford the smallest slur on his good name.

" A very sound fellow," his employers said, and " Integrity beyond question, thank goodness." And they reminded each other he had been a dark horse out of McEwen's stable.

This was Sir Reginald McEwen, that trainer of young

promise to whom the country owed more than it guessed. In his private capacity he lent a hand to those who had come to grief, and it was in this way that he had met the young Ross. When Gerald was sixteen he had become implicated with a gang of young mobsters with no respect for law or order, and had been caught by the police when acting as a look-out man while the more active members of the gang broke into a warehouse. Ironically, he was the only captive, but it came out in court that the other three were well known to the police, and a well-meaning magistrate sent him to Borstal for three years " to keep him out of mischief." He had no parents, no human ties, had been clapped at the age of fourteen into a dead-end job, which he lost when he was taken by the police. The magistrate addressed a little homily to the boy and Gerald disappeared for three years. When he was released he had his first stroke of good fortune. McEwen took an interest in him, discerned great possibilities and started him on what had turned out to be an honourable and distinguished career. The past, said McEwen, should be ignored, so far as possible forgotten. Not even Sally, whom he had married, knew of the Borstal episode. That marriage had been highly successful, his elder boy was about to sit for an Eton scholarship, his employers thought highly of him, everything, in short, seemed set for a hopeful future, and now someone, whose name he had never previously heard, had loomed up on the horizon with the age-old threat, Your money or your life.

It couldn't be money, he hadn't got it. The Government didn't overpay its scientists, and he had no private means. Sally had a little, but he didn't intend to touch that. So, it must be his life, and that meant Sally and the boys, his work and all his hope. There was no one to whom he could turn for advice, because they were all dead, McEwen who had helped him, the chaplain, the governor of the prison, even the magistrate who had sentenced him, every man Jack of them gone, and with them all the links that bound him to Borstal. Ah, but he hadn't allowed for Teddy Lane. He re-read the letter, as Alice and Julia and Harmsworth Ames had done, but nothing could alter the unmistakable meaning. Somehow (and precisely how didn't matter) this fellow, Lane, had unearthed the truth and meant to profit by it. Gerald stared out of the window. It would not have surprised him to find the sky obscured by a thick yellow cloud, but the day was as bright as a daisy's eye.

Life's unreasonable, he thought desperately, no sense, no logic. Good chaps get killed in air crashes, die of pneumonia, get drowned, run over, murdered by terrorists in obscure corners of the world. But Teddy Lane won't die. Not he. You can count on that. And then, like a cloud no bigger than a man's hand, came the thought :

Why shouldn't he die ?

CHAPTER TWO

RENDEZVOUS FOR DEATH

MRS. TEMPEST, believing there's no sense in postponing the unpleasant, arrived at Ellison Mansions rather before her time on Friday evening, and found them very much what she had anticipated. The building, which was old and smoke-begrimed, was tucked away in a cul-de-sac, and the general impression she gained was that the people who lodged there lived their drab existence in another kind of cul-de-sac. There was no porter on duty, since it was after half-past five, and the management employed no night porter. Probably, thought Mrs. Tempest, with a twisted lip, that was deliberate. They would be discreetly blind and dumb to the conduct of their tenants, probably wouldn't even object to murder so long as it was tactfully engineered and the good name of the place wasn't involved.

Afterwards it occurred to her that this was the first time the actual word had gone through her mind.

The door of No. 12 was opened in reply to her ring by a man who might have been created to fit his surroundings. Julia was to see a considerable deterioration in the Teddy Lane she had known ten years before ; he wore a suit that had never been made for him, and his smile and his air of false *bonhomie* were as meretricious as his surroundings. He led her into a darkish room, furnished without taste and indifferently clean.

" A glass of sherry," he suggested. He had a bottle and some glasses on a tray.

Mrs. Tempest refused. " No, thank you."

Teddy shrugged. " It's not poisoned." But even the semblance of a smile vanished from his eyes.

" I hardly imagined it was, Mr. Lane. I should be of very little assistance to you dead. On the contrary, I should prove a considerable embarrassment. And now perhaps you will be kind enough to explain your reason for inviting me here."

" Do take some sherry," urged Teddy, smoothly. " Honestly, it's quite drinkable. The others will be here in a few minutes."

" The others ? " He had caught her off guard there, and secretly he smiled.

" I did say a party, didn't I ? " he murmured. " Anyway, it's a very select gathering."

" Am I right in supposing we shall all be strangers to each other ? " she suggested.

" Shall we say people who all have something in common ? "

" Meaning that in some way or another they are all in your power ? But surely you're not proposing to share your knowledge with anyone else ? That would instantly destroy its value."

" There's safety in numbers," said poor deluded Teddy Lane, and at once she thought : " He's afraid," and that gave her a sense of reassurance. Her quick mind instantly began to work. The years of struggle had given her the capacity to plan swiftly, to make the best of hard circumstances, and now her intelligence began darting this way and that, like the forked tongue of a snake. Anyone who came to this party must be Teddy's enemy. What was there to be gained from that ?

Teddy was answering her question. " I shan't give you away," he promised, quite gaily. " Not, that is, if you're prepared to co-operate."

Then the front door bell rang again and he went into the minute hall to see who had arrived. Mrs. Tempest heard him say, " Oh hallo, have you introduced yourselves ? Come in, Julia. Lovely to see you again. There's only one more person to come and then the party can begin."

Thanking her lucky stars that this was one of the Fridays when Charles travelled down to his constituency to meet his supporters face to face and do his best to solve their individual problems, Julia had put on a very plain black suit and a tiny black hat with a diamond spray ; she wore very high-heeled shoes that accentuated her slender height, and she looked, thought Gerald Ross, like a million dollars as she strolled into the dingy hall and paused, her heart beating like a gong, wondering if she could reach No. 12 without being seen. Gerald himself had just arrived and entered the lift when he saw her. His first impulse was to shut the gate and shoot up without being recognised. Then he wondered, " What on earth is Julia Silk doing here ? Surely not Mr. Lane, too ? " He called softly, " Julia ! " and she turned in a flash.

" Why, Gerald, fancy seeing you here ! It's a bit off your beaten track, isn't it ? Or are you planning to blow the whole place skyhigh ? "

" I might do worse," countered Gerald, grimly. " And if Charles knew where you were to-night there'd be murder. You must be crazy—or don't you know the reputation of the place ? "

" Do you suppose I'm here for fun ? " demanded Julia, and he said in a gentler voice : " Oh Julia, not you, too ? Not No. 12 ? "

She nodded. " How did you know ? You don't mean that you . . . ? "

" Why else ? " He clashed the gate to, and they began to rise. " You know, it's quite incredible."

" Oh, the whole thing's incredible. I keep feeling I shall suddenly wake up, but, of course, I know I shan't really."

As the lift creaked its way upstairs he murmured tentatively, " Julia, I don't want to seem prying but—couldn't you have confided in Charles ? "

" Could you confide in Sally ? "

" Good God, no ! " The words shot out of him.

Julia shrugged. " You see ? We're in the same boat. What I'm beginning to wonder is—who else is going to be in it ? I thought it would just be Teddy and me."

" You know him then ? "

" I shouldn't be here if I didn't. Oh Gerald, it all seems so unfair. One does something reckless and—oh, wrong, I suppose—but something other people are doing all the time, and then years later, when you've almost forgotten and you feel you've paid anyhow, another bill's presented."

" At compound interest. I know. And the alternative to paying it . . ."

" Oh, there isn't any alternative," said Julia.

" Only bankruptcy."

" So it's just as bad for you. Gerald, why did he wait so long ? "

" Perhaps he's only just found out ; or only just realised there's money in it."

" Or perhaps he's become desperate, like animals that are perfectly harmless unless they're starving."

" If you're destroyed by a wild beast I don't see that it helps to know it's starving," retorted Gerald, bitterly. He had never been precisely handsome, but he had inherited an air of distinction from the father who had never owned him. His own life had been so hard, he had worked so furiously to overcome its early disadvantages and make it the sound, the worth-while affair it had become, that he felt a murderous hate of the unknown Teddy Lane surge in his breast. A wild beast, Julia had said—a cobra, thought Gerald, swaying its idiot head, waiting for the moment to strike.

Downstairs someone pressed the lift button. " Someone else for the party ? " hazarded Gerald. " Julia—I suppose you are sure you have to go through with this ? "

" Quite sure," said Julia, briefly. Because, though Charles loved her and was kind and understanding, mud sticks, and he'd never be able to forget that she had spent one night with Teddy Lane and the next in his arms. He could tell himself a hundred times that the meeting had been innocent, but— could he ever be perfectly sure ? Since Julia loved her husband and son more than herself, more than life, she felt she would stick at nothing to preserve Charles from this knowledge.

The lift stopped at the sixth floor and they got out. " I wonder how many of us there are going to be," murmured Gerald, ringing the bell and hearing the lift start to descend.

" One more anyway." Julia stooped and picked up a small fine linen handkerchief lying on the threshold of Teddy's flat. " A woman—and the sort of woman who can't afford pub-licity any more than ourselves," she decided, tucking the handkerchief into her pocket. You learned a lot from hand-kerchiefs. This one was very simple, very faintly perfumed. In a way, it was a comfort to know there would be one other woman there.

The door of the flat opened and there was Teddy, with his sharp alert face and narrowed eyes, and nothing left of his early charm but a veneer that barely concealed the sudden, bitter rage he felt at the sight of them. For, without a word being spoken, they emphasised the gulf that yawned between his furtive, grabbing existence and their honourable lives. Ah, but it hadn't always been like that, he thought, or they wouldn't be here now. They'd have to dance to his piping, whether they liked it or not.

But he could put on an act almost as well as she, and he offered his hand, remarking, " Oh hallo, have you introduced yourselves ? etc. etc."

" We've been meeting in other people's houses for some years," Gerald told him drily. " I don't think you mentioned it was going to be a party."

" Oh surely," Teddy looked surprised as he led them into the living-room where Mrs. Tempest sat in a dusty armchair, " I said it was a reunion."

" Since I have never met either of your visitors before we can hardly be said to be re-united," Alice Tempest observed. She recognised Julia at once from various photographs that had appeared in the society press. She had no notion who Gerald might be, except that he certainly was not Sir Charles. But she felt a stab of relief at the sight of him. He didn't look the kind of man to knuckle under tamely. And the plan that was already beginning to form in her mind was strengthened by the fact that he, too, was involved in the situation.

Julia came towards her, holding out the handkerchief. " Is this yours ? We found it on the mat."

" How careless of me ! Thank you." She looked at Teddy. " Are you expecting any more guests ? "

" Only one." Teddy was pouring sherry. Julia took her glass and put it on the mantelpiece. Gerald waved his away. Mrs. Tempest was thinking, " What on earth can such a man have on people like these ? " and Gerald and Julia were thinking the same about her.

Teddy tossed off his glass and said conversationally, indicating Julia (they all noticed how careful he was not to mention names), " We worked together during the war, you know."

" I didn't," said Alice Tempest. " How should I ? "

Teddy frowned. Such a pity when people were deliberately ungracious. Julia thought, with a pang of hope, " She isn't going to make things easy for him." But she wondered what Teddy expected to get from her. Julia knew, if Gerald didn't, that Alice's clothes were the result of careful planning and reconstruction, and a woman who has no money for new clothes hasn't much, as a rule, for blackmailers. Alice was watching Julia. It hurt her to think that Teddy, that little worm, should have this lovely creature in his power.

" She walks in beauty like the night," she reflected, turning as always in moments of pain to the poets she knew and loved so well. She spoke on impulse :

" My dear, I am going to say something you may think most impertinent. Why don't you confide in your husband ? "

Before Julia could reply Teddy cut in, " Why, come to that, don't you confide in your son ? Or you," he turned to Gerald, " in your employers ? The answer is the same in each case, and yet they say two heads are better than one."

" Don't you believe it," said a new voice, and Harmsworth Ames came marching in, sartorially perfect as a tailor's dummy, for all his immense size, carrying the inevitable silk umbrella on his arm. Like Mr. Chamberlain, he was never seen without it. " A secret shared by more than one person soon ceases to be a secret."

" How did you get in ? " exclaimed Teddy, momentarily taken aback.

" Found the door ajar and thought perhaps it had been left for me." He accepted the sherry Teddy automatically offered and sipped it. " Planning a mass murder ? " he suggested, setting the glass down. " Beats me why fellows go to such lengths to get poison when you can buy stuff like this."

Teddy burned with resentment. " You needn't talk as though I were a dishonest grocer," he snapped.

" No ? Now that's just what I should have thought you were." His gaze, cool and scornful, swept the room. "Best Mixed, that's what we are. Best Rich Mixed, you hope."

He took it for granted that everyone would know who he was, and he recognised the two younger members of the party. Mrs. Tempest might be any one of a great army of pleasant well-bred women you could meet on Tuesday and forget on Wednesday, or so he thought then. Like Julia, he was surprised to find her here. He wouldn't have supposed she was worth Teddy Lane's while.

As for his fellow-victims, each was conscious of a new element in the gathering since his arrival. Pit him against Teddy Lane and the most sanguine would hardly venture a fiver on Teddy. He was a man it would be difficult to overlook in any company. A great nose dominated the face, the eyes were dark caves under beetling crags, the mouth shut fast and relentless as a dungeon. He stared at the thin figure of Teddy Lane, who at once became shabbier, shoddier, more frail than before. He nodded towards his fellow-victims.

" Your bodyguard ? " he suggested to Teddy. " Maybe you're wise." He took his hand out of his pocket, and showed them all the wicked little automatic lying in his huge palm. " I had a feeling this might come in useful, but, speaking as an experienced counsel, I wouldn't advise anyone to commit a murder with three witnesses. One of 'em 'ud be bound to crack."

Teddy found his voice. " I had a notion you might prove violent," he said. " That's why I asked my other visitors to come a little earlier than you."

" Lucky for me, I dare say," said Harmsworth Ames. " Always awkward being found alone in a flat with a body."

" If you are serious," said Alice Tempest, " may I assure you of my hearty co-operation." She sent Teddy a sidelong glance. Co-operation was his word, wasn't it ? Well, let him make what he liked of that.

Julia exclaimed, " But he wasn't—serious, I mean. You can't shoot people out of hand."

Ames turned with a smile as menacing as a thunderstorm. " Only thing to do with a rat. Still, it looks as though I'll have to figure out some other way of getting rid of him."

" You of all men," rebuked Teddy Lane, " should know how dangerous murder is. You couldn't hope to get away with it."

" No ? Ever occur to you that having a lot of scoundrels through your hands is an education in itself ? Listen ! Nobody knew I was coming here to-day. Nobody saw me arrive, and I'll see to it no one sees me go ; no one likely to tell against me, that is. All I had to do was put back the hands of that clock of yours, shatter the face with a bullet —after I'd put one through you, of course—and it might be a couple of days before anyone noticed you weren't going around as usual. When the police did come in, the inference 'ud be you were shot at four-thirty by a chap who wasn't as good at the job as he'd like, and if questions had been asked, well, I've got three or four witness to swear to where I was at half-past four. You know," he smiled at Teddy quite benevolently, " you should stick to chaps of your own size, unless you want a quick funeral."

" Nice of you to warn me," laughed Teddy, but his hands

weren't quite sure of themselves. " But don't forget there are three witnesses to what you've just threatened."

Ames tipped back his huge head and roared with laughter. " Don't you believe it. A chap isn't a witness till he's in the box, and you must be even crazier than I thought if you suppose anyone present is going to volunteer information in your interest." He glanced at the other three. " Any reason why we shouldn't sit down ? " He picked up a chair and dropped into it with a thud. " Now you may have plenty of time on your hands, but the rest of us are busy folk. Put your cards on the table, and watch us trump them."

" It's perfectly simple," said Teddy. " I'm in the uncomfortable position of not being able to pay my way without a little help, and I thought we might strike a bargain."

" Ever think of working ? " asked Gerald Ross, drily.

Ames turned an immense sardonically amused face over his shoulder.

" Don't do the chap an injustice. He's put in a hell of a lot more work getting us together here this afternoon than any honest employer would get out of him. I've been in my job for nearly thirty years," he went on reflectively, " and I still don't know how it's done—his sort of game, I mean." He butted his head in Teddy's direction. " A vocation, I suppose. Or perhaps that type's born with an extra ear. What I do know is that if he hadn't got something on each of us we shouldn't be here this afternoon, we should be in the police court giving evidence to his detriment."

" You can't bring any charge against me," Teddy assured him contemptuously. " I simply suggested you should come along for a drink."

" Don't pull that one on me," Ames advised him. " I could make mincemeat of it quicker than I could of you. Still, the fact is you have got something on each of us, enough, you hope, to compel us to keep you in comfort for the rest of your days. Speaking for myself, you couldn't be more wrong. There are better ways of stopping your mouth."

" But perhaps," murmured Teddy, " more expensive ones."

" I never had much use for these cheap outfits. By the way, what figure did you have in mind ? Just for the record, mark you."

" I don't want to insult you by mentioning too low a sum." Teddy had recovered his suavity. " You've all got such a lot to lose. How does five hundred pounds strike you ? "

" Five hundred too much," was Ames's prompt retort.

" Speaking for myself," said Mrs. Tempest, " such a sum is quite out of the question. My income, which is exceedingly small, has to be stretched to meet my bare expenses."

" But you have connections, shall we say ? who are more fortunately placed. Your son . . ."

" If my son is to be brought into this I could have saved myself the disagreeable experience of coming here this afternoon. Believe me, Mr.—er—Lane, if any action of mine can prevent his learning the facts that have so disastrously come into your possession, any action whatsoever, I shall not hesitate. And please understand that so far as I am concerned there are no limits to the risks I am prepared to run. So far as trying to obtain help in any other direction is concerned," she added in tones of disgust, " I would as soon rob a poor-box."

Ames grinned. If she'd been his client he would have trembled for her neck, but as an ally she could scarcely be bettered.

" Well, you've heard this lady's view," he remarked cheerfully. " How about the others ? "

" I'm in the same position," said Julia at once. " I have no money at all."

" I always understood your husband, Julia . . ."

" My husband doesn't come into this," exclaimed Julia, sharply.

" Mr. Lane seems to have been rather haphazard in his choice," commented Gerald by way of good measure. " With the exception of yourself," and he bowed to Ames, " not one of us would be able to provide the financial support he's after, even if we had the will."

Teddy shrugged that aside. " Even if your salary doesn't run to an ability to pay your debts, there's your father-in-law . . ."

Gerald drew a sharp breath. John Edgecumbe hadn't been too enthusiastic about the match for his daughter from the start ; if he had known the facts he would have moved heaven and earth to prevent the marriage, and though Sally would have gone through with it in any case, because she was in love, it would have deprived her children of that background that should be theirs by right and the privileges accompanying it that every child should enjoy. His recollection of his own wretched childhood had made him the more resolved that his own sons should have a family standing foursquare behind them.

Teddy followed up his advantage. " I was accused just now of wasting time," he pointed out, " but if any of you had found any alternative you would hardly be here now."

" There's always an alternative," insisted Ames. " You know what mine was. I shall have to change my plans a little, but my intention remains firm. Any man who provides food for a rat is an enemy of the community."

" If it is any consolation," put in Alice Tempest, " I have no intention of providing a single crumb for our rat."

Ames put out his hand. " You and I 'ud make a good team. How about the others ? "

Gerald said harshly, " Don't let there be any mistake about it. I've met Lane's sort before. If we don't put up in cash *or* kind, he'll ruin us all."

" Thank Heaven for a gleam of common sense," Teddy sighed.

" If we follow up what this gentleman has just said, it leads to the obvious conclusion that we must discover some effective way of ensuring your silence," continued Mrs. Tempest, addressing Teddy direct. " I don't wish to jump anyone else's claim, but I have a plan in mind . . ."

" Perhaps you'll tell us," murmured Teddy, politely.

" I think it would be wiser to consult my allies, if I may call them that, before taking any action. You have so many aces up your sleeve it would be folly to strengthen your hand still further. So long as it's agreed that we come to no individual arrangement with you before we have an opportunity of discussing the situation *in camera*, well, frankly I can see no point in prolonging the interview."

" Very nicely put," agreed Ames. " Well, Lane, here's your last chance. Are you going to hand back any evidence you may have ? "

" Over my dead body," replied Teddy theatrically.

" It looks as though that's what it might come to. Well, that's curtains for Act One. In Act Two we'll meet to discuss this lady's proposal, and with any luck Act Three will end in curtains for Teddy Lane. All agreed ? Then let's go."

Teddy, feeling like a man who, paddling happily in a millpond, suddenly sees Niagara just ahead and knows he will only avoid being swept over by paddling madly for the bank, cried in a loud high voice, " You must all be out of your minds. What you're saying amounts to a threat of murder."

" Even the law permits judicial murder in the community's interest," Ames pointed out. " And we're all agreed the community will be a lot safer when you're tucked up cosily under your tombstone."

" You talk as if planning a murder was no more difficult than arranging a tea-party." Teddy was shocked to find he was shouting. " You won't feel so fine when you're all in the dock."

" Who's going to put us there ? Not you, because you'll be in the mortuary, and even if anything should involve any one of us in your death your ghost will be surprised to learn you've committed suicide. Well, why not ? You're dead broke, aren't you, in every sense of the word. You can't pay your rent, you've no friends, no job, no prospects, in fact, you're an absolute pauper."

Julia's illogical heart turned over in sudden compassion. Because it was true, every word of it. What had Teddy got to show for more than half a century of existence ? She had Charles and Johnny, Gerald had his work, his wife and his boys, Mrs. Tempest clearly had a son who was all her life to her, Ames had his career and his reputation—only Teddy was absolutely down-and-out. She felt sorry as she'd have felt sorry for a man begging in the gutter. Let social workers say it was his own fault, she couldn't pass judgment on him. A hungry man is a hungry man, whether it's his own fault or someone else's, and if, by giving him his five hundred pounds, she could have assured him an honest ending to his miserable tale of days, she'd have strained every nerve to get the money.

She felt a powerful hand on her arm. " Leopards don't change their spots," Ames advised her, " and rats don't change their natures. One rat allowed to live can father about eight hundred in a year, if you get my meaning, what with grand-children and great-grandchildren and so forth, or so I've been told. You have to think of the community. Now, if there's nothing more anyone has to say I propose we go out and look for some place where we can breathe."

The two women rose at once, collecting bags and gloves, Mrs. Tempest cool and pitiless, Julia near to tears. " Know whose shoes I wouldn't care to be wearing ? " Ames inquired casually of their discomfited host. " Yours. And know why ? I'll tell you. Because you've said good-bye to any peace you ever knew. From now on you're never going to be sure what's going to happen to-morrow, and while you're wondering, the odds are it'll happen to-night. Take my tip and don't go around by yourself after dark."

"I've been told it's surprising how many fatal accidents take place on the platforms of underground stations," put in Gerald Ross, as hard as Mrs. Tempest. "People pressing and pushing. It could easily happen, you know."

"In your place, Mr. Lane," contributed Alice, "I should be very careful about sampling anonymous boxes of chocolates."

"In fact," wound up Ames in high good humour, "in your place I'd be inclined to ask for police protection. I'm sure you could easily think up some good story."

Only Julia said nothing. Julia was remembering Teddy as he'd been ten years ago, taking her duty, encouraging her in her hour of terror, saying, Don't lose heart, chaps do turn up months afterwards, and anyone married to you would have every incentive. And now—Ames was right, when he said a rat, with rat's eyes, narrow and bright, a rat's teeth, pointed and pitiless, a scourge to the community. She choked back a sob.

"By the way," Teddy was elaborately casual, "I can allow you a week to find the money. If I don't hear from you by Friday next you'll know what to expect."

"We won't keep you in suspense," promised Ames. "You'll get our ultimatum before Friday, and after that I don't think you'll have any need to worry ever any more."

After the front door had closed behind him Ames said with a shade of regret, "I'm not sure my original plan wasn't the best. If I'd stayed behind and plugged him, it's a hundred to one I'd never be identified."

"It would be putting too much responsibility on our shoulders," Mrs. Tempest pointed out. "I can't swear no one saw me enter, and I am told the police are a very intelligent body of men. If I were questioned . . ." She paused. "No, I think an accident would be a far more satisfactory solution. If any of us become openly involved we might so easily pull all the others in after us."

"That's true," said Gerald. "We're like climbers, all roped together. If they get one of us the odds are they get us all."

Julia said, "What was your plan?" and Mrs. Tempest replied composedly, "I think we should do nothing in too much of a hurry. I suggest that you all come to tea with me to-morrow—the address is 10 Hunter Street. We have until next Friday, and that should be plenty of time. My daily woman isn't on the premises on Saturday afternoon. And it will give us all time to weigh the position : circumstances have changed considerably in the last hour. For instance, I had no notion I should have three allies, and I dare say the same is true for everyone else."

Here the lift reached their floor, and Mrs. Tempest and Julia got in. On Ames's suggestion the two men walked down separately, so that if they should meet anyone they wouldn't be connected in his or her mind. Once in the street they went their independent ways, agreeing to come together the following afternoon.

Teddy Lane heard the whine of the descending lift, and remained standing in his little dark hall. He felt dazed and bruised ; the meeting had not gone at all as he had anticipated. There had been something terrifying about Mrs. Tempest's calm attitude ; he believed she really would run him down in a car or put poison in his tea and never lose a wink of sleep. She was like the man in the Bible who sold everything he possessed to buy the pearl of great price, and such people are unconquerable. A little later he heard the lift come whining up again and stop at his floor. Steps approached his flat, and in sudden panic he leaned forward and switched off the light. Then, as someone pressed the bell, he put out his hand and the man on the other side of the door heard the bolt being softly shot. He went on ringing for another minute or so, but Teddy never stirred. He wasn't going to make things as simple for them as all that.

And presently the footsteps moved away and the lift went down again.

It was some time later that the telephone began to ring. He put out his hand, then let it fall to his side. You didn't catch old birds as easily as all that. Let them think what they pleased, that he had gone out, anything. For the next week—he knew that now—he'd got to be more careful than he had been in his whole life. But, by Heaven, they should pay for their defiance. He was shaken by the rage of a weak man. None of them would have any compunction, except Julia. Julia was different. He must concentrate on her.

Downstairs in the basement the porter said to his wife, " Whatever's up with Number 12 ? Bolting himself in like that ? Did he think I was coming to put a knife in him ? "

" Got someone there, I expect," said Mrs. Moxon, cosily. And winked.

" He could answer the telephone, couldn't he ? "

His wife chuckled gustily. " Got better things to do, I'd say. Give over worrying, Stan. He can look after himself."

" Well, I don't like it," grumbled Moxon. " You mark my words, he'll be found in the river at the end of the week, and we don't want any mucking police round here."

CHAPTER THREE

AFTERMATH OF A PARTY

MRS. TEMPEST'S tea-party was conducted with a decorum and charm that increased Ames's respect for her. He congratulated himself in private that he only had Teddy Lane against him though that was bad enough. But this woman, who, for all her pleasing manners and competent small-talk, was about as harmless as a black mamba, would be infinitely worse. When the cups had been put on one side and the plates cleared, Alice Tempest outlined her plan.

" I am taking for granted," said she, " that we are at one in our agreement that Mr. Lane must not be allowed to put any of his threats into action. As to how he is to be prevented, that must be the concern of whoever draws the Black Death."

" The Black Death ? " repeated Ames, in a perplexed voice.

" It's a plan I had in mind. Naturally, if anyone has an alternative I shall be perfectly prepared to abandon mine. My suggestion is that, since we are all in this dilemma together, we should each take an equal risk. It won't be safe to count on providence coming to our aid, that, I fear, only happens in fairy-tales; the initiative must be taken by one of us, and, of course, the question is which."

" I am prepared," began Ames, but the look on her face stopped him in mid-flight.

" I think it is equally important that none of us shall know the name of the member of our party who becomes responsible for—putting out Mr. Lane's light is, I believe, the modern way of phrasing it. Therefore, to secure anonymity . . ."

25

"I have it," exclaimed the Q.C. "You're going to suggest we draw lots."

"As I have said, if anyone has any other proposal . . ."

But they all shook their heads.

"I don't see how the idea can be bettered," Ames acknowledged. "What's this Black Death?"

"I have here four counters in opaque envelopes; I suggest that we should each draw one, and whoever draws the black counter shall hold him or herself responsible for silencing Mr. Lane."

Julia found her voice. "It's murder," she whispered.

Ames turned in a flash. "Who's used that word? This lady specifically said silencing Mr. Lane. The simplest way to do that would be to pay his demands, two thousand pounds in all. I don't say I couldn't find two thousand pounds without much difficulty, but I assure you that if I draw the final counter that won't be my solution of the problem. However, it will be left to the enterprise and possibly the conscience of the favoured individual to pick his own way. The main thing is that it will effectually keep the fellow quiet."

Gerald Ross said slowly, "He can hardly utter threats without something to back them up. Blackmailers always have documents of some sort; if we could get those away from him I hardly think anyone would be likely to accept his bare word."

"I don't know, of course, your particular predicament," said Mrs. Tempest, courteously, "but, so far as I'm concerned, it is less simple. A private letter or paper is perhaps easily dealt with; where an official record is concerned . . ."

She broke off as Gerald nodded sharply. "My own position," he agreed.

Ames glanced at him quizzically. Scratch a Russian and you find a Tartar, they'd said when he was a boy. Scratch an apparently irreproachable Government servant and you found—what? a secret criminal? a traitor? Who was to say? For the first time it occurred to him that it might be even less in the country's interests to preserve one of the victims than to pander to the demands of their oppressor.

"Old sins have long shadows," quoted Julia. "But—I must say this—something's happened to him, to Teddy, I mean. He wasn't always like this. He was generous—and kind."

" People dying of cancer or tuberculosis weren't always like that either," Ames reminded her hardily. " But once the disease has developed, then you've got to take drastic steps to destroy it. I haven't any particular feeling about Lane as an individual ; only in his activities he's a danger, and in one way or another his fangs must be drawn. I think we should clarify the position to the extent of putting it on record among ourselves that we are not making a murder compact. If Lane should die as a result of any action taken by one of our party, then that person and that person alone must accept responsibility. We're in a spot," he added more colloquially, " and we may as well accept the fact. We've got to trust each other and if X decides the best plan is to go to the police and get Lane pulled in (though I fancy the chap's right when he says he's covered himself there), then only X's affairs can be made public to the authorities."

" We get you," said Gerald. " All the same, I doubt if the police would be a very clever solution. As our hostess has already reminded us, they're a very intelligent and conscientious body of men, and the odds are they'd winkle the truth out of any one of us, in spite of all our good intentions. I believe refusing to answer the police's reasonable questions is an indictable offence," he added.

" Are you seeking Counsel's opinion ? " murmured Ames. He went on, without waiting for a reply, " We want to be careful that none of us becomes an accessory before the fact. Now, I don't know whether any of the rest of you noticed a black japanned box in Lane's room. I take it that's his version of the Bank of England. If we could get our hands on the contents of that we might be able to shut his mouth for the duration."

" In short," said Gerald, " take a leaf out of his book."

" People in our position can't afford all the luxuries," the Q.C. reminded him, drily. " I agree it would be better if we could chase him underground, but for amateurs that's not so easy. Speaking for myself," he added, with a shrug of his enormous shoulders, " if I draw the fatal counter I'm prepared to shoot it out with the fellow, if need be." The expression on his face said that you could say your prayers for Teddy Lane if that happened, assuming you were religiously inclined.

Gerald nodded his assent. Teddy wouldn't have much fun if he found himself up against this fellow, Ames reflected ; he hadn't any fears where Mrs. Tempest was concerned, either, but Julia Silk was a different cup of tea. Although she said, " I agree not to implicate any of you, whatever happens," she was ashy pale, and he knew that a chain's only as strong as its weakest link. Here, he told himself grimly, was the weakest link. Women were always incalculable, but he would back Mrs. Tempest as readily as himself to steel her heart against pity. He did not know the nature of Lane's hold over this beautiful creature, but he could guess it was an emotional one. Some women became embittered and positively Amazonian in circumstances involving a one-time lover ; this girl would be compassionate. She wouldn't want to sacrifice her husband, would wish to be loyal to her allies, but she couldn't help being sorry for their common enemy. Inevitably she would remember him in kindlier times. The rest of them were more fortunate in that they had never met any other Teddy Lane than the contemptible little black-mailer of yesterday. He glanced at Mrs. Tempest ; he saw that she could read his mind, share his wish that the affair was between the two of them. There'd be no fear of weakening then.

She spoke next. " If no one else has any point to raise, shall we draw for the Black Death ? " She put the four envelopes on the table. " I will draw last. They are all precisely similar, but in case any doubts should be felt, I should prefer to be the last."

" Point is," murmured Ames, " who's to be the first ? "

Eventually they decided on alphabetical order, and in turn Ames, Gerald and Julia took their envelopes, thrusting them into pocket or bag without a second glance. Mrs. Tempest composedly took the one that remained.

" Since it's improbable we shall be meeting again," she said, " and in any case it would be wisest to avoid any such contingency, may I take this opportunity of wishing good luck to whoever may need it."

Ames rose to his tremendous height. " That'll be our Mr. Lane." She was a clever woman, hadn't asked their names or offered her own. He supposed it wouldn't be difficult to find out who she was, now that they knew her address, but anonymity seemed to him desirable for every reason. He would have agreed with Arthur Crook, that unconventional lawyer and sleuth (and at this stage it never occurred to anyone that before the affair was closed Crook would be drawn to the centre of the stage), that there are times when nothing's so advantageous as a little healthy ignorance.

He took up his hat and held out his hand. The others followed suit. When they had all gone, and the china was washed and stacked, Mrs. Tempest picked up her envelope and stood staring at it for some time. Then she slit it open and let the little disc pour slowly into her palm. There was no change in her expression, no relief and no apprehension. She might have known which one it would be. After a moment she opened a drawer and tossed it in. There was almost a week to go, and a good deal can happen in a week.

Julia hailed a taxi at the corner of the street and opened her envelope as she was driven home. When she saw the colour of the little counter as it rolled into her hand her face turned as white as paper. For it was as black as a sparrow's eye. She lay with her hands folded, wondering what she should do next.

She hadn't the least idea.

When Harmsworth Ames saw that his counter was the Black Death he knew a stab of relief. As soon as he got back to his chambers he rang up a man called Plunkett and gave him his instructions.

"This chap's name is Lane and he lives in Ellison Mansions," he said. "What I really want is his head on a charger before Friday next, but just to be going on with I want him hunted and harried, so that he's afraid to sleep, afraid to cross the road, afraid to open a newspaper or open the door."

"In fact," said Plunkett, unmoved, "everything short of murder."

"We must hope it won't come to that," said Ames cheerfully. "But he's in my road and he's got to get out. I'm on a case that I don't intend to lose and he's in the middle of the picture. If you can drive him into the country or, better still, into the river, that'll suit my book to a T. You know the old torture of never letting a man sleep? Well, there's your cue. No need to get on the windy side of the law or push him off a bridge. If you do your job properly he'll jump off of his own accord."

Gerald Ross was the last of the four to open the envelope, and his first reaction was one of gratitude that Julia at least hadn't drawn the Black Death. He felt none of Ames' stolid conviction, none of Mrs. Tempest's suppressed passion or Julia's naked fear. His thoughts ran :

Teddy Lane's a menace to any decent person who happens to get in his power. Take myself. I'm doing useful work, essential work not only for myself but for generations to come. I've got a wife and children who deserve the very best ; and this chap threatens all that. You cut a cancer out of the living flesh without a qualm, and Lane's a cancer in the body politic.

He didn't for a moment suppose they four were his only victims. You only had to look at Teddy to see he hadn't done a stroke of real work for years ; by now, of course, he was completely unemployable. All over the country hearts would offer up thanksgiving to hear he'd met with some fatal accident. The only question was just what sort of accident would be best.

" What's the governor got on his mind ? " one workman asked another.

The second shrugged. " Don't ask me. Some new way to kill us off, I suppose. Well, he's the boss. He should know."

Mrs. Tempest drew back the curtains at ten o'clock and went to bed. Alone of the four she slept calmly. No doubts gnawed at her mind, she was taking no chances.

All four of them had drawn the Black Death and even Teddy Lane couldn't hope to win at such colossal odds.

CHAPTER FOUR

JOURNEY INTO FEAR

WHEN TEDDY woke on Saturday morning he lay for some time with his eyes closed. He knew that some black shadow threatened him but so long as he kept his eyes shut he felt, childishly, that he could keep it at bay. The arrival of the post, however, made him turn over and sit up, stretching wearily. Even then he had an instant's respite before the recollection of yesterday's calamitous meeting came rushing into his mind. It was like a tidal wave, he couldn't stem it, or mitigate the violence of its assault. The situation resolved itself into five words.

His life was in danger !

He could (and did) tell himself over and over again that it was absurd, that he was getting worked up over a possibility that was itself impossible, but he couldn't convince his fear that it no longer existed. He recalled Mrs. Tempest's fanatical composure, Ames' unconcealed intention to have his life—-he really did believe that if only he and Ames had been in the flat the Q.C. would have carried out his threat. He could tell himself as often as he pleased that it was murder, and eminent men draw the line at that, but back came the reply —Ames was the exception, Ames would take the chance. He'd taken chances enough already, and what would there be, when the man had gone through the place and removed the only piece of evidence linking his successful life to Teddy's tawdry existence, to point to Harmsworth Ames as the criminal ? When he planned the party it had never occurred to him that his four victims would band themselves together. He had been living, shabbily, it is true, but still keeping alive on the fruits of his illicit knowledge for many years. There had been sidelines, of course ; he'd played the Black Market, come in with Morell, scrabbled for the price of a pint wherever it could be picked up without too much danger to himself, but now (here he changed the metaphor) he had overcalled his hand. Not only would he not get the money, he wouldn't be allowed even to keep the wretched thing that was still his, his pitiable life. Automatically he picked up his letters and glanced through them. There was a card from Morell, another threat though a decently veiled one. He tossed it into the waste-paper basket. Morell could wait ; he, at least, wouldn't dare go too far, he had too much to lose. The others were different. He toyed with the idea of writing to them all and cancelling his proposal, but even his poor common sense knew it was too late in the day for that. They wouldn't trust him, and in two cases at least it was more than a matter of mere documents.

He couldn't make up his mind if he'd be safer in his flat or in the street. Suppose he kept his door locked, didn't answer any bells, let the telephone ring its head off, stayed away from windows—why, I might as well be in the grave, cried Teddy in anguish. And the grave was where he most feared to be.

When he nerved himself to look out of the window he knew his terrors were justified. A man was leaning against the lamp-post on the other side of the road. As Teddy watched him, fascinated, the fellow drew out a packet of cigarettes, put one in his mouth, and lighted it with deliberation. The first match apparently was insufficient, because after a moment he struck another. As he did so he turned casually and stared in Teddy's direction. Teddy shrank back behind a curtain. He knew the man wasn't just filling in time or waiting for a pal; he was waiting for him, Teddy, to emerge. Quite what he would do then Teddy couldn't formulate even to himself, but—accidents happen so quickly, and where there aren't witnesses who's to say where the fault lies? Anyhow, it wouldn't be any satisfaction to a dead man to know his killer was going to be censured by a coroner. And, reflected Teddy an instant later, there would be a witness. The striking of the second match was part of a code. He's there, it meant. Or, Look out, he'll soon be coming down. Well, thought Teddy, shuddering violently, he wouldn't. And since he didn't propose to go out there was no reason why he shouldn't lock his front-door, was there? And seeing his head ached like nobody's business and the sun was coming through the pane with a heat quite unsuitable for the time of year, there was nothing, peculiar—was there?—in pulling down the blind. So he pulled it; and he locked the door and because, now he'd shut out the sun, he felt quite cold, shivering, in fact, he breakfasted from the whisky-bottle, and wasted a lot of time trying to think of someone who might help him in this appalling plight. But the Teddy Lanes of life can't afford luxuries like friends, and there wasn't anyone.

Soon after he had drawn the blind the man leaning against the lamp-post was joined by another to whom he said, " Cheero, Len, thought you were never coming."

" Bumper trouble," said Len. " All right now though."

Then the two got into a little black car and went off for a day at Brighton. They had neither of them ever heard of Teddy Lane.

He had to go out after lunch because he'd finished the whisky, and when he came back he found Moxon talking to a stranger. Both gave him a most curious glance as he passed, and while he was waiting for the lift the porter strolled across to say, " Feeling all right, Mr. Lane? "

" Any reason why I shouldn't? " snapped Teddy.

" I just wondered," said Moxon. " I was trying to get you last night."

" Last night ? " Teddy ad-libbed frantically. " Oh, I was out."

" Funny about that," said Moxon elaborately. " I could have sworn there was a light on when I first rang. And then it went out. Funny, wasn't it ? "

" Unless one of the mice you let loose in the flats is clever enough to operate the switch, you must have been seeing things," retorted Teddy violently. " I tell you I was out. What did you want anyway ? " he added.

" Just to remind you you owe three weeks' milk," said Moxon. " Chap's getting tired of waiting."

Teddy didn't believe a word of it. Moxon, the lazy hound, hadn't come upstairs after hours to ask for a few shillings for the milk. He'd come because someone had tipped him off. The torture had begun and already he saw, though as yet only dimly, that he was never going to know an hour's true peace again so long as he lived.

" Who was that chap you were talking to just now, when I came in ? " he asked abruptly.

Moxon looked startled. " No one you know. Matter of fact, it was someone asking if there were any vacant flats."

Again, Teddy didn't believe a word of it.

" I told him," Moxon went on, " there might be one any minute."

" Who's going ? " He felt his mouth as dry as a rose-bed in a drought.

Moxon shrugged. " Could be anyone. People go so sudden sometimes, don't they ? "

Teddy knew he was in a bad way, reading second meanings into the simplest expression. All the same, had it been so innocent ? *He went off very sudden*, people said to each other. *Funeral was Thursday.* It could be—couldn't it ?—that this time next week people would be saying just the same about him.

" Why did you look at me ? " he demanded truculently.

Moxon shrugged. " I don't recall that we did. Still, it might as easy be you as anyone, mightn't it ? Easier than some."

" What do you mean by that ? "

" What's biting you ? " asked Moxon curiously. " He wasn't a bum bailiff, if that's what you're afraid of."

" Why should I ? " Teddy stuttered.

" Never can tell, and I thought, being a bit short these days . . ."

" I don't owe you anything, do I ? " demanded Teddy.

" That's according to how you look at things. No, I suppose you couldn't say you *owe* me anything."

Teddy knew what that meant. Porters expected regular tips, though why they should, considering they were paid for their jobs, Teddy could never understand. Still, it didn't do to fall foul of them so he straightened his face and asked, " No registered letter came for me to-day, I suppose ? "

Moxon looked at him with such contempt that Teddy felt himself flush scarlet. Expecting a chap of my experience to buy that one ? asked that look. The lift came down at last and Teddy yanked the doors open. " I can take myself up," he said, sharply.

" There's no charge," returned Moxon in bland tones. " Besides, you were going to give me the money for the milkman. He won't go on delivering without you pay him."

Teddy found the money with an ill grace. " I've got a bad headache," he announced. " I don't want any visitors and I don't want any telephone calls put through."

" I see, sir," agreed Moxon, in mock respectful tones. " About that letter, the one you were expecting. If that should come, do you want that brought up right away ? "

" Yes," said Teddy feebly. " Of course, it may not come to-day."

Moxon smiled again. He knew it wasn't coming to-day or any day. All the same, he wondered what had happened to the tenant of No. 12. Look at the way he noticed the stranger, who certainly hadn't paid nearly so much attention to Teddy, whom he'd never seen before and wouldn't recognise if he saw him again.

Teddy went into his flat and locked the door. He peeped through the blind, but there was no one leaning against the lamp-post now. He opened the bottle of whisky and took a shot just to steady his nerves ; then he went to lie down. But he had to keep getting up and going into the other room to make sure the fellow hadn't come back. But he didn't, and so at last Saturday drew to its close.

On Sunday the sun came out early, and Teddy haunted the window. There wasn't anyone leaning against the lamp-post this morning, but an old man whom he'd never seen before was selling flowers just opposite. Teddy bore his presence there as long as he could, then in a sudden access of defiance he marched out and bought a bunch of wilting daffodils.

" New pitch for you, isn't it ? " he suggested.

The old man behaved as though he'd been insulted. " What's that to do with you ? Got a right to be here, haven't I ? "

" I never said you hadn't." Teddy was taken aback. " I only thought I hadn't seen you before."

" Chap's got to get a living somehow, hasn't he ? " demanded the old 'un belligerently. " Got as much right on this corner as anyone. Is that all you came down for, to pry ? "

" I asked you a perfectly civil question," protested Teddy, feeling his nerves jumping like fleas on a Spanish veranda. " If you've got a guilty conscience . . ."

" Who said I had a guilty conscience ? What are you trying to do ? Rob an old man of his livelihood ? "

Teddy snatched up the daffodils and fled. But his suspicions were sharpened by the interview. Because it wasn't natural, was it, to take offence unless there was something queer going on ? Coming in, he encountered Moxon and Mrs. Moxon emerging in their Sunday clothes, and on an impulse he stopped and said, " Oh, just a minute."

Moxon looked indignant. Bertha strolled on, smiling to herself.

" What about it ? " asked the porter in surly tones.

" That old man over there—he's never been here before."

" What of it ? It's not a crime to sell flowers."

" I believe he's a phony."

" Why don't you get in touch with the police then ? Telephone hasn't been cut off yet, has it ? "

Teddy rushed past him into the flat. It was a plot, he was convinced of it, and they were all in it. all leagued against him. The flat looked shoddier than usual. The woman who " did " for him had been away the last day or two, influenza, she said. Everything was smeared with a film of dust, greasy and joyless. He thought, If I could get out of here, and then Why not ? But he knew the answers to that. One was that he wouldn't get far, not without one of his enemies getting on his track, that is, and the other was that he couldn't afford it. Paying the milkman had brought him down to a bare three pounds. He'd had to pay for the whisky, nobody trusted you any more. He felt his fury against the quartet rise till it was like a fire ; he shot out his arms foolishly as

35

though they were all in the room with him, and he was knocking them down like ninepins. Then the telephone began to ring. It rang and rang. Someone must have dialled the number and laid the receiver down to reiterate its shrill summons until the tormented subscriber at the other end lost patience. This happened pretty soon in Teddy's case. He snatched up the receiver.

" Who are you ? Who do you want ? "

" Mr. Lane ? Good afternoon. How are you, Mr. Lane ? " The voice was pleasantly crisp.

" I'm perfectly well," replied Teddy, choking over the words. " Who are you ? "

" That's good," said the voice. " Make the most of it. You haven't much longer."

" I don't know what you mean," stammered Teddy, terror striking into his vitals.

" You will," said the voice. And the telephone went dead.

He sat there a long time with the instrument in his hand before he realised he hadn't hung up. He replaced the receiver oh, so carefully, not making a sound, as though he could deceive the enemy into believing he wasn't there. That didn't make sense, of course, but his mind was in such a whirl he wasn't capable of logical thought. He couldn't rest. He marched up and down the living-room till the tenant in the flat below got a walking-stick and thumped on the ceiling. But it didn't make any difference to Teddy Lane. He didn't even hear.

" You haven't much longer," said the voice over and over again, as clearly as if the speaker were actually in the room.

" I don't know what you mean," repeated Teddy Lane, and like a gramophone record back came the answer : " You will."

He generally went to a cinema on Sunday afternoons ; it helped to while away the interminable hours, but to-day he stopped at home. If his enemy knew of his habit he'd be waiting on the corner, and what better place than a dark cinema to drive a silent knife into a man's ribs, or slash him with a razor or—oh, there were a dozen ways of perpetrating a crime, with all the fools round him intent on the screen or on making surreptitious love in the darkness.

" If I stay here," he repeated, like someone re-reading a letter he already knows by heart, " if I don't answer the telephone or open the door, if I refuse to accept parcels, never take a free drink . . ." It was no good. He couldn't quieten his nerves. There was only one thing that could do that, and his supplies were running dangerously short. He didn't suppose Morell would let him have any more without payment and he couldn't pay. He was like some wretched beast in a trap, or that anguished creature in the Pit and the Pendulum who saw the walls of his cell slowly advancing and knew that presently they would crush him to a horrible death. He even had a crazy moment when he thought the best way might be to put himself beyond the reach of his tormentors once and for all, but he got no further than considering that. Because paradoxically while young Edward Lane, fresh from school and filled with hope, had not been afraid of the imminence of death, Teddy Lane, thirty-five years later, shuddered at the mere contemplation of the word. Death—the inescapable foe of all men. Well, it might come, but not at his own hands. He succumbed to his temptation, administered a shot of his drug, and sank into merciful darkness.

It was a little after six when he was awakened by a sound, and starting up heard the ringing of his front door bell. He sprang from the bed in a frenzy of terror. Had he remembered to lock the front door ? He couldn't absolutely recall. It was quite dark now, and he dared not put on a light for fear of advertising his presence in the flat. Moving silently in his socks he stole into the little lobby. There was a light visible under the door from the passage outside ; he stood waiting, scarcely daring to breathe. The bell rang again, then a third time, and still Teddy made no sign. At length a hand lifted the letter-box. He saw a white card come slowly through the aperture ; he had to struggle with himself not to dash forward and snatch it away. Inch by inch it appeared, fell on the mat, the bell pealed once more and then the feet went down the stairs. It seemed ages before the skulking man found the courage to move forward and examine his communication. It proved to be a plain white card on which had been carefully printed the message :

In the midst of life we are in death.
Prepare to meet thy God.

Abruptly he laughed aloud. If that was the best they could do he needn't be so scared. Did they really expect him to take this childish, semi-hysterical warning seriously ? Suddenly he decided to go across the road to The Bunch of Grapes and find a little society there. He generally went in on Sundays on his way back from the pictures ; they knew him all right, though not to the extent of letting him chalk up a drink. Still, at all events he'd hear a human voice, feel himself part of a normal world. He sluiced cold water over his face, smoothed his hair, tied his shoes and went out. It was a chilly evening and no one seemed to be lurking on the pavement. In the bar he saw another fellow from the flats, a man called Prentice. He didn't know him very well, but he had to talk to someone so he went up with a casual word.

" Come to celebrate your approaching end ? " laughed Prentice. (He was rather a foolish fellow really.)

Teddy nearly fell over his own feet.

" My end ? "

" Didn't you get one, too ? " He put his hand in his pocket, and pulled out a card, the precise twin of the one Teddy had found in his hall. " That crazy fellow, Dawlish, has been making a round. You must know him."

Teddy shook his head. He never knew anyone who couldn't be some use to him ; even Prentice had his uses, once or twice he had been known to buy Teddy a drink.

" I fell for it like a sucker," Prentice confessed ruefully. " I was expecting a visitor, so I opened the door. Took me twenty minutes to get rid of him. Chap's really a fanatic. Carries a sandwich board at the seaside on Bank Holidays. The wicked shall be turned into hell. You know the sort of thing."

" To tell you the truth," said Teddy inaccurately, " I didn't give the thing a second thought. I imagined it was some sort of advertisement."

" You missed something," Prentice assured him grimly. " He had even me a bit shaken before he was through. Honestly, I wouldn't be surprised to meet a chap on the stairs who put out his hand and said, ' Good evening. I was just coming to call. My name is Death.' "

" That's a silly sort of joke," said Teddy uneasily.

" It's not a joke at all. Still, as I said, Dawlish has a bee in his bonnet. A bee ? A whole hive of them. He insisted on going into statistics before I got rid of him, you know the sort of thing, one child in every four will either die young, die on the scaffold or end in an asylum. For all I know it's true. Anyway, according to his arithmetic, at least one person in our block is likely to die within the week."

" How does he work that out ? " Teddy blurted the words before he could stop himself.

" Don't ask me. All the same, Lane, old boy, he was impressive. It might be you, he said, stabbing a finger at me like the Recording Angel. Had you thought of that ? And would you be ready ? I headed him off, naturally, but, on my sam, the chap's perfectly right."

" I don't know what you're talking about." Teddy's voice was as sharp as a saw.

" Seen the evening paper ? Well, take the front page at random. Charter plane drops into the sea, six dead. Woman found stabbed in railway siding. Arsenic suspicion in lonely cottage mystery. Runaway lorry kills child. See what I mean ? That was Dawlish's point, too. These things are happening all the time to somebody. None of the passengers in that charter plane expected to come down in the sea ; that woman in the siding may have had a date for to-night ; the kid who was killed by the lorry may have been anticipating a birthday party to-morrow. Makes you think, doesn't it ? I mean, during the next twenty-four hours it might be you or me."

" I can tell you one thing," snapped Teddy. " It won't be me. I shall see to that."

Prentice wagged his head. " Rash man," he murmured. " Setting yourself up against the gods."

Teddy slammed down his glass and marched out. As he crossed the street someone caught his arm, nearly pulling him off his balance.

" What the devil . . . ? " he began, panic-stricken.

" Excuse me, sir," said a whining voice, " if you've a minute . . ."

" I haven't," proclaimed Teddy, trying to shake himself free.

" You wouldn't like to have my death on your conscience," the voice insisted.

" Your death ? " The word brought him up short.

" I'm hungry," said the man simply. " I haven't had a meal all day."

" There's the National Assistance Board, isn't there ? " demanded Teddy, knowing very little about the subject.

" Not on a Sunday. Put yourself in my place . . ."

" Why the devil should I ? "

" If you knew what it was to be born unlucky," whined the man, who was practically invisible in the thin drizzle of rain that had begun to fall while Teddy was in the Bunch of Grapes . . .

" Do you suppose everyone's lucky ? " Teddy was shaken with the violent rage of the weak man. " Besides, how do you know you'd be any better off if you could change places with me ? Perhaps I'm less lucky even than you."

" Oh, I wouldn't say that, sir. You've got a roof, I dare say, and something to eat. . . ."

Teddy laughed abruptly. " So you'd like to change places with me ? Would you really ? Suppose I told you I had only a week to live ? "

" Well, of course you might have a new set of troubles just ahead—we can't tell, can we ?—but you wouldn't have to wonder where next month's rent was coming from."

Teddy took a sudden step forward. An instant later he felt an arm round his neck and he was jerked back. In a flash he thought, This is it. Dawlish was right, Prentice was right, it could be to-night and it could be you. The suddenness of the attack had taken him completely by surprise, he stumbled and his head hit the kerb. For an instant everything went dark. Then a voice said, " I say. Lucky for you I was there. That lorry . . ."

" Lorry ? " said Teddy in a faraway voice. " I never saw a lorry."

" I know you didn't, but you were standing right in its path. It went round the corner there. The driver ought to be had up for dangerous driving. Don't believe it even stopped. Wait a minute and I'll see."

His footsteps vanished in the mist. Teddy stayed where he was, the chill rain soaking slowly through his clothes. His head was ringing. Had there been a lorry ? How was it he hadn't seen it ? Of course. No lights. But in that case how had the other chap seen it ? There's nothing wrong with my hearing, he thought resentfully, unaware that he was speaking aloud.

A different voice answered him. It was Prentice, who had just come out of The Bunch of Grapes.

" What on earth's up, old chap ? "

" Lorry," said Teddy indistinctly. " Nearly bowled me over. If it hadn't been for that chap . . ."

" What chap ? "

" Some fellow trying to make a touch. Saved my life really."

Prentice looked down at him quizzically. " Where did *you* start to-night ? " he demanded. " There's no lorry here."

" It went round the corner."

" Where did it come from ? "

Teddy stared. What a damfool question. " Up there, of course."

" That's a cul-de-sac. It can't have been coming from there. Look here, Lane, you'd better get to bed. I'll give you a hand."

" You don't believe there was a lorry ? " Now he was angry again.

" Of course there wasn't a lorry. Any more than there was another chap. . . ."

" There was another chap all right." But suddenly he felt sick. Prentice had spoken the truth. No lorry could have been coming down the street. That meant the fellow had invented it and . . .

" Wait till that fellow comes back," he said truculently. " Fellow who pulled me out of its path, I mean."

" I'll be waiting here till to-morrow morning if I do. Do pull yourself together, old boy, and get back to your flat before you're run in for being D. and D. There's no lorry and no other man."

Visited by a sudden appalling suspicion Teddy thrust his hand into his breast pocket. It was as he suspected. His note-case was gone. So it had all been a hoax, the chap was just a common or garden sneak-thief, he'd been had. Or— was it really as simple as that ? Did his enemies mean to ensure that he couldn't get away from London ? Or was it just the beginning of the torture ? He didn't know. He shook Prentice's hand off his arm and went into the Mansions. Thank goodness he'd only taken one of his three pounds into the public-house. He wasn't quite destitute.

As he shut his door behind him the first thing he saw was the card lying beside the telephone.

> In the midst of life we are in death.
> Prepare to meet thy God.

CHAPTER FIVE

THE WHEEL SPINS

THERE WAS A MAN leaning against the lamp-post again the next morning, but Teddy paid no attention to him. There was usually someone there, and if he had been put to watch Teddy Lane, then let him have a run for his money. That Monday morning was fine and gay, with blue skies and plumy clouds. Teddy dressed with particular care and went down the stairs. He avoided the lift, remembering that they sometimes go wrong and pitch people into shafts ; anyway, he didn't want to meet Moxon. He didn't, in point of fact, see Moxon, but the porter saw him and as he crossed the hall nodded towards a tall broad-shouldered stranger who was easing his shoulders against the wall. Teddy glanced at him suspiciously—the stranger, that is—the time had come when he hadn't an ounce of trust to spare for anyone—but the man paid no heed, and Teddy hurried out into the sunshine. He set off briskly in the direction of Piccadilly and presently the clear air and the sense of a new day began to dispel his terrors. He decided to stop at Blackie's Coffee House for a cup of their famous brew, while he glanced through the paper. All manner of people migrated to Blackie's, and in time past it had proved if not a happy certainly a prosperous hunting-ground for him. Once he had eavesdropped on a conversation between two women who naturally hadn't imagined they were overheard, and his profits from that had kept him quite comfortably for nearly six months. He knew, if amateurs did not, that it's never safe to go by appearances ; smart people may be broke, demure ones be rakes or ne'er-do-wells. Who, for example, would suspect Alice Tempest of cherishing a secret worth, at a conservative estimate, five hundred pounds ? Teddy had wisdom of a kind ; when a victim had paid his price he was thereafter immune. Like lightning, Teddy never struck twice in the same place.

He had almost reached Blackie's when something happened that dispelled all his new-found assurance. He had stopped at one of the new pedestrian crossings, where the traffic came briskly up and down. He let more than one chance of crossing go by ; he liked to hold up some large and important car, it gave him a momentary sense of power. So that he teetered on the kerb until he saw an imposing vehicle bearing down upon him. Then casually, hand upflung, he sauntered into the road.

Someone gave a shout and he glanced up. To his horror he realised that the juggernaut wasn't going to stop. It was coming straight at him ; he took a frantic leap backward and stumbled in the gutter. Someone caught his arm.

" You must be tired of life," observed a sour voice.

Teddy didn't speak ; his eyes were on the big car that had been compelled to stop by the lights, and his heart seemed to fall through his body, for he saw the huge shoulders, the powerful hands, the black hat worn aslant.

" Ames ! " he whispered to himself. " He meant to get me."

" I don't know what you're talking about," ejaculated the man at his side. " But if you want to get out why don't you jump off a bridge like a gentleman ? It's bad enough driving in London traffic as it is."

" He made a dead set at me," cried Teddy, hotly, shaking off the delaying arm. Then, as he lifted his eyes, he knew a fresh throb of terror. For this was the man who had been hanging about in the hall of the Mansions not an hour ago ! He was convinced of it. He'd been trailing him, and you could be sure he had no good purpose in mind in doing that.

" Let go my arm," he exclaimed, wrenching ineffectually at the other man's hand. " Why are you persecuting me ? "

" There's gratitude for you. I save your perishing life and that's all you have to say. Chaps like you shouldn't go out without their keepers."

" I saw you just now," insisted Teddy. " You were in the hall." It occurred to him that most likely this was also his assailant of the night before. The theft of the wallet had been an act. And he was pretty sure this was the man who had telephoned and told him he hadn't got much time left.

The man shrugged. " Barmy. Haven't you got anyone to look after you ? "

A second man detached himself from the little crowd that had collected on the spot. " I am a doctor," he said. " Perhaps I can be of assistance. I'm going along to the hospital now." He gestured towards his car that was parked in a side-turning.

" I don't want any hospital," cried Teddy. " I'm perfectly well."

And at once, like some malicious parrot repeating what it has once heard, an echo rang in his brain. " Make the most of it. You haven't much time left."

" He tried to do for himself," put in a paper-seller from his pitch at the corner.

" I simply tried to cross the road," Teddy protested.

" He hung about for ages waiting for a big car," volunteered a woman passer-by. Oh, they were all against him. " Ought to be shut up," she added.

Shut up! Nothing would suit his enemies better. Clap him into a cell and get him certified. Not that he believed this fellow was a doctor, of course. He simply wanted to coax Teddy into his car and whirl him off somewhere where no one could guess his whereabouts. He took advantage of a momentary change of lights to dash across the road and mingle with the crowd by the park gates. He was terrified of feeling a hand on his shoulder, even of seeing a policeman loom up, but he reached Blackie's and got inside without any further trouble. The café was particularly full that morning. The only empty seat he could see was at a small table near the wall ; one of the two chairs was already occupied by a woman reading a newspaper. All that could be seen of her was a neat round black hat with a little grey feather in it. Teddy pulled out the opposite chair and sat down. She paid no attention to him at all, simply went on reading her paper. He ordered coffee and biscuits and pulled out his cigarette-case. The waitress brought the woman her coffee and she, without taking her eyes off the sheet that hung between them, fumbled in her bag and brought out a little tube of white pellets. But she didn't tip any of them into her cup, just sat there, her eyes glued to the newspaper. Teddy pulled *his* paper out of his pocket and stared at it, without seeing anything. He was still badly shaken by what had just happened. In due course his coffee came, and the waitress set it down alongside the other cup. He was just going to move it closer to himself when he saw a large capable hand come stealing round the side of the newspaper the woman held, and in the hand was the uncorked phial of white tablets. He watched in a sort of fascination. The tube tilted, three or four pellets slid into the cup nearest him, then the hand was withdrawn. Teddy was staggered by the neatness and audacity of it. He didn't know what was in the phial, but he felt sure it was something he didn't want in his cup of coffee. Putting out his hand he swiftly changed the position of the cups. The head behind the newspaper moved ; beneath the little black hat he saw a squarish white forehead and grey eyes as direct as—as torpedoes, he thought vaguely. And then before she could remove the paper entirely or take up her cup he was on his feet, with an incoherent mutter, the coffee and biscuits untouched, the cigarette unsmoked, and was retracing his way hotfoot between the tables. Because it hadn't been an accident, she hadn't in her absorption tipped the pellets into the wrong cup (as naturally she would pretend if he accused her), it was a deliberate attempt against his life. He was convinced of it. He dropped a shilling at the cash-desk as he hurried out.

" Why didn't I realise from the start ? " he muttered. Mrs. Tempest, that's who it was. Those hard grey eyes, that resolute glance belonged to the most ruthless of his enemies. Not that he really blamed himself for not recognising her at once. For one thing, he hadn't anticipated finding her there, and for another he had only seen her once, and she had looked like scores of other women of her age and build. In fact, he could have passed her in the street without being sure of her identity. But not now, not now that he was the victim of a monstrous plot. Two attempts on his life within the hour couldn't be mere coincidence. His hands shook so he was afraid of attracting attention, so he hurriedly bought a midday edition and leaned against the park railings staring at it. He didn't see a word on the printed sheet, he was wondering what on earth he'd better do next.

" Feeling better ? " inquired a voice in his ear, and there was his original persecutor, the man who had so absurdly claimed to have saved his life, caught up with him again. " Hadn't you better go home in a taxi ? You might have another turn, and next time you mightn't be so lucky."

Teddy dropped the paper and said brutally, " Who the hell are you ? "

The man's brows lifted. " My name's Plunkett, if that means anything to you."

It didn't, naturally, and one of the chap's strong points was that, like Mrs. Tempest, he looked like so many other people. Like those enterprising beasts, certain hares and stone martens who turn white in winter and resume a brown coat in the spring, he melted into his surroundings. Keep him on the run, Ames had said, and that was precisely what he was doing. A policeman came by and in an agony of nervous irritation Teddy turned to him.

"Can't you stop this chap from annoying me ? " he asked.

"What's the trouble ? " inquired the bobby, stolidly.

"Gentleman nearly got himself run over just now," said Plunkett in an equally stolid tone. " He's not well."

Teddy couldn't see his own face, didn't realise how his features were working, though he could feel the sweat tingling on his brow.

"I'd be all right if you'd leave me alone," he declared.

A woman walked past, without a glance for the little group, a woman in a small round black hat with a neat little grey feather at one side ; she behaved as though none of them existed, but Teddy knew her at once. She was the woman who had shared his table at Blackie's. And he knew, too, why she had chosen a seat in the farther corner of the room and kept the paper in front of her face. Because she had obviously been in some appalling accident quite recently. There was a scar twisting her mouth, giving her a hideous lopsided appearance. At close quarters she was no more like Mrs. Tempest than the policeman.

"Chap's right," thought Teddy, panic-stricken. " I am ill. If I'm not careful I shall develop persecution mania, and we all know where that ends." Chaps either went off their rockers (even in his thoughts Teddy employed the slang terms of his youth) or they started trying to get their own back, and found themselves in the dock on a murder charge.

The two men with him had also been struck by that disfigured face, and it distracted their attention from himself for an instant. Taking advantage of that, he twisted like an eel and vanished down the steps of the underground station. The constable shrugged.

"So long as he can keep his feet there's nothing I can do about it," he said.

Plunkett nodded. He didn't follow Teddy down the steps ; he knew where he was going—back to Ellison Mansions. He hailed a taxi and gave the driver the address.

Teddy hurried down the steps and waited by the automatic machines, feeling for the necessary coppers. The Tempest episode had shaken him more than he liked to admit. Because if he could make one mistake, why not two ? Was he, then, absolutely certain it had been Harmsworth Ames in the car ? Might he not have been deceived by another surface likeness ? After all, he reminded himself he hadn't actually seen the fellow's face, only the immense shoulders, the slouched black hat, the ostentatious car, characteristic of the man. But was that enough ? And suppose he had been wrong ? Suppose he was panicking for nothing ? The telephone call might have been a poor sort of practical joke; the card was explained by Dawlish's fanaticism.

To his surprise he saw an unoccupied telephone box and he hurried into it and dialled Ames's number. A voice, that certainly didn't belong to the Q.C., said curtly that Mr. Ames was out of town, was not expected back before tomorrow. Teddy stammered something about an appointment that morning, but the voice said there was a mistake, Mr. Ames had left London early the day before. Teddy hung up. He didn't leave a name. Only a private matter, he said. Nothing important really. He didn't get a ticket, after all, remembering Gerald Ross's warning about accidents on tube platforms, and travelled back by bus. There was another man leaning against the lamp-post, but by now Teddy had decided he'd been hypersensitive, there was always someone there, not likely to be anything to do with him. When he had seen Teddy go inside the flats Plunkett straightened himself and went down to the corner where he bought some cigarettes and wondered how long before the next move.

Moxon was in the hall when Teddy entered and he said at once, " Parcel come for you, Mr. Lane. I've got it here," and handed it over. It was a square box and there was nothing to show from the outside where it had come from or who was the sender. He opened it in his flat to discover a pound of chocolates from the most famous shop in town. He flipped off the lid ; the sight of them made his mouth water, they were so glossy, so decorative with their crystallised violets and rose-leaves. There was no card inside the box, and the label had been written by hand, in printed capitals, which was surely suspicious in itself. He remembered Alice Tempest —would he ever get the woman out of his mind ?—warning him against chocolates sent through the post. He took one out of the box and examined it carefully. It wasn't difficult, he'd been given to understand, to drill a minute hole in the bottom and squirt in a little poison. Then you filled up the hole with chocolate, and it wouldn't be obvious to anyone who wasn't looking for clues that it had been tampered with.

He examined three or four of the sweets but he could find nothing to justify his suspicion. All the same, that didn't mean he was going to be caught so easily. Because there was some reason for sending them, and he was pretty sure it wasn't love. No one felt like that about Teddy Lane. No, it would be one of the four, and the only question was—which ? It was a woman's trick, and he didn't believe Mrs. Tempest would go to Jay & Jessop. Julia, on the other hand, regularly bought chocolates there ; and didn't they say no woman made a worse enemy than one who had been a previous lover ?

Someone had been rattling the letter-box for some instants, but he had been too much engrossed with the chocolates to hear. Now the flap was lifted and a voice called wheezily, " Mr. Lane. Mr. Lane, ain't you in ? "

He drew a deep breath of relief. He recognised the voice as belonging to the old crone who cleaned the place for him in a desultory fashion. He opened the door and she came marching in like a brisk old beetle.

" Mr. Moxon told me you was here," she said. " Well, you 'aven't wasted much time keeping the place clean, I must say."

Teddy muttered something about hoping she was better, and she said, " Dessay I shall get over it." She hung her old coat and hat on a peg, shuffled into carpet slippers and came into the living-room.

" Coo ! Look at them ! " Her greedy old eyes were fixed on the chocolates. " Someone's loving you to-day, Mr. Lane."

She wants one, thought Teddy. He couldn't tell her they might be poisoned, she'd be like all the rest, think he was going crazy. And if he refused, she'd think he was mean.

" Help yourself," he suggested, watching her intently. She spooned up three or four in her crooked old fingers and thrust them into her mouth.

" I'm not feeling any too good myself this morning," Teddy explained. " Just give this room a lick and a polish and wash the crocks and that'll do."

He went into the bedroom and shut the door. The more he thought about it the more probable it seemed that Julia had sent the box. She was the only one of the four who knew what a sweet tooth he had. At the Ambulance Station she used to give him half her sweet ration and her share of the sugar at tea-time. Mrs. Tempest wouldn't know, neither of the men would know. So it had to be Julia. He couldn't be sure if it was old love or wounded vanity that struck like a physical chill at the thought that she, too, wouldn't stop short of murder.

He was still considering this, shocked and dejected, when the handle of the door turned. " I'm going now, Mr. Lane," said the old woman's voice. " To tell you the truth, I've come over queer all of a sudden, and your own place is best when you feel like that."

Teddy was aghast. He didn't doubt for an instant that this sudden change was due to the chocolates. Suppose she died, he wondered, trembling, would he be held responsible ? How was I to know they'd been tampered with ? he asked himself angrily. He encouraged the old woman to go home. Much the best place, he said heartily. Thank goodness he hadn't tasted the sweets. As soon as Mrs. Carr had changed back into her downtrodden shoes and replaced her travesty of a hat on her grey head, he sent her down in the lift, causing her to think, Fancy, he has got a heart after all. Opening the door for me and everything. Teddy's main preoccupation had been to see her off the premises. He gave her five minutes' start, and then, wrapping the chocolates in their brown paper covering, he tucked the parcel under his arm and came cautiously down the stairs. He knew that at this hour Moxon would be having what Bertha Moxon called his tea and unscrupulous brewers labelled beer. Hurrying on his way Teddy reached Cambridge Circus, turned into a by-street and found himself outside a chemist's shop with the name, P. Morell over the door. It was a narrow, shoddy little place, very appropriate to Morell. Teddy had got his hand on the door and the man behind the counter had actually seen him before he realised that this was no place for him to seek advice at the present time. He had made his way here as instinctively as a homing pigeon, so full of apprehensions about his own physical safety that he had forgotten his intention to avoid Morell like poison until he was in a position to straighten things out. As the phrase " like poison " passed through his mind, he gave a start. There it was again, the fatal word. It looked as though he couldn't get away from it.

Morell had a customer, but he jerked his head at Teddy which meant that he'd be free in a minute. Teddy looked at a lot of patent mixtures, aperients and digestive remedies and innocent sleeping-tablets. The customer was one of the fussy kind, asking innumerable questions, but at last even she went. Morell threw open a door at the back of the shop.

" Come in here ! " and, as Teddy obeyed, he shut the door and said sharply : " Well, I hope you've come to square things up. It's about time."

Teddy had been thinking fast during the minute or so he had had to wait. He knew Morell to be unreasonable, ungenerous and ruthless. Somehow he had got to jolly him along, make him think everything was all right.

" I've got some news for you," he announced importantly.

" News can wait," said Morell in curt tones. " I want the money."

" Oh—the money." The phrase slipped out before Teddy could amend it. " This is what you'll want to hear." He leaned forward, his expression very intent. " I believe I've touched a new source of supply—fellow called Lloyd."

Even Morell in his present mood couldn't pretend that wasn't pretty important. With the authorities working twenty-four hours a day to put down the drug traffic it was becoming increasingly difficult to lay hands on sufficient illicit supplies to cope with the demand. If Teddy really had found a new source and wasn't bluffing—and Morell had as little faith in his partner as Teddy himself—then it might be wise to relegate the question of the money outstanding to some more convenient time.

" You're sure it's safe ? " he demanded.

Teddy shrugged. " There's always a soupçon of risk, but if you want to be safe you'll have to wait till you're on your death-bed." He was startled to hear himself say the words. It was as if he couldn't escape that fatal word.

" How far has it gone ? " asked Morell.

" I've had to pay out in advance," said Teddy slowly. " I should have either the stuff or the money (if the deal falls through, that is) by Saturday."

Morell sent him a keen, sly look. " It sounds a bit fishy to me. Sure you've haven't walked into an ambush ? "

That was precisely what Teddy felt he had done, though not in the circumstances Morell envisaged.

" I've told you," he said in a more irritable voice, " it's a chance. But we can't afford not to take chances. To hear you one would imagine cocaine grew on trees."

" Quiet," said Morell in a low furious tone. " Do you want to get us both jugged ? The very word's dynamite."

" I didn't imagine you had a pick-up machine in your wall," murmured Teddy, smoothly. He felt suddenly in command of the situation. He had contacts Morell couldn't hope to achieve, and in his furtive way he went about a good deal, and he knew to a nicety how to peddle the minute packets in bars and cinemas and at cocktail parties given for the purpose. There were other ways, too, of passing it. Inside playing cards, for instance; experts could insert a pinch of the stuff between the two parts of the card and only certain of the cards were treated. They'd tried all kinds of dodges, mixing pellets with the genuine article in tubes of aspirin, the drugged tablets bearing a minute distinguishing mark known to the purchaser. It was the most paying racket in which Teddy had ever been engaged, much more paying than black market butter or smuggled nylons.

Morell accepted the situation with mistrust. " We must hope for the best," he said, " but, I warn you, if you were thinking of double-crossing me it wouldn't be healthy."

" What would you do ? " asked Teddy, with a chuckle. " Go to the police ? I don't think so. You'd get ten years."

Morell turned an ugly whitish colour. " Is that a threat ? " He came closer and put a hand on Teddy's arm. " Don't forget you'd be in the same boat."

" Perhaps I can swim," Teddy murmured.

Morell knew what that meant. He might turn King's Evidence, and get off with a light sentence, might even pass the buck altogether. The police were getting properly rattled about the increase in the drug traffic. It was spreading in all classes of the community, slipping back, they feared, to the hectic twenties when even the young became addicts. No, thought Morell, deliberately, he's right. I can't afford to get on the wrong side of him. Best thing would be to cut clear. But that was more easy to say than to perform. Still, Teddy had no actual evidence, simply his word against Morell's. So far as the latter knew the police had nothing on him. Morell plumped for diplomacy.

" No sense upsetting the boat," he murmured. " What have you got under your arm ? "

" Something I'd like you to have a look at," said Teddy easily. He unwrapped the box. " These came through the post this morning, no letter, no card. And I don't believe in taking unnecessary risks."

" Can't you take a guess where they come from ? " asked Morell bluntly.

" That's just the point," said Teddy in slow tones. " I can. And seeing that women have no sense of morality . . ."

Crook wouldn't have agreed with him there. He'd have said of course they have a moral code, but it's a type that drives men scatty.

" Sure it's a woman ? How about the husband ? "

Teddy coloured up at the insolent tone. He'd sunk pretty low, and he knew it, but he still resented the fact that a man, like Morell, who had come up from the gutter (in Teddy's outdated phrase) should be in a position to address him in that tone of voice.

" There's no question of the husband being involved," he said haughtily. " But I'd like some reassurance these haven't been tampered with."

Morell laughed, an unpleasant sound. " Can't be too careful," he agreed, " especially a valuable life like yours."

Teddy drew a breath so sharp it was almost a whistle. Valuable ? His life ? Why, it scarcely amounted to more than permission to breathe, and any minute now even that permission might be withdrawn.

" I'll come back to-night for the verdict," he said as carelessly as he could, but Morell, casually putting the box down, said : " Better wait till the morning. Or I'll ring you. No sense your attracting attention coming here twice in one day."

Teddy blundered out into the sunshine. It was a lovely morning with a hot sun and the streets were full of hawkers' barrows blazing with colour. Two women went past, one saying with the cheerful pessimism of her kind, " We shall have to pay for this, you mark my words." And again the casual phrase gnawed at his vitals. Wherever he looked, it seemed to him danger beckoned.

" I must get away from London," he thought in a panic. The country might not promise absolute security, but surely if he kept away from cliff-tops and didn't go sailing or swimming, if he avoided solitary paths and deep woods, refused drinks from strangers and lifts from large handsome men in large handsome cars, turned a deaf ear to elderly women who has lost Fido or Rover, and refused to provide anyone with a

light or tell some phony foreigner the time.—" Why," exclaimed Teddy, the tears actually coming into his eyes, " I
don't believe there's any safety anywhere."

And like an answer the voice of someone going past said
clearly, " Safe as the grave." That was coincidence again,
but it shook him. Because it did begin to look as though
the grave might be the only solution, and though he didn't
believe any of the claptrap his clergyman father had preached
steadfastly for half a century, he was terrified of death.

CHAPTER SIX

SOCIABLE DEATH

THE AFTERNOON was comparatively quiet. No one rang up,
but at four o'clock the silence was punctured by a commercial
traveller selling crematorium premiums. Twelve payments
and you could be burned without further expense to your
relatives.

Teddy said coldly he had no relatives and he wasn't proposing to pass out to suit a society that, he asserted libellously,
lived by exploiting the dead.

" Better be sure than sorry," urged the man, not in the
least put out by Teddy's attitude. He looked rather as
though he had been dug up for the express purpose of going
round and putting terror in the hearts of still-living men.
" No one can tell when the call will come. It might even be
to-night."

Teddy wasn't as disturbed as he would have been a week
ago. He didn't believe it was coincidence that someone should
try to sell him burial rights on the instalment plan, he was
sure it was part of his tormentor's plot to break his nerve.
There was no message from Morell, but late that evening the
telephone rang and he answered the summons, thinking it
probably was the chemist. But it was a woman's voice at the
other end of the line. He recognised it at once, and almost
wept with relief because it wasn't one of the four. Lucille
Morton was a woman of practically his own age with whom
he had been associated in various ways for a number of years.
They had shamelessly made use of each other as occasion

demanded. Because she might be able to help him now
Teddy made his voice cordial and flattering.

" Why, darling, how are you ? I haven't heard from you
in an age."

" Does that mean the chockies never arrived ? "

He was so much relieved that he began to laugh. " So
that's where they came from ? " But the next moment he
was angry. Why couldn't the fool have put in a card and
saved him all this anguish ? But he knew she liked to play
at being coy, which wasn't suitable in a woman of fifty.

" Do you mean to say those silly people didn't put my note
in ? I was wondering why you hadn't rung me up."

He thought cynically he might have guessed. Nobody
gave you anything, not even a box of chocolates, without
expecting a return.

" Something cooking ? " he asked.

" Oh, just a cocktail party to-morrow night. I thought it
might amuse you to come with me."

He understood now. Lucille Morton had had her share of
social success in the days when she wouldn't have crossed the
road to speak to Teddy Lane, but she was rising fifty now,
had played her cards badly, let two husbands slip through her
fingers, but was still scornful of women who went to parties
alone or dined and did a theatre with another woman. Fortunately she had plenty of money ; she could afford to buy
her favours. It seemed to Teddy she might prove the answer
to his sordid prayer. He needed money to get away, and
he'd got to get away for a few days to give himself a chance
to pull himself together. It wouldn't be the first time Lucille
had made him one of those loans that are never repaid. So
now he said sweetly, " Heaven, darling. What time shall
I call for you ? "

When he had rung off he thought with a stab of relief that
now he needn't revisit Morell. The chocolates were O.K. He
dismissed them from his mind and began to calculate how
much he could touch the old girl for. Even a tenner would
be better than nothing. Or he might stumble on something
good at the party. He never refused invitations like these,
even when they only arrived at the eleventh hour. You never
knew what contacts you might make.

He called for her the following evening in a taxi for which,
both understood, she would pay. It had been a quiet day, so
quiet that his suspicions were aroused. True, he had stayed

indoors and told Moxon he had a migraine, didn't want any calls put through and all visitors to be intercepted, but it seemed odd that these simple precautions should win him so much temporary relief. He looked round him cautiously as he came down soon after six o'clock, but no one seemed to be hanging about, and the taxi-driver wasn't a thug in disguise. Lucille greeted him with her usual shrill exuberance, asked how he was getting on without waiting for an answer, and said, " Gadding about as usual, I suppose. What a thing it is to be a gay bachelor," for she was as *vieux jeu* as Teddy himself.

Teddy said it was swings and roundabouts and everyone was in the doldrums just now, anyway, but he was careful not to overdo it. He wanted her to ask him back for a snack, and then he could open his campaign. The party was like all the others he had ever been to with her, crowded because nowadays people gladly accepted practically any invitation, life had got so dull and money was so tight, and as soon as she recognised someone she knew Lucille swam away from him like a rather hippy goldfish, and Teddy looked round with a glance that would have made a razor seem blunt. His earlier experience as a gigolo, paid escort, dancing-partner, however you liked to call it, stood him in good stead. He had been bred to believe that you had to sing for your supper, particularly if your tastes were oysters and champagne, and he sang with all his heart and so successfully that his hostess, who had thought him a dreadful little man at first sight, even a bit down-at-heel, changed her views. Probably he was only eccentric, she decided. Teddy had a nice line of patter, and at parties like these there were always solitary women who come in the hope that something exciting will happen ; for the most part they spend the evening propping a wall and looking unnaturally bright. Teddy was Heaven's gift to all such ; he brought them drinks and reminisced and made them feel they really had immense capacities that somehow life hadn't given them a chance to develop. His hostess felt grateful to him for the trouble he was taking ; it couldn't be much fun for him. However, he netted a couple of in-vitations for parties a week hence, and was just noting details of the second in his little diary when a buoyant voice at his elbow exclaimed, " I say, don't you want a drink ? "

He turned quickly, fear never far away, and saw an attrac-tive girl of about eighteen, carrying a glass in each hand.

" I'm supposed to be helping to look after people," she

confided. " No, this glass, I've been drinking out of the other." She saw him take the glass and went on, " I suppose you know everybody here. I've never been to a cocktail party before."

She laughed as she spoke ; she wasn't a beauty but she had a clear complexion and lovely teeth ; her hair gleamed from brushing, not from something out of a bottle. She made Teddy feel shop-soiled, bargain basement : a second-hand feeling. But he drove that out, and said, " You mustn't waste your opportunities, you know."

" I came with my cousin," she confided. " His wife couldn't make it, and I was dying to test a theory of mine, so I made Sandy bring me."

" What theory ? " He finished the drink and took another from a tray a waiter was offering. The girl did the same, but he saw that she sipped cautiously. Obviously she wasn't accustomed to alcohol and didn't mean to make a fool of herself.

" We were talking about murder," she said, and Teddy started and a little of the drink slopped over on to the floor. " I told Sandy I was sure it wasn't as difficult as people make out."

" Oh, I've always understood murder *per se* was simple enough," Teddy agreed. " It's not getting found out that's hard."

" Well, but my idea—anyway, see what you think of it. You wait till your enemy and you get asked to the same party—you couldn't do it in your own house, I quite see that—and you take some sleeping tablets with you, enough for a fatal dose. You'd crush them, I think, unless you could get them in very minute pellets and could be certain they'd melt, but personally I'm all for crushing them. Well, you wait for your opportunity and presently you put your powder into a drink, and you offer the glass to the person you mean to get rid of. Nobody suspects there's anything wrong—look how you took the drink I gave you. It never occurred to you it might be poisoned, did it ? "

" It did not." He smiled. " But then you're not my enemy. If I thought you had it in for me for any reason I should be a lot more careful."

" I'd thought of that." Her eagerness was rather charming. " Naturally I wouldn't bring it you myself. I should tell someone, someone like me, that is, if you understand what I mean, to take it across. Naturally it wouldn't be one of those sudden poisons ; you wouldn't want the person to drop dead on the spot. The odds are he'd never know he'd been murdered. He'd go home and go to sleep and just not wake up again. And everyone would think he'd committed suicide."

" Always assuming he had a motive."

" Oh, practically anyone can cook that up. Suppose it was you, for instance. You might be in debt or in trouble with the police, or your wife might have left you ; or, say, you were being blackmailed and couldn't pay up and didn't dare go to the police. Besides, haven't you noticed there's always someone who comes forward to say you've been very depressed lately, and as your real enemy would make a point of not even speaking to you at the party he'd never be suspected at all."

" You seem to have thought of everything," Teddy congratulated her. " What made you pick me as a victim ? "

" I didn't," acknowledged the girl, candidly. " Sandy put the glass into my hand and said : ' Give it to that chap with the Leander tie leaning against the mantelpiece. Don't let anyone else have it.' " She laughed joyously. " If someone had tried to take it from me I suppose I should have had to upset it, and that would have annoyed my hostess."

Teddy laughed at her enthusiasm. Actually, he wasn't wearing a Leander tie, but it was like enough for anyone but an expert to make the mistake. It didn't do to wear the real thing at a party like this ; you might get asked inconvenient questions, and as it happened there was a chap with the genuine article among the guests.

" You make it all sound very sinister," he said.

" Have I made your flesh creep ? Do you begin to wonder —shall I really wake up to-morrow ? "

" Of course not. But you're a very neat little actress. You'd probably do well on the stage."

" Oh no ! " She seemed not merely surprised, but actually scornful of the idea. " I'm studying for my science degree. Then Sandy's going to winkle me in at the foot of the ladder."

Teddy sighed. He couldn't understand women these days. A girl like this should be thinking about having a good time. She spoke again. " There's Sandy raising his eyebrows at me. That means it's time for me to go. Good-bye. If you wake up dead in the morning you'll know what's happened, won't you ? "

She held out her hand, and then he watched her neatly threading her way across the room. The man she called Sandy was waiting by the door, and he half-turned as she came up. For the first time Teddy saw his face, and the shock, the disbelief, the sheer terror made him stumble, the little glass fell out of his hand and rolled on to the floor where a scornful waiter picked it up. Because Sandy was Gerald Ross, who now met his eyes with a stony gaze as though they'd never set eyes on one another before.

"Hold up," said a voice in his ear, and he knew they thought he was drunk. He tried to speak, but even to himself his voice was unfamiliar. He tried to move, but his feet seemed to be on roller-skates, they slipped about and when he moved his arms they struck against someone standing near. He wanted to shout, Clear the way! Clear the way! I've got to get back at once, I've been poisoned. Poisoned, do you understand ? *Poisoned !*

He saw Lucille coming towards him across the room. Her face was furious with disgust. She said in a loud voice, " I told you you shouldn't come out so soon after flu. They'll get you a taxi. You must go straight home."

But she didn't offer to come with him.

When he spoke his voice was furry as velvet. " Feeling faint," he buzzed. " Heat of the room. Got to get back." He executed a sort of dive into the company.

" You'll be better in the fresh air," insisted Lucille, and he saw two or three of the nearer guests exchange glances he could interpret without any trouble at all.

Anger rose in him like milk frothing up in a saucepan. " I've been poisoned," he shouted.

Lucille looked as if she should have killed him where he stood. He thought confusedly that any hope of borrowing money in that direction could be abandoned. Not that he'd need money unless he acted pretty fast.

" Nonsense, Teddy," she said clearly. " You don't know what you're saying. I'll find Mrs. Latham and explain you've been taken bad. Now go straight to bed and get that man of yours to ring up a doctor."

Somehow he got out of the room ; a manservant gave him a hat and he managed to snatch it, though it was waving about like something in a goldfish bowl, and he clapped it anyhow on his head and pushed forward as though an army were barring his way. The servant said, " Shall I call you a taxi, sir ? " but he shook his head and thrust past, against the rushing tides and the bells ringing in his ears and the anonymous army that tried to prevent his escape, and there was a clash, and that was the front door closing, and at last, at last he was alone in the dark. He ran into the dark as if it were a familiar house that would put walls all round him.

He hadn't gone far, reeling all over the road, when a policeman popped up from nowhere and asked him if he was all right.

" Bit faint," muttered Teddy. If he told this chap the truth, that he'd been poisoned, they'd run him in for being intoxicated and by the time the doctors got round to the truth he'd be dead, or as good as. So, " Of course I'm all right," insisted Teddy Lane. And anyway, he told himself, this wasn't a real policeman, any more than the taxi, that would turn round the corner in another minute, would be a genuine taxi.

As he thought this the taxi turned the corner, and was immediately hailed by the policeman. Just like a play, reflected Teddy Lane, all the characters jumping in on their cues. Only, as it happened, he wasn't accepting his part, didn't mean to tie up with the plot. So, when the policeman said, " Gentleman taken poorly " and then, to Teddy: " What's your address, sir ? " instead of stepping meekly into the cab Teddy reared back, exclaiming, " I don't want any taxi. Don't be so damned officious ! "

The taxi-driver said briskly, " And I don't want any trouble, if that's the way it is," and stepped on the accelerator.

Teddy stared after him, deeply perplexed. Was that line in the script ? If you didn't know the whole world was your enemy and in a plot to murder you, you'd say the fellow was genuine.

Somehow, shaking off the constable, he got himself home and up by the lift. He mixed himself a dose of mustard and water, and the effect of that almost knocked him out for two hours. But he ensured there was no poison, and precious little else, left inside him.

As he lurched out of the bathroom he saw an envelope on the mat and gingerly picked it up. Inside was a sheet of black paper with red letters on it. The letters wavered and blinked at him.

Have You made your Will?

they inquired.

" It worked beautifully," said Gerald Ross's cousin, as they made their way back from the party. " If there had been any poison in the glass he'd be found dead in the morning. I told you I was sure everything would go smoothly."

" If ever you put the idea into practice," Gerald murmured, " be sure you get the right man. I told you the chap in the Leander tie. I didn't even know the other fellow was there."

He said it in a meditative voice of so much meaning that his young cousin looked at him in surprise.

" You said that as though you knew the other one. You didn't, did you ? "

Gerald laughed. " What I was thinking was that if ever I wanted to poop a chap off you've given me quite a useful idea of the way it could be done," he said.

Teddy woke the next day as weak as a cat ; though it was quite early the telephone was ringing.

" What happened to you last night ? " asked Morell's voice. " I thought you were coming in for the report on the chocolates."

" Oh, I had to go out," said Teddy as airily as he could manage. " Anyhow, I found out where they came from, so I knew they were O.K."

" Didn't occur to you you might let me know and save me the trouble of doing a post-mortem ? No, it wouldn't, of course. Never mind. Let it ride. I wanted a word with you about what you were saying when you were in last."

Teddy felt his face stiffen. " That's O.K.," he said sharply.

" Any developments ? "

" Not yet. I told you, the end of the week."

" That's all very well," grumbled Morell, " but are you sure you're not being taken for a ride ? "

" I tell you, it'll be all right."

" Who is this fellow ? Where did you meet him ? "

" You don't expect me to tell you that on the telephone, do you ? I tell you, you've nothing to worry about."

" I'll look in tonight," said Morell, but Teddy said in desperate tones : " It won't be any good. I shall be away."

" Leaving London ? "

" I didn't say that. Just that I shall be out. Besides, I don't think it would be wise for you to come round."

" How come ? " Morell's voice was thick with suspicion. Even the distortion due to a poor line couldn't muffle that.

" If this thing comes off, as of course it will, the less we're seen together the better."

" A bit late in the day to think of that, isn't it ? "

" You know what we agreed—this stuff's dynamite. I don't want to feel an official hand on my shoulder . . ."

" Getting cold feet ? " sneered Morell.

" From all I get out of it," cried Teddy in desperation, " I'm beginning to wonder if the game's worth the candle."

" My feelings exactly," returned Morell. " So far as our partnership's concerned, that is. You're about as reliable as a box of live matches."

Teddy rang off and sat there, on the edge of a fake Jacobean chest, white and sick, like an old monkey, not knowing where to turn. There was no hope of touching Lucille now ; she was mad about last night, and who else was there ? Who else ? Who else ? Who else ?

The answer was—No one. He'd even lost faith in himself, so that, though he might cry with the Psalmist, Mine enemies encompass me on every side, he could find no consolation as David had done, because for him there really was no one. It was a dreadful realisation and it left him stunned for a time. Presently he pulled himself together and brewed some black coffee and while he was drinking this Moxon came thumping at the door, with a large registered envelope in his hand.

" Second time I come up," he announced sulkily. " First time you was out to the wide." And he added, " Why don't you see a doctor, Mr. Lane ? First thing you know you'll find yourself in an ambulance."

" You must have been a raven in a previous incarnation," said Teddy, signing for the envelope. " This all there was ? "

" Ain't it enough ? " the porter demanded, and when Teddy opened it, it was. Because the envelope was stuffed with one-pound notes, fifty of them, with a bit of paper folded round them. The message on the paper was typewritten. It said :

I want you to take this and give yourself a holiday. You must realise you're on the verge of a breakdown and if you don't want to collapse you'll take my advice and

go away for a bit. Don't try and telephone, I am going
away myself.

There was no signature, but there wasn't a shadow of doubt
in his mind as to who had sent the money. Lucille had had
pretensions to journalism in her time—just my scribbling, she
would say, with an airy gesture and eyes as jealous as the little
Yellow God's—and she never wrote if she could help it.
Faulty education, darling, she'd tell you. The typewriter and
the telephone are my best friends. It was entirely typical
of her not even to have put her initials to the paper ; after
what happened last night she wouldn't want to take any
chances, and it's an uncharitable world, and people can be
quite unkind about women who are no longer young who send
money to men.
    Teddy crumpled up the bit of paper and threw it in the
basket. He had no illusions as to why the money had been
sent to him, any more than he believed Lucille was going away
herself. The obvious fact was that she had been humiliated
almost beyond endurance by his behaviour at last night's
party, wouldn't (in her own mind, at least) be able to live it
down for weeks to come, but felt it would be easier with
Teddy out of the way. It was significant that she hadn't
rung up to find out if he were really ill. Not that Teddy cared.
Suddenly a way of escape had appeared before him, he was
like the ram that got out of the thicket, his head whirled.
He knew where he'd go, a little place called Stonemarten;
he'd stayed at the hotel there some years ago and it had been
comfortable and comparatively cheap. There wouldn't be
a soul there he knew, and fifty pounds would keep him there
for several weeks at this time of the year. The season didn't
begin till June. When he came back there'd still be time to
deal with the four. In fact, he might put his threats into
action from Stonemarten, if they didn't brass up. Much
safer for him that way. He began to whistle " *Is you is or
is you ain't my baby ?* " always a sign that he was in good
spirits.
    It never occurred to him that it might suit anyone besides
Lucille Morton to have him out of town.

CHAPTER SEVEN

STILL FULL of jubilation he packed a small case, in which he secreted forty of the precious fifty pounds, gave Moxon ten shillings with a lordly air and instructions to tell visitors that he'd suddenly been called out of London, and wasn't quite sure when he'd be back, and came out into the spring sunlight.

" You don't want to forget your mac," Moxon called after him, but Teddy laughed. He wasn't going to be caught out in the rain this time, not he. But he remembered to shout back a reminder to stop the milk.

Moxon, not nearly so grateful for the ten shillings as you'd have expected, said sullenly it was too late to stop it that day ; his shrug inquired what was half a pint of milk to him ? It wasn't anything to Teddy either. Having money to throw about went to his head like wine. He took a taxi to Victoria and bought a first-class return ticket to Stonemarten. He hadn't much sense, poor Teddy Lane, and he quite forgot that money can't cure all ills. The terrors of the last few days no longer assailed him ; he didn't even wonder if he was being followed, so he didn't see Plunkett stroll along to a telephone booth and ask for further instructions.

Teddy thoroughly enjoyed the first part of the journey. He bought a paper—he'd left the *Record* in the flat but he got a lurid *Morning Pictorial* with immense headlines :

MANIAC KILLER AT LARGE ?
DEAD WOMAN IN
TRAIN MYSTERY

The police believe that Mrs. Elsie Lees, whose murdered body was found in a train in a siding, was the victim of a maniac. From recent information it is hoped to make an arrest shortly.

Teddy flipped the page over. Maniacal killers didn't bother him. It was perfectly obvious, he thought, that the chap was a sexual fiend, with a yen against women. And whatever

63

Teddy might be it wasn't a woman. No, the killers he feared were the normal kind. He bought a ticket for the first lunch and promised himself half a bottle of wine with it, and settled comfortably in the window corner. No one else invaded his carriage—worth while going first class for the privacy it bought you, he decided—and the paper was unusually interesting, printing all manner of items you never found in the *Record*. Quite soon the steward came along the corridor chanting "First lunch, please. Take your seats for first lunch," and he threw down the paper and went along to the dining-car. The food was better than he had anticipated, and the wine (he decided critically) more than drinkable.

He was rather annoyed on his return to find that someone had invaded his carriage, an ordinary sort of chap in a raincoat, wearing a bowler hat and reading a newspaper. There was nothing outwardly objectionable about him—Teddy had to admit that—but well, Teddy preferred his solitude. From behind the cover of his *Pictorial* he surveyed the intruder. He had a glossy black moustache, and glossy black hair that looked like an advertisement for haircream; he had long hands with big wrists, and he wore horn-rimmed glasses. Probably a commercial, thought Teddy, travelling on expenses, and he knew the irrational annoyance of a man who has had to pay for his ticket against a chap who was probably travelling at someone else's expense.

After several glances the stranger suddenly looked up. " I see they think this chap's somewhere in our neighbourhood," he remarked.

Teddy was so startled he could only say feebly, "Which chap ? "

" The one who did for that poor woman they found in the siding. Mind you, it's easier for the police if they say it's a maniac, and they may well be right." He spoke very seriously. " But it makes it more difficult for them. No motive, you see. Mind you, I know in law there doesn't have to be a motive, but naturally the public expects one. I mean to say, suppose you were suddenly to stick a knife into me and then hop it, who's likely to suspect you ? You've never seen me before—have you ? "

Teddy shook his head.

" That's what I mean. No reason why they should ever cotton on to you."

" Why on earth should I want to stick a knife into you ? "

asked Teddy reasonably, though to himself he thought any chap who started a silly conversation like this with a stranger was asking for trouble.

"That's my point. Answer is, of course, there's no reason. But if you're mad you're not a reasoning being. There's nothing to tie this unfortunate woman up with any killer, not so far as the police can find out. Funny thing about these maniacs," he went on chattily, "according to what a doctor in my paper says, as often as not they don't know what they've done. Run berserk for an hour, say, do for some poor wretch they've never set eyes on before, and then hey presto! they're back where they were before, nice respectable little men going back to nice respectable little suburban homes, kissing the wife and the kids, helping with the washing-up afterwards —yes, and reading about the case in the paper next day and saying, just like you or me might, 'well, there's a shocking thing.' Makes you think, don't it?"

"You seem to think a lot about it," agreed Teddy, who was beginning to feel ill-at-ease—practically anything upset him these days. "A bit morbid, I'd say."

"Oh well." The stranger smoothed his black moustache. "You might say it was my trade."

"Your trade!" Teddy sounded stupefied.

"I'm connected with a very high-class undertaker's business," the stranger explained. "A mute, really. A lot more interesting than p'raps it sounds. The things we see, going into the best houses as we do. Widows and widowers all in black, and practically dancing for joy because they're free, before the last clod's broken over the coffin. Oh yes, we could tell some funny stories, but, of course, that's not our job," he added primly. "Mum's the word's our motto. What we're there for is to clear away the remains, not to ask how they come to *be* remains."

Teddy felt as though his compartment had been invaded by a ghoul; while another part of his mind was saying, "What chances these fellows must have. The bereaved wouldn't think of them as human . . ." He paused a moment, deep in reverie. What a chance to milk the survivors, he thought. He wondered if his companion had ever thought along similar lines.

"Yours must be an entrancing life," he said with heavy irony, but the other returned in grave tones: "Well, it's like any business, isn't it? Ups and downs. But between you and me I have sometimes wondered just who we were burying. F'r instance, we got a call this morning to measure for a gentleman very highly thought of in his neighbourhood, very highly indeed. Mind you, I don't say a word against him. He may be everything they think, but—there's always the chance, isn't there, he could be the one ? " And he tapped his newspaper again.

" Come to that," exclaimed Teddy, eager to put a stop to the conversation, " there's nothing to show, is there, it wasn't you ? or me ? " he added, feeling he'd rather overplayed his hand, " except that we could probably produce alibis."

" Well, to tell you the truth I don't think I could. I was thinking that when I read the paper. But it seems to me that, in ten years, say, because if this chap's a maniac the odds are this isn't the first time he's broken out, someone would have a suspicion. Bennett's acting a bit queer to-day, they'd say —Bennett's my name, you understand. It's different for these fellows that don't make friends. I've always had a very nice circle, very nice indeed, and my wife and I entertain quite a bit. No, I'd say quite definitely I was in the clear."

" Perhaps," said Teddy wanting to put an end to this, " he isn't mad, after all."

But nothing silenced the persistent Mr. Bennett. " I suppose in a sense you could say all murderers are mad, though not, I grant you, according to the law. I read of a chap once who thought it was his duty to blot out someone who was a burden on the community, one of these big business men who, they say, are responsible for slumps and high prices and all that. Well, you might say he was mad, but the court didn't think so. I don't know anything about this Mrs. Lees, but say she had some secret in her life that made X—best to call him X, don't you agree ?—feel the world 'ud be a better place without her. No," he put up a big hand as though to stem Teddy's instinctive protests, " don't tell me that's against the law, I know it, but say there was a chap arguing along those lines, then the odds are he won't break out again. Makes it difficult for the police."

" Well, that's their job, isn't it ? " said Teddy rather disagreeably. " If nobody ever broke the law they'd be queueing up for the dole." He half-rose as if to leave the carriage. But the stranger had stretched a long leg in front of the door, almost, thought Teddy beginning to feel appalled, as though he didn't intend to be deprived of his audience.

" To my mind," Mr. Bennett went on moving as slowly and monotonously as a crippled worm, " that sort of maniac's more dangerous than the other kind. In the sense that he knows what he's doing, and he knows it's wrong—illegal, that is. The end justifying the means—a very dangerous doctrine exposed by St. Paul."

" I'm not interested in St. Paul," Teddy assured him. " And to tell you the truth, I'm not interested in this conversation. I've not been well—influenza . . ."

The stranger looked delighted. " A very depressive illness, often leaving alarming symptoms. I thought the minute I set eyes on you—he looks low. Something on his mind, I said. That's really why I entered into conversation with you. Take his mind *off* his worry, I thought."

" And I suppose you imagine that your sort of conversation would cheer up a man who was a bit below par ? " said Teddy, rudely. " I can assure you I'm not interested in your theories, and I'm not interested in murder."

" That's the point," said Mr. Bennett, by no means deterred. " Could you call it murder ? A man who kills an enemy in war-time is regarded as a hero. You've fought yourself, perhaps ? "

" In the 1914 war," agreed Teddy.

" And no doubt you killed some Germans ? "

" I shouldn't be surprised. As a matter of fact, it's so long ago . . ."

" You mean, those deaths are no longer on your conscience ? "

" They were never on my conscience. It was my job . . ."

" Precisely. But suppose X considers murder to be his job ? "

" Then the sooner the police lay hands on him the better."

" I suppose so. I wonder if you remember what you were doing on Monday night when this poor woman was killed ? "

Teddy stared. " Monday ? " For the moment he couldn't remember.

" You see ? The odds are you haven't got an alibi."

" Why the hell should I want one ? If you're going round England looking for men who can't remember on the spur of the minute what they were doing on Monday night . . . you're going to have your work cut out. Now you tell me something. Have you ever been in a lunatic asylum ? "

" As a matter of fact, I haven't," the man assured him

without a trace of offence in his voice. " Though, come to think of it, lunatics must be buried like anyone else. It's not like murderers that lie under prison-flags and not even a headstone to mark the place. What's it like ? "

" What's what like ? "

" An asylum. Been in one lately, perhaps ? "

" I've never been inside one of those places."

" No ? That's funny, that really is. I mean, why bring up the matter without some special reason ? Not that it surprises me exactly. I noticed from the minute you came into the carriage there was something abnormal about you. For instance, you didn't like finding me here, did you ? "

" If you want to know," snapped Teddy, " I like my own company."

" I wonder why. Perhaps you feel safer by yourself."

" To tell you the truth, I do."

" Really. Most interesting. Have you paused to wonder why that should be so ? Because that in itself is abnormal. Now, take me. I was delighted when you returned, simply delighted. Mind you, I knew someone was travelling in the carriage, because I saw the bag in the rack. Mr. Lane, isn't it ? Oh yes, there's a label on the bag, and I took the liberty . . ."

" Who the hell are you ? " shouted Teddy, goaded beyond control.

" I told you—my name's Bennett. I see you're going to stay at Stonemarten. We buried someone from that inn once—a tragic affair really, a double funeral. Husband and wife, quite elderly people, killed in a road accident. The daughter looked after everything, a very stylish interment, and a nice piece of statuary put up later. *Oh death, where is thy sting ?* That did seem to me a *leetle*—but then perhaps she meant it."

" What are you trying to do ? " asked Teddy thickly. " Poison every association for me ? Anyway, I don't believe you ever went near the pub. I don't believe you're in the undertaker's business either. You're simply here to try and finish me off."

" Well, really, Mr. Lane, what a thing to say ! What could have put that idea into your head ? " And then a really shocking thing happened. He tittered. " I wonder when that idea occurred to you."

" Seeing you've been talking of murder ever since I set eyes on you. . . ."

" Oh, everyone likes a good murder. Let's see, you change at Woolston, don't you, for the loop line ? A very old-fashioned little railway, not many people travel on it, I find. If you like a carriage to yourself, Mr. Lane, it ought to suit you down to the ground, yes, right down to the ground."

A new and appalling fear was rising in Teddy's heart. He looked across the carriage ; the stranger had reinforced his control of the exit by putting both legs across the door and crossing them at the ankle.

" You seem to know a lot about it," he muttered.

" Oh, I've often gone on that line," said the stranger. " In fact, I've often thought there could hardly be a better setting for a crime. The train not only stops at every station, it stops between most of them. You'd only have to ensure there was no one in the adjoining carriage—a perfectly simple thing to do as that train's always half-empty—and then you'd simply have to lean forward—like this (he suited the action to the word), make some friendly remark (your victim wouldn't be suspicious because you'd be a stranger, no reason why you should cherish animosity), you might even offer the loan of your paper, like this "—and on the words he rose and came half across the carriage, his lips stretched in a horrid smile under the glossy black moustache. " Then, as your hands met, you'd leap—like this . . ."

" Stand back," shouted Teddy. " Here, guard . . ." He stretched his hand frantically and caught the safety chain, tugging at it until his hand was indented by the impression of the links. He felt a hand at his throat and uttered a strangled scream.

At the same moment the train ran into the long tunnel before Woolston.

The train clanked to a stop, and the guard came hurrying along the corridor. When he reached the carriage Teddy was wrenching at his necktie. His companion was nowhere to be seen.

" What's wrong, sir ? " asked the guard, looking grim.

" A homicidal lunatic," said Teddy, frantically. " *The* homicidal lunatic most likely, the one the police are after. He attacked me just as the train went into the tunnel."

" Were you able to see where he went ? " asked the guard.

" I had my hands full seeing he didn't strangle me," Teddy

protested. " I suppose he bolted when he saw me pull the chain. He can't have got far, though," he added. " He's a distinctive looking chap, a big black moustache and black hair, wearing a raincoat and a bowler hat. Must have got on during the first lunch. I found him here when I came back."

" You'd be able to identify him again ? " said the guard.

" Of course. He's been talking to me for—well, it seemed like hours, ever since I came back from lunch. I spotted there was something queer about him almost at once, but I thought I might be able to stall him till we got into Woolston."

" You mean, you thought he was a lunatic ? "

" He kept on and on about this woman—Mrs. Lees—how it was probably done and the sort of chap who did it. Well, look at that." He pointed to the newspaper the stranger had left in the carriage when he disappeared. " That's not mine."

" Bought at the station from the look of it," said the guard. " No delivery marks on it. Well, that won't help us much." He turned to a subordinate who had accompanied him. " Better search the train, Joe. Do you feel up to coming along with us, sir ? "

" You'd better try and contact the police, hadn't you ? " Teddy suggested. " There's not much doubt you've got the killer on board." By this time he really believed it.

" You can leave that to us, sir," said the guard. So the search began. Carriage by carriage they traversed the length of the train, looked in the vans, the dining-car, even in the lavatories, but nowhere was there any sign of a man answering to the description of the one they sought. Teddy became flustered.

" This is nonsense," he said. " The chap was there—unless he managed to slip off the train after I'd given the alarm."

The guard sent for the ticket collector. " Did you see another passenger in this gentleman's carriage ?" he inquired.

" He wasn't here then," protested Teddy. " I tell you, I found him when I came back from lunch. He must be somewhere." He began to inspect the carriages again. Suddenly he stopped. He'd seen a face he recognised.

" That's the man," he cried hysterically. " Of course. Why didn't I think of it before ? "

" This gentleman hasn't got a black moustache," protested the guard.

" He's wearing a raincoat, isn't he ? And you'll probably find the moustache in his pocket."

70

"Good Lord!" said Plunkett. "You again? What's the idea? Are you trying to trail me?" He turned to the guard. "The chap's nuts," he said frankly. "Tried to chuck himself under a car the first time I set eyes on him, and when I pulled him away he as good as accused me of murdering him."

"He's still saying it," said the guard stolidly.

"It's true." Teddy heard his voice going up in a shrill scream. "You were travelling in my carriage—in disguise —and . . ."

"How was I disguised? As an organ-grinder's monkey?"

"This gentleman's wearing a cap," the guard pointed out. "You said a bowler."

"It was a bowler," Teddy insisted. "He's probably chucked that into the tunnel."

"I don't know who you are," said Plunkett woodenly, "but I'm damn' sure you shouldn't be going about alone. Is there a doctor on the train?"

"Is this the gentleman you think strangled that woman they found?" the guard demanded.

"No. No. I don't think that, not any more. Oh, but don't you see," he pleaded desperately, watching incredulity strengthen in the eyes of the onlookers, "that's what he wanted me to think. And he did make an attack on me. . . . If I hadn't pulled the chain he'd probably have succeeded."

"All right," said Plunkett, obligingly. "So I tried to murder you. Any special reason?"

"You've been following me about for days. You hope to drive me out of my mind. . . ."

"What for? I don't run an asylum, you know."

"You said you were a mute." Teddy was almost weeping. "In the undertaker's business. Not that I believed a word. . . ."

It was becoming increasingly obvious that nobody believed a word Teddy was saying, either. The guard took down his name and address. It was second nature to Teddy to give a false one. He couldn't deny his name, it was on his baggage for all to see, but the address was that of the hotel where he meant to stay, so he said he lived in one of the more prominent suburbs. It wasn't likely, he thought, they'd be able to trace him there. Plunkett also gave his address— the correct one. Because he had nothing to fear. He was simply a passenger going to Woolston on business—not under- taker's business, of course. That, he implied, was part of

71

Teddy's hallucination. For an appalling moment it seemed as though he might be held for police investigation, but eventually they let him go. Stonemarten was quite near, and it would be simple to telephone to the hotel and ask to be advised if Teddy suddenly decided to leave.

But Teddy wasn't going to Stonemarten now. No fear. Someone else in red whiskers and a Glengarry would probably be waiting on the next train to push him out of a window or slash him with a razor. He got into the train, because he knew Plunkett would be watching him, and so Plunkett was. But the little train stood in a bay and just as it was pulling out Teddy picked up his bag and sneaked out on the further platform. There was a slow train going to London and he got on to that. Plunkett did not realise what had happened; for once, Teddy had scored. Plunkett saw his quarry board the train and stopped to send a telegram. It didn't occur to him that Teddy would go back to London. He did think he might alight at some intermediate station on the route, and he watched like a hawk every time the train stopped. He couldn't walk up and down and keep an eye on Teddy, because there was no corridor. When the train drew up at Stonemarten he noticed that Teddy didn't alight, but he imagined he intended to try and throw dust in his pursuer's eyes by going on another station or so and changing his temporary address. He had travelled to the end of the line before he discovered his mistake. As soon as he did so he tried to communicate with Ames, but without success.

There was a small sequel to these events that went unchronicled. The following morning a gang of three railway workers, walking through the Woolston Tunnel, picked up a crushed black bowler hat with no name in it, and no signs of identification.

" The chap this belonged to must have had it on his perishing head when he stuck it out of the perishing window," observed the first.

" Perishing lucky his perishing head wasn't in it," suggested the second.

The third said nothing. They chucked it into a clump of weeds growing near the line and a day or two later some kids found it and knocked it into some sort of shape and played with it for a bit till one of them got the idea of using it for a bird-bath. It pretty soon leaked and they lost interest in it, and it was crammed into a garbage tin and carried off to the rubbish tip. Nobody connected it with Teddy Lane's hysterical story because nobody believed that anyway. The authorities soon discovered he'd given a false address and though Plunkett could have put them right it didn't suit his book to do so. Because by that time the less you knew about Teddy Lane's affairs the better, unless you were the unnatural kind that likes policemen nosing into your business. Teddy was going to make the headlines, after all, and it was surprising how much damage he was going to do when he was out of the running for good and all.

But that came later. When he slipped out of the train in the bay and boarded a slow train to London he had no notion how matters were going to shape during the next twenty-four hours. He couldn't rest even now, because he couldn't be absolutely certain Plunkett hadn't detected his ruse. Up and down the corridors he prowled, staring in at all the windows, and constantly turning an anguished face over his shoulder, darting like a bird or a serpent, in case his enemy was creeping up behind him. People inside the carriages rustled their papers angrily ; they thought he was one of those pests prowling in search of some woman travelling unaccompanied. One wife even remarked to her husband, " It's enough to make you nervous of going anywhere alone. It wouldn't surprise me to learn he was the man who killed that poor Mrs. Lees. They haven't got him yet, have they ? "

CHAPTER EIGHT

DEATH IN A DARK SUIT

AT VICTORIA Teddy mounted a bus, taking the front seat, and then thought he'd have done better to go at the back where he could see the faces of the passengers as they mounted. He'd thought first that if he went in front nobody could identify him, but he was beginning to think it didn't matter much what he did, they'd get him in the end, but he didn't realise yet how soon. Someone mounted the stairs and sat at the back and Teddy trembled, already anticipating a knife between the shoulder-blades. He thought of going inside, but that meant walking down the bus and exposing himself to a possible enemy. He was so keyed up that he didn't even hear the conductor mount to the top deck, and when the man tapped him on the shoulder he let out a shrill scream like a rabbit.

" Here, what's biting you ? " asked the man in amazement.

" Coming up like that," panted Teddy. " If I'd had a weak heart . . ."

" If you got a weak heart you didn't ought to be on the top platform," retorted the man who was as unsympathetic as everybody else.

Teddy took his ticket and crouched in his seat. To add to the rest of the miseries of this endless day a steady spiteful rain now began to fall, obliterating even familiar landmarks. Teddy stared out of the mottled windows, seeing his own reflection broken and hazy in the wet light. Somehow the vision shocked him it looked so pale, so haggard, so—out of this world. The phrase had a charnel ring. Suddenly he put his hands over his trembling face. He felt absolutely lost, was afraid to stay on the bus, was afraid to get off, thought he'd never realised before what a disadvantage it was to live in a cul-de-sac, where your enemy might be waiting for you in the streaming dark at the end of the street, knowing you'd no way of escape, remembered with shocking effect lines he'd learnt at school and never read since that came surging back into his mind, making him shiver anew.

74

> *" Like one that on a lonesome road*
> *Doth walk in fear and dread,*
> *And having once turned round walks on,*
> *And turns no more his head ;*
> *Because he knows a frightful fiend*
> *Doth close behind him tread."*

But he had to dismount, of course, when it came to his corner. The malign conductor, under the pretence of giving him a hand, tried to shove him under the wheel in the muddy gutter ; he staggered and almost lost his footing.

" What are you trying to do ? " he demanded. " Murder me ? "

The conductor gave as good as he got. " You've no right to be travelling on my bus in your state," he said, " and if you was to put yourself underneath it, it wouldn't be much loss to anyone."

There was so much truth in this that Teddy found himself without words. He crossed the road shakily and went down the cul-de-sac to the Mansions, expecting at every instant that some dark figure would leap out of the blackness and bear him to the ground. But nothing happened and he stumbled into the entrance of the Mansions.

Though it was long past his duty hours Moxon was moving about and pushed a pasty inquisitive face through the swing door to see who it was.

" Well, look 'oo's 'ere ! " he exclaimed. " Thought you was going to be away for an indefinite period."

" Plans changed suddenly," Teddy mumbled. " Met a chap . . . Been any messages for me ? "

" I'll say," said Moxon. " Mind you, I think you'd ha' done better to lie low for a bit. Not very nice for us having the police making inquiries."

" The police ! " He turned a sort of chalky yellow. " What did they want ? "

" Ho, they weren't going to confide in me. Just said they wanted a word with you when convenient and when would you be back. I told them I couldn't say, and there was no forwarding address."

Teddy leaned against the wall. " Wonder what they want," he murmured, forcing a smile. He couldn't afford to *seem* licked, whatever he might feel. A new thought occurred to him. " What time was this ? "

" 'Bout a couple of hours after you went."

Teddy nodded as though that confirmed some inward suspicion. Actually it left him completely in the dark. Moxon was watching him narrowly. Funny about that money, he was thinking. He never earned it. Never done a stroke of work since he's been here.

Teddy straightened himself. " Well, I suppose if it's anything important they'll call again. Anyone else ? "

" Only the lady," said Moxon casually.

" Lady ? Which—who was that ? "

" She didn't leave no name. Just wanted to know when you'd be back. I couldn't tell you, I said. I think Mr. Lane's gone out of town. ' His milk's on the step,' she said, quick as a knife. I do 'ate a sharp woman," he added in parentheses. " As soon live with a darning-needle. That don't mean he's coming back to-day, I told her. The milk come before there was time to cancel. I meant to go up and collect it," he continued meditatively. " I 'ate waste. Still, now you're back it'll be useful, won't it ? "

" Are you sure the lady didn't leave a name ? " Teddy insisted.

" She didn't leave nothing," said Moxon with unmistakable meaning, " and it's no good asking me what she looked like because I didn't see her proper. I was out at the back when she come, seeing to the furnace, and being mucky I wasn't going to show myself in the front hall. She called out to know about you and I just popped my head round the door. She was wearing one of these mackintoshes—rain started about midday here—and I wouldn't know her again if I was to see her. Seemed proper put out you wasn't here," he added. " I did ask about a message but she said ' No, she'd get in touch.' "

That was all Moxon could tell him, so wearily Teddy took himself up to his flat. There was the inevitable letter on the mat, and at first he thought he wouldn't even look at it, but curiosity got the better of him, so he picked it up and it was from Julia. It announced that she'd be coming that evening to settle her account with him, and she hoped he'd see to it there was no one to interrupt them. His head cleared a little. That sounded as though she'd got the money, and once he had that he could clear the ground with Morell, explain that the mythical Lloyd hadn't been able to lay hands on the stuff after all, had gone to ground, drawn in his horns, anything, and it seemed to him that capitulation on Julia's part pointed to similar action on the part of the other three.

Since she proposed coming to-night it was hardly likely she had been the visitor of the afternoon, which only left Mrs. Tempest—or so he thought until it suddenly occurred to him that it might have been Lucille, wanting to make sure he had really gone. He snatched up the receiver and dialled her number.

" Hallo, darling," he said, automatically adjusting his voice. " Teddy here. I say . . ."

" What do you want ? " The words came like shots from a toy pistol—crack, crack, crack.

" Just wondering if you looked in on me this afternoon," said Teddy.

" Looked in on you ? Why on earth should I ? After the way you let me down last night I wonder you've the nerve to ring me up at all."

" I wanted to thank you for your generosity," he explained. " Those fifty pounds may save my life yet."

" Fifty pounds ? I don't know what you're talking about. I haven't sent you fifty pounds and I don't intend to, what's more. As for saving your life, I haven't the least interest in it."

She was in a towering rage. Teddy winced even at the end of the line. He hung up very gently. The conversation had started a fresh hare. If she hadn't sent the money, who had ? And then he remembered the mysterious policeman, and was convinced it was all part of a trick. He was going to be run in for stealing the money—he didn't quite understand how it was to be worked—but of course if he was in jug he couldn't be much danger to the Big Four. He opened his case and looked at the wad of notes. They were single pounds and there was nothing, so far as he could see, to distinguish them. Pound notes can't be traced, that's why they're sterling currency on the Black Market. Teddy knew all about that. Still, there was Moxon ; he'd signed for the registered letter. Teddy's signature was for the porter's benefit, so that a dishonest tenant couldn't say subsequently he had never seen the package. Besides, he didn't believe any of the four would approach the police. It was probably some trivial affair like not renewing his wireless licence. His thoughts returned to this afternoon's visitor. It seemed clear it must be Mrs. Tempest. Surely, he argued, she wouldn't have come in person unless she realised she was defeated and meant to pay his price. All the same, his uneasiness remained. He decided that what he wanted was some coffee, very hot and sweet, so he put on the percolator and carried in the little bottle of milk from the mat, reflecting characteristically that Moxon probably watered it, it looked as though it had been messed about and in London you could not put it on to the tits who were supposed to open country milk bottles for their own refreshment, and shook open the copy of the *Record* that had arrived that morning. He always read the obituaries first, then the Personal and then glanced through the headlines. Almost the first name he saw to-night was his own. He sat staring, aghast and afraid. The fear was like a living thing in the room with him, with icy hands and a face to chill you to the marrow.

LANE. Suddenly, in London, Edward Lane, aged 56. No mourning, no letters, no flowers.

It was sheer coincidence, of course. There must be scores of Edward Lanes in the world, and a good many of those would be living in London. No doubt there were at least half a dozen in the telephone book. But there was no getting away from it, it had given him a nasty jolt. He was still staring at the entry when the telephone began to ring. He went into the hall and lifted the instrument mechanically.

" Mr. Lane ? " said a voice, and he knew it at once, even though he might make a mistake about a woman at a table in Blackie's. This was Mrs. Tempest. " So you changed your mind ? "

" Changed . . . ? "

" The porter said you had gone away for a long week-end, but I was sure he must be wrong. You had too many important thing to keep you in London for that to be true."

He said lamely, " So it was you who came this afternoon. Why did you want to see me ? "

She asked, " Is it so unlikely ? You can't already have forgotten last Friday." Then her voice changed a little, and she asked, " Have you seen this morning's *Record* ? "

He stiffened, and fear leaned over his shoulder. " Yes. Is that your idea of a practical joke ? "

" Hardly a joke," she corrected him.

" What else would you call it ? It isn't true."

" Not yet. But you must have noticed that I left the date blank. By this time to-morrow no one will be able to deny it, not any of it, and the *Record* will be able to claim once again —First with the News."

He couldn't rest, couldn't settle to anything. He wasn't even sure in his own mind if she was in earnest. He had known from the instant of meeting her that she was his real danger, far more to be feared than Ames or young Ross, who were public men, in a sense, and couldn't take the same risks. And naturally she was far more perilous than Julia. Thinking of his one-time love reminded him of her letter. He read it through again, then dropped it on the table. But he wasn't much consoled. Because even if she paid up there was no guarantee that he could get away. He'd tried once already —and look at the result. Here he was back in his hole, with snakes swarming all round him, falling from the ceiling, peering up through the floorboards, he thought wildly. Still—how about a cruise ? They might follow you on a train, trail you in the street, but a cruise lasting several weeks ought to be safe. With Julia's five hundred, which characteristically he already thought of as being virtually in his pocket, he could afford to stay away a long time, three or four months. England had about had it, anyhow. All this talk about austerity and sacrifice—he'd heard it as a young man and in those days he'd been had for a sucker all right. But not now, not any more. Chaps had to look out for themselves these days. He bent to turn down the gas under the percolator. The coffee would have to simmer for a few minutes, so while he waited he shook out the evening paper he had bought at Victoria, and the little draught he made blew Julia's letter into the waste-paper basket. On the front page—this was a day of news and encounters and shocks of every kind—he saw a paragraph that interested him very much indeed. It was headed :

Reprieved Murderer Dies After Almost Forty Years

and informed anyone who might care for the information that George Tempest, found guilty of the murder of a 17-year-old girl nearly forty years ago, and believed to have served a longer consecutive period of detention than any other inmate of an institution, had died at Clifftown. Teddy sat for some time wondering how this would affect the widow. She hadn't breathed a word when she telephoned. Did she assume she was less under his thumb than before ? He smiled grimly. Oh, she might think she had scored by inserting the obituary notice, but she should learn with whom the last laugh lay. He unlocked the shabby black deed-box and took out the verbatim reports of the trial. The pin fastening them was brown with age and he had some difficulty in pulling it out. There were two photographs inset in the closely-printed columns, one of a good-looking but unstable man of about forty and the other of an eager girl. He stared at the latter, trying to find in this happy creature some trace of the steadfast icy woman who had been in this room less than a week ago. He glanced through the details of the case. It was hardly surprising that a mother would be at pains to prevent a beloved only child from realising the sort of man his father had been. It wouldn't do Dr. Henry Tempest any good when the truth was known. For by now Teddy had no mercy. Mrs. Tempest had overplayed her hand when she caused the obituary notice to appear in the *Record*. *No mourning, no flowers, no letters.* She had intended the words not as a warning to friends but as a statement. There would be no mourners for unwanted Teddy Lane, nobody would send flowers, there was no one who would write. On the contrary, there'd be jubilation. *That little worm dead ! God's in His Heaven, all's right with the world.* Teddy's face went dark with anger and misery. But he could pay her back in her own coin. Taking a large envelope from the drawer of his table he addressed it to Dr. Henry Tempest, then realised he didn't know the fellow's address, didn't even know in which part of the country he practised. Still, that didn't matter. Any Public Library would supply a Medical Directory that would tell him all he needed to know. And anyhow he'd missed to-night's post.

Suddenly he remembered the coffee and snatched it off the gas-ring. He was just in time, it was exactly how he liked it. He put on some milk to boil, found sugar and a cup and saucer, and at that moment the door-bell rang.

Automatically he removed the saucepan from the flame, thinking : Which ? Mrs. Tempest ? Ames ? the anonymous police officer ? And then he relaxed. Of course, it would be Julia. She had said she would be coming to-night. Just in time for a cup of coffee. He added a second cup to the tray, remembering as he did so the innumerable times they had drunk coffee together in the past. Suddenly the years came rushing back, and with them a sudden quite irrelevant surge of tenderness. Dear Julia! How sweet she had been in the old days—and how little either had suspected they would ever come to this. Still, he had no bitterness against her. She was going to pay up, and then he'd leave London, after he'd laid his series of mines (he didn't mean to let his victims off, even though he himself might have disappeared), and his terrors would stay behind in the empty flat.

The bell rang a second time, and he called, " Coming, Julia. Coming, my sweet ! " and put the milk saucepan back on the little flame. Then he hurried through the little lobby and drew the bolts and threw open the door, crying, " Come in, it's all set," in a voice no one had heard from him for years.

The next instant he was wondering, " How could I be such a fool? Coming, my sweet, indeed!" For though he might feel a momentary softening, even a romantic thrill, it was obvious in that first glance that there was nothing kind, nothing tender, about to-night's visitor. Indeed, nothing less like the Julia of his dreams could be imagined. He stood spellbound for a moment, surveying the beautifully-cut black suit with a narrow pin stripe, the handsome hand-made shoes, the black hat pulled a little over one eye, and was shaken with anger because he was so shabby, so poor, so cowed. Between the hat brim and the coat collar the face was like a flint. It was hard to believe there had ever been even a semblance of good fellowship between the pair of them.

" May I come in ? "

The voice matched the icy face, the scornful eyes.

" Looks like death," thought Teddy, stepping backwards and desperately trying to recover his poise.

And Death was just who it was.

CHAPTER NINE

A NICE CUP OF COFFEE

IT WAS HARDLY to be expected that Teddy would recognise his visitor in this guise. In any case, he felt shaken and lost, as if someone had suddenly knocked him off his feet. The illusion that he was about to recapture a Julia who probably only existed now in his imagination, had been so strong that the reality made him feel stupid and helpless. It had been a nightmare of a day, the sort a man experiences in dreams and wakes with a sob of relief to find isn't true, after all. Only—this *was* true. There had been his attempt at escape (and what hopes had buoyed him up *then* !) ; his terrifying encounter in the train ; his slow return, haunted every step of the way ; Moxon's news about his two visitors, who were equally unwelcome and probably equally dangerous (though which of the four had had the temerity to approach the police he couldn't imagine. Again it never passed through his mind that it might have been someone else. The police had nothing on him, had they ? Not likely. Teddy Lane wasn't born yesterday—and wouldn't, though as yet he didn't know the fact, be alive to-morrow.)

Thoughts darted about in his mind like rats, scurry, scurry, he couldn't keep his eyes on all of them. He put one hand to his forehead. Oh, why had Death elected to come to-night ?

Death was watching him, puzzled and sceptical.

" You hadn't forgotten I was coming ? I did warn you . . ."

" Of course not. I've had a busy day. Only just got in. I don't know why we're standing in the hall." He led the way into the living-room. Julia's letter winked at him from the waste-paper basket.

" Then—you aren't expecting anyone else, are you ? "

So he wasn't the only apprehensive person in the world, reflected Teddy. He tried to make a small joke.

" Not anxious to be found in my company ? How times change ! "

But Death's expression remained immovable.

" I'll let the porter know," said Teddy, grasping at the opportunity of an instant's privacy to compose his anguished features, fix a formal smile on that pale trembling face, where it sat like an amateur comedian's moustache, insecurely fixed.

Moxon, as might have been expected, was surly and unco-operative.

" It's nothing to me if you've got the King of the Cannibal Islands there," he said. " I'm off duty. It's a quarter to eight. Or hadn't you noticed ? "

Teddy hung up with a sigh. Somehow it seemed important to let Moxon know someone was here. All the same, it was extraordinary how desolate and solitary he felt. Surely he should be used to taking a lonely stance by this time. It was years since he'd really had a friend. Couldn't afford them and that was the fact. He came back to find the milk in the saucepan bubbling up, and quickly he took it off.

" Black, I seem to recall," he murmured turning with that false smile to his visitor. His hand shook a very little as he poured out the coffee, but he didn't suppose Death noticed. Anybody can spill a teaspoonful into a saucer when the atten-tion is distracted. He passed the cup over, and then he had another moment's respite, because the telephone rang and he had to hurry out and answer it.

" Help yourself to cigarettes," he called out.

" Mr. Lane ? " said a voice he didn't recognise.

" Who's that ? " Most likely his tormentor again, he thought.

" I called this afternoon. I understood from the porter you expected to be away for some time."

" I changed my plans," said Teddy as haughtily as he could manage. " Who are you ? You didn't leave a name."

" I'm afraid you didn't get my message. I asked the porter to tell you the police would like a word with you."

" Not to-night," said Teddy quickly. " I've got a friend. You'll find the chain up if you do come," he added unwisely.

" Be careful," the voice enjoined him. " It's never safe to make an enemy of the police. I'll get in touch to-morrow."

Teddy hung up the receiver and stood swaying a little. So it wasn't a trick on Moxon's part, as he'd been trying to persuade himself. Someone had dragged the authorities in ! Then light broke. It was another fake, of course. It wasn't the real police, not the real police, not—the—real—— Ah, but suppose it was ? He was rattled all right now.

" But they haven't got anything on me," he exclaimed.

" Who are you talking to ? " asked Death from the inner room.

" Myself," said Teddy promptly, resuming that bright, ghastly smile.

> " I often talks to myself, I says,
> I talks to myself, says I.
> For I like to hear a clever man talk
> And a clever man reply."

He had hoped for an answering smile, something to break through the black fog in which they were labouring, but there was nothing.

" I don't want to keep you," said Death, " particularly as it sounds as though you had another visitor on the way. . . ."

" Nonsense," said Teddy sharply. " Just a practical joke."

" Are you sure ? " asked Death. " It seems rather late in the day for that. Anyway, I prefer not to take the risk. Besides, it's late."

" Must think of your good name," agreed Teddy, refusing to take offence. " Not that anyone else is coming, of course."

He picked up his coffee-cup and began to gulp down the contents. It was too hot, and it almost scalded his throat.

" Our business won't take long," Teddy went on. " The cards are on the table already." He spoke with a certain defiance which seemed rather wasted on his audience.

Well, that might be true, but when it came to playing them they found themselves at cross-purposes. Their exchanges snapped out like conversation on a stage, question and answer, comment and cross-comment. The subject, of course, was money. All Teddy's conversations nowadays centred round that point—sordid or fascinating according to the way you looked at it.

" If you hand over the money as arranged there'll be no need for me to keep you. I can see you're in a hurry."

" That's the point. I haven't got it."

" You haven't got it ? " Had he expected that answer ? " Then why . . . ? "

" You talk as if money grew on trees. The fact is, I haven't been able to raise it. I explained my position . . ."

" I'm not interested in your position, but—others might be, don't you think ? "

The atmosphere became more electric than before. " Is

that a threat? Where's the sense of that? What do you stand to gain? You can't get blood from a stone or money from an empty purse."

"Then perhaps you will explain what you do propose?"

This was the moment for a bold stroke. Teddy and Death stared at each other across the phony fumed oak table.

"I propose you should cut your losses. Regard the whole affair as a speculation that hasn't come off. Speculators always take a chance, and this time the luck has gone against you. Can't you see it that way?"

Teddy gave a short laugh.

"You mean, this is a complete get-out? You're not simply postponing payment?"

"I can't give you what I haven't got, and I can't hold out any hopes that I'm likely suddenly to stumble on a new source of money. . . ."

But it wasn't going to be as simple as that, because when you have taken immense risks and put yourself on the wrong side of the law (which has an uncanny way of digging out uncomfortable truths once it goes to work), you don't say good-bye to your anticipated profits with a casual kiss-your-hand gesture. Teddy knew that much, though there was a great deal he didn't know and would never have time to find out.

"I warn you, I mean what I say."

Teddy was showing signs of passion, but he controlled himself and satisfied himself by shrugging his shoulders. He said meaningly, "I could do a bit of damaging talking, you know. Had you thought of that?"

"Of course I'd thought of that. Why else do you suppose I'm here to-night?"

Teddy sighed; he was feeling so exhausted he could scarcely maintain his part of the struggle. He muttered something about wanting a handkerchief and slipped into his bedroom where he kept the whisky handy for breakfast. He poured himself a stiff dose and drank it neat. He was feeling all at sea, thinking confusedly, "This can't be happening to me, not to Teddy Lane, who started with such high hopes, and good friends once and a good name." Where had he gone wrong, taken the crooked path? He tried to look over his shoulder, but the past was a blur. He took another shot of whisky. He had had nothing to eat since his lunch—how long ago? It seemed like a week. He couldn't do himself justice when he was so worn out. Why couldn't Death wait till to-morrow ?

To-morrow, he repeated. To-morrow is another day To-morrow and to-morrow and to-morrow . . . and all our yesterdays have lighted fools the way to dusty death. There it was again, the word he couldn't escape. He looked at the whisky bottle. Better not, perhaps. It was almost empty now. Besides, he still had a visitor, hadn't he ? There was a fight of some sort going on.

" Fighting for my life," he said aloud, in a thick voice. A valuable life like yours. He started. Who had said that ? Of course. That chap, Morell. Morell meant trouble, they all meant trouble, come to that. Like playing Puss in a corner, with all the corners occupied and you by yourself in the middle, chased by the cat. He sat on the edge of his bed, and waited for the faintness to pass.

A voice called from a long way off, " If I see the porter on my way out shall I send him up ? "

Porter ? Moxon ? Up here ? What the deuce for ? He put out his hand as if to push away a dark curtain that obscured his sight. Hell, it was dark, wasn't it ? For an appalled instant he thought he was dying, everything was so shapeless, so remote. Then the room came back to him—or had he come back to the room ?

He looked round. He must have walked in from his bedroom. Except for himself the room was empty !

He felt dazed. Surely there'd been a visitor—he had been expecting someone. He lurched over to the table, fell into his chair. Julia's letter stared up at him from the basket. Of course—Julia. Dear Julia. Kind Julia. But not any more. There wasn't any more kindness in the world. It was like the butter ration, say. You got a little and then you went to the larder and there was no more there. Finished. Like Teddy Lane, Teddy Lane who'd expected life to be a treasure chest and had discovered it was only a garbage can, full of offal and old bones. Old bones. Rattle his bones over the stones, he's only a pauper—only a pauper—how true. Somebody giggled.

" Who's there ? " he called sharply, but nobody answered.

Oh well, if there had been anyone he had gone now. Nothing to sit up for. He staggered back to his bedroom. His head pressed in the dingy pillow, something nagged his mind. What was it ? Oh yes—he hadn't heard the door shut, so perhaps someone was still there.

He lifted his head. " Julia ! " he called.

But no one answered.

There was a sound, though, a familiar sound. Yes—the lift was coming up. Someone for him ? Somebody had telephoned—a long time ago ? Or had that been a dream ? He listened.

No one rang the bell, so it must have been a visitor for the chap in No. 11. He sighed and dropped his head again, and suddenly the light went out.

A power-cut ? A funny time to have it, he thought vaguely. Still, more sensible really, when people had gone to bed. What was the time ? He'd forgotten to look and now the light was out. Kind of someone really to save him the trouble.

And not knowing that, so far as he was concerned, the lights had gone out for ever, Teddy Lane fell into the eternal dark.

It hadn't all been a dream, though. Someone had brought the lift up to the sixth floor, and the person who stepped out had come to visit Teddy Lane. Death, emerging from the dark little lobby, missed the newcomer by a matter of seconds. There was no time for subtlety. Just above the sixth floor were the attics, large cupboards with sloping roofs, lit by a single skylight, where tenants could keep their baggage and where Moxon had stored the flotsam and jetsam of years. Death stole noiselessly up the uncarpeted stairs and was concealed in a patch of shadow as the lift gates opened and Teddy Lane's second visitor of the evening stepped out.

No matter what Teddy had said, this one appeared to be awaited, for without any hesitation the newcomer pushed open the door, that Death had pulled to but dared not close for fear of self-betrayal and softly shut the door from within. An instant later the light went out. Death waited no longer. Stealing down, past the closed doors of the other flats, scarcely daring to breathe lest one should flash open, peering cautiously over the banisters lest Moxon should have taken it into his head to hang about the hall, Death escaped into the rain and the cheerless night.

A little later Teddy Lane's second visitor emerged from the darkened flat and also retreated, unperceived. Upstairs the silence was suddenly broken by the sound of the telephone. Ting-a-ling, ting-a-ling, it rang, until the caller grew tired and hung up. Then the silence came down for good on the unlighted room where Teddy Lane slept his wretched life away.

CHAPTER TEN

BLACK FRIDAY

It was half-past eight that Thursday night when Julia reached home to find an unnerved Charles in the hall.

" What on earth's happened ? " he demanded, as she closed the door. For her face was paper-white and there were dark shadows under her eyes. She hadn't been looking herself for some days past, but this was the end.

" How you startled me ! " exclaimed Julia. " What's happened ? Has there been a fire in the House ? I thought you always sat till about eleven." There was a disagreeable flavour about that, as though she had known she would be late for some particular reason and hadn't intended to confide in him.

" Special Welsh Bill," he said briefly. " Anyway, I arranged to be paired in the unlikely event of a Division. But where on earth have you been ? "

" The old old story," said Julia. " Don't look so Jove-like, Charles. I took the car out for a run—it was a lovely morning and how could I guess it would turn into such a wretched afternoon ?—and I had a breakdown."

" Where's the car ? " asked Charles.

" I left her at Barnards. We've been limping home at a pace that would make a snail look like a Derby runner."

" What's wrong with her ? "

" Broken fan-belt."

Charles whistled. " Good grief, Ju, you don't do things by halves. How did you manage to coax her along at all ? "

" I couldn't have done anything by myself and unfortunately I'd taken the short cut by the Beacon . . ."

" The Beacon ? " Charles interrupted. " What on earth were you doing down there ?"

" I had a sudden yearning for sea-air, so I thought I'd go to Rowlhampton and take in Liz Harding on the way."

" Liz Harding ? But she's in Cannes."

" I know. The lucky thing." She spoke with unusual

passion, as if being in Cannes approximated to being in Paradise. Perhaps, thought Charles uneasily, in her present mood it did. " Characteristically I'd forgotten that. Anyway, she was only a peg. I wanted a day off. Have you ever noticed, Charles, that in London you never escape the tyranny of the clock ? You're always aware what time it is and what you ought to be doing and how impossible it's going to be to fit everything in ? But directly you're free of London then it's perfectly obvious to you that clocks are simply mechanical devices for man's convenience, and you don't need to be bound by them at all."

" It's perfectly obvious to me," said Charles, " that you could use a drink. Come in here and I'll mix you one."

She came in, drooping, Julia who never failed or faltered, and his heart misgave him afresh.

" Any special reason for picking Rowlhampton ? " he asked, trying to make his tone light. But he hadn't Julia's advantages. She'd been a actress and she hadn't forgotten her art, though she had ceased to practise it professionally years ago. She knew he was bothered and, worse than bothered, suspicious. She was so tired that all she longed for was to lie down and drift away into sleep (as Teddy Lane was sleeping now). But she'd got to wait a little. She couldn't confide in him, take comfort from him as the prayer-book said ; she was in much too deep for that.

" It was wonderful air," she told him, taking the glass he handed her. " And all those beautiful Regency houses on the front."

" If you want Regency," said Charles, " you needn't go farther than Regent's Park. But assuming you must have sea air, why the late arrival ? Or did you spend the afternoon sitting in the Beacon short-cut waiting for help ? "

" It seemed like that," Julia confessed. She finished the drink in a rush and held out the glass. " Yes, darling, another please. I began to wonder if I should spend the night there."

" From the look of you, you might have met a murderer," commented Charles rather brutally. " I take it you didn't."

She shivered. " I believe I've got a chill. No, of course not. A delightful young man on a motor-cycle."

" Who put the car right for you ? "

" Well, no, he wasn't a professional magician. But he made it possible for me to drive her back—very slowly."

" What made you go off the main road anyhow ? "

" I thought I could avoid Blind Man's Corner. You know what that's like, and this is early closing day for that part of the world and those huge buses come sailing round every five minutes. Yes, I know they all have ace drivers, but it's very unnerving just the same. Anyhow I couldn't guess the fan-belt was going to break, could I ? "

" I hope you took her into the first garage you passed."

" I didn't dare," said Julia candidly. " They wouldn't have let me bring her home. The young man warned me of that."

" Your luck with young men is phenomenal," her husband congratulated her, trying to import a rather lighter note into the conversation. " You were fortunate to meet anyone on that short cut. It's death to cars."

" Oh, I think he was in a hurry too. For one appalling minute I thought he wasn't going to stop. He kept looking at his wrist-watch as if he had a date, too."

" Too ? "

" Well, we don't usually dine at 8.30," improvised Julia swiftly. " It was lucky for me he understood about cars, but he said in the army you learned a lot and were paid for learning so he couldn't see what chaps belly-ached about. Yes, Charles, that was his expression."

" I only hope you didn't land him in for a court-martial," returned Charles a little grimly. He wasn't a fool ; he knew there was a whole lot Julia wasn't telling him but he knew too there was no sense trying to force her. She was frightened, that was the fact, and he'd never seen Julia frightened before.

" Anyway, he got me going and I gave him a pound and he said well, that'll oil the sergeant-major's tongue, may as well spend it, no sense keeping it the way things are, and he shot off, really like an arrow from a bow. He was out of sight in a minute, and I tooled very slowly home, stopping every now and again to give her a chance to get her breath. And—well, here I am."

" You might," suggested Charles, " have telephoned."

" I did. That is—I tried. Anyway, it was too late . . ."

" Too late for what ? "

" Too late to prevent Cook making the soufflé."

Charles nodded. She hadn't meant that. Too late, she'd said. Too late for what ? He hadn't a notion.

" You don't look fit for anything but bed," he told her drily.

" I don't feel fit for much else. It's a bother about the car. I'm going to the hairdresser to-morrow."

" Thank Heaven she's in dry dock," said Charles sincerely. " You must have been picked up for illegal parking by every constable on the beat. What's wrong with taxis ? "

" It seems silly to take a taxi when you've got a car."

" Far cheaper than paying your fines," Charles told her pretty drily.

She picked up her bag and trailed towards the staircase. " Too bad to desert you the one night you're home."

" That's all right," said Charles. " I've plenty to do. By the way, I ran into Ross this evening."

" Into Gerald ? " She recovered herself in an instant. " Where did you meet him ? He's not much of a society man."

" He asked after you."

" Well, that was nice of him." She laughed, a bit tinnily. " Darling, why should you sound so surprised ? After all, we have known each other for years. It's natural he should ask after me. It can't be the first time."

" No," agreed Charles, pushing open the bedroom door for her. " But—this seemed special, as if he was—afraid."

" Afraid ? "

" Yes. That something was wrong, I mean. ' How's Julia ? ' he said. ' She's all right. So far as I know,' I told him, and I saw something, a suggestion that perhaps I didn't know much. Julia, if there is anything . . ."

Julia threw down her hat and pulled off her shoes. " Darling, aren't we getting melodramatic ? "

" Well, why not ? Life can be pretty melodramatic. I know. Probably you do, too."

That stung her. Because it was true. Six months ago she'd have laughed at the idea that she might find herself in her present position. Stagey ! she'd have said. Not very good stage at that. Still—Gerald !

" I promise you you're imagining what doesn't exist," she said. " Why, one thinks of Gerald and Sally like bread-and-butter and ham and eggs and—and Charles and Julia."

" I didn't mean that sort of thing particularly," said Charles. " But—there isn't anything else on your mind, Ju ? If so you'd do much better to share it with me."

" Darling," she assured him, " I've got absolutely nothing

to tell you. Oh dear, I do hope you didn't put ideas into Gerald's head. You know what a sensitive plant he is—comes of being an orphan, I suppose."

" I didn't know he was an orphan," said Charles. " As a child, I mean."

" Well, I don't know a lot about him," Julia confessed, " but I did once hear him say that a home and security was every child's birthright, and only those who had had to do without them realised their value."

" Rum chap," murmured Charles. He didn't feel exactly happy about Julia, because knowing her and loving her as he did he could see there was something wrong, but it didn't concern Gerald Ross. She had convinced him of that. He wasn't a fool by any manner of means, but naturally he never suspected the truth, didn't come within miles of it. Still, you could scarcely blame him for that.

After he had gone, Julia lay wondering how she could suggest his sleeping in his dressing-room without reawakening his suspicions. She'd never made a similar proposal to him ; now and again it had fallen out that they were separated, but it had all been perfectly natural. To-night, after what he had said about Gerald Ross, the suspicions she had lulled might start fermenting again. Well, then, she couldn't ask him, because Charles was worth a million Teddy Lanes, and a good many Geralds. She had been struck by a fear that had leapt full-grown into her mind while they were speaking that she might talk in her sleep. Did people ever know ? And suppose she actually uttered Gerald's name ? It was too dangerous. She must contrive somehow to keep awake. But Charles settled everything quite simply by saying she looked like death —and instantly she sheered away from *that* phrase—and he thought he'd sleep in the dressing-room and give her an opportunity to get nine hours.

" Which is what you need," he told her.

" What happens to women whose husbands fail them ?" she murmured. " If anything happened to you, Charles, it would be like being decapitated."

" Nothing's going to happen. It wouldn't surprise me if you were running a temperature, and if you are you'll cancel your date with the hairdresser, if it means your going round looking like the Witch of Endor for the next week."

But next morning she hadn't a trace of temperature. With

the light she seemed to have recovered her balance. She went off to Pierre in a taxi, and nobody noticed anything unusual about her. They called her another taxi, without even asking, as she came out, and she stopped it by the tube station and said she would walk across the park. She was taking no chances. Taxis at Ellison Mansions were unusual enough for their occupants to be noticed, particularly visitors like Julia Silk. The day that had begun with cloud had dissolved into soft sweeping rain as she came up from the tube station but that was an advantage really, because it meant she could hide behind her umbrella. A number of people were taking shelter under the porch of the Mansions, so she didn't attract any special attention ; she had taken care to wear a little dark hat with a veil and as she ducked through the crowd she felt perfectly anonymous. It never occurred to her there might be anyone there who recognised her and could even guess why she had come.

The lift was not available, but on the whole that was an advantage. Julia slipped softly up the stairs. There seemed a general air of tension, but she supposed that was due to her own sense of panic. She had reached the fifth floor and was turning the corner of the last flight when she heard voices from the landing above.

" Tell your chaps to bring the ambulance to the back entrance," said a cockney voice she did not recognise. " You know how it is in a place like this. Let it get about there's a corpse on the premises . . ."

A corpse ! She came to a dead stop. It never occurred to her they could be discussing anyone except Teddy Lane.

" They'll have to know," said a very different voice, cool, rather disgusted. " Still, I dare say they won't mind."

" Suicides get a place a bad name," whined the first voice.

" I shouldn't have thought that need trouble you much," said the other unsympathetically. " You'd better be prepared to attend the inquest," he added.

Another voice, also cockney but of a quite different timbre, asked when the inquest was likely to be.

" This afternoon if it can be squeezed in," said the man who was obviously a doctor. " Coroners don't like their week-ends mucked up any more than anyone else. What relatives has the chap got ? You'd better get in touch."

" I wouldn't know," said the voice. " I'm only the porter here."

" Well, I suppose there'll be letters or papers of some kind. If they can't be contacted you can presumably give evidence of identification."

" I've only got his word for it that his name was Lane at all," Moxon objected.

" Any reason to suppose it wasn't ? Then don't try and make difficulties, man."

" And you'll give the certificate ? " asked Moxon.

" We don't know what he died of, not officially, not till after the inquest. Oh, some form of drug administered as an opiate, but whether he took it himself . . ."

" Of course he took it himself. He was in deep enough."

" Deep ? "

" Broke, if you ask me. And then there was that policeman what came round yesterday afternoon. Oh, he'd had it and he knew it. Don't surprise me in the least."

" You'll be able to tell the court that, when you're asked," said the doctor crisply. " By the way, I've notified the police. Well, suicide's a form of murder, you know, according to their rules."

Obviously he was coming downstairs. Julia turned, panic-stricken, and slipped away again. So it was all over. Teddy Lane was dead. The danger had disappeared and she could breathe again. They could all breathe again, Gerald and she and the woman in Hunter Street, and probably a dozen others. But instead of the relief she anticipated she felt her heart as heavy as a rock in her breast. Poor Teddy Lane ! A little worm, Charles would have said, but when worms get stamped on you can't help remembering that even for them life had some value. She wondered if it would be safe to send flowers. He had been her enemy, nothing could change that, but he'd been a human being, too, who had somehow gone wrong ; in the end he was to have nothing, not even the privacy of a family funeral. And at *his* burial there would be no mourners, no friends, only a reporter or two sniffing round for a reason. Not that that would be hard to find. He'd been threatening them—Gerald and Ames and the woman in Hunter Street, as well as herself—but obviously someone had been threatening him and he hadn't been able to take it, as they said.

Presently she would feel a sense of release, but not yet, not yet. Pay a few moments' tribute to the memory of some-one who had once, long ago, been gentle, been kind.

It was still raining, and she paused on the step to open

her umbrella. She was quite oblivious of the little crowd still gathered in the hall and was totally unprepared for the hand on her arm and the voice that said in her ear, " There's a tea-shop on the corner. Go there and buy yourself a cup of coffee. And wait for me. I shan't be more than a minute."

She didn't look round to see who spoke to her, didn't even think of arguing or refusing. She went out like an automaton, walked into the teashop and picked up a tray. There were eight or nine people moving along the self-service counter, collecting buns and cakes and beans on toast ; she moved with them, thinking, " What a fool I was to believe I could get away so easily. When flies get into webs Providence doesn't shrivel the web to let the fly escape. Even if the spider dies the victims aren't set free."

Someone nudged her sharply from the back, and she looked up to realise that she was being addressed.

" Tea or coffee ? " demanded the woman behind the counter.

" Oh—coffee, please."

" With or without ? "

Jula stared. " With or without what ? "

The woman sighed with impatience. " Sugar, of course."

" Without, please. And black coffee."

" Black ? "

" Yes, please."

The woman put down the cup she had already half-filled with milk and muttering to herself got another.

" It'll be extra," she warned Julia, but Julia only looked at her uncomprehendingly. She took the cup, and a friendly little man put a saucer on her tray. " Spoon in the rack at the end," he whispered.

" You don't want a spoon if you don't take sugar," remarked the woman in a loud voice, and sniffed.

Julia moved on like one in a daze. The clerk at the cash-desk glanced at her cup.

" Bovril ? "

" Coffee."

" Coffee ? Black ? Fivepence."

Julia put the money down and took the tray to a small table in the corner that fortunately was unoccupied, and two or three minutes later Mrs. Tempest joined her, bearing a tray on which were a cup of coffee and a bun and butter.

" Clever of you to get a table to ourselves," she remarked

composedly, though in fact her heart was thumping away like a sledge-hammer. " Please tell me what's happened."

" He's dead," said Julia flatly. " Is that what you expected ? "

" To-day is Black Friday. I had to be sure."

" That the person responsible was going to honour the agreement ? That means—you knew I drew the Black Death."

" Yes," said Mrs. Tempest. " When did it happen ? "

" I—I don't know," whispered Julia. " The police are there now, I think."

" I see." Mrs. Tempest stirred sugar into her coffee. " What made you come back ? "

" Come back ? "

" If he's dead now he must have been—disposed of—last night or early this morning. As a matter of fact, they think it was last night. I've been listening to gossip for quite a long time."

" Weren't you afraid someone would notice you ? "

" The best of looking like everyone else is that you're virtually invisible. Now, no one who had once seen you could ever forget."

Julia instinctively put up a hand to shield her face. " I came because I had to be sure that it was going to be all right. Don't you see, I had to come ? Last night . . ." She stopped.

" You were going to say ? " prompted Mrs. Tempest.

" Nothing."

" Perhaps you're wise. Years ago I was at a murder trial, and I heard a counsel say the best defence was, I don't know, I wasn't there, I don't remember. Because if you don't remember you can't tell them anything, can you ? "

Julia dropped her hand. Her eyes were wide with terror. " Why are you saying this to me ? "

" I thought it such excellent advice. I thought, if ever I found myself in similar circumstances, it would be worth acting upon. I don't remember—not anything. You do understand, don't you ? " She pushed away her cup. " I wonder what they make this coffee of," she observed. " I believe in the Boer War they used egg-shells and acorns. At all events, that is what an aunt of mine used to say. I think we'd better not leave together." There was no change whatsoever in the cool voice. " You never know who may be watching us. I suppose the news will be in the late editions."

And, gathering gloves and purse, she rose and, every inch a lady as Crook would have said, she went quietly out.

It was a representative of the Gas Board, come to empty the meter, who was responsible for Teddy being found as soon as he was. Having rung twice, and recalling that on a previous occasion he had been unable to get in, he called to Moxon, who was delivering a parcel on the floor below, " Any chance of getting at the meter in No. 12 ? Chap's had the usual card warning him we were coming but—nothing doing. Gentleman must be out."

" I'll let you in with the pass-key," offered Moxon, obligingly.

The other looked a little dubious. " Suppose he's in ? "

" If he's in he'd open the door, wouldn't he, unless he was ' out,' " retorted the porter, wittily. " Matter of fact, you'll probably find the bolt's up. Whether he's going in fear of his life or it's just the bailiffs, search me ..." He produced the key as he spoke, and opened the door of the flat. " O.K.," he remarked cheerily. " Come on, mate, it's all right, you don't have to worry about him. He owes a month's rent, anyway." It might have been Teddy Lane's epitaph.

The meter supplied gas to the small fire and ring in the living-room. Hot water, such as it was, was included in the rent and was the cause of many of Moxon's complaints. These blasted furnaces ... A little to the gasman's surprise the porter followed him into the room. The storm of the previous night had blown the communicating door between this and the bedroom ajar, and both men could see the supine figure of Teddy Lane lying sprawled on the bed, still fully clothed.

" 'Ere, I say," expostulated the meter-reader, who was clearly a nervous type, " 'e is in. Look there."

Moxon threw Teddy the most cursory of glances. " Sleeping it off," he said. " Well, I ask you——" he had reached the threshold of the bedroom and stood inhaling. " Look at that." He indicated the whisky bottle that was practically empty. " A man's best friend ..."

But his companion had not moved. " Don't much like the way he's lying," he said. " Besides, he's sleeping it off very quiet. I was in A.R P. in the war, and we saw a lot of chaps looking like that, after raids, and they all went the same way home. Mortuary," he added in explanatory tones.

" You're too sensitive for this job, mate," Moxon told him. " Still, just to please you . . ."

He walked carelessly into Teddy's room. " Man to empty the meter, Mr. Lane," he announced in loud tones.

Teddy didn't stir. Moxon bent a little, his expression changed. " Crumbs," he said. " Here, mate, come in a minute."

The other sidled through the door, approached the bedside. After a moment he said, " Best get the police, 'adn't you ? "

" Wait a minute. We can't be sure . . ."

" Can't we ? I can. He's had it, mate." He glanced round. " How about a doctor ? "

Moxon looked dubious. " Don't know that he ever had one. Wait a minute, though, we don't want the police if we can help it. There's a chap called Allen on the ground floor. He is—or was—a doctor."

Allen was in and only took a glance at Teddy to confirm the gasman's verdict. " If you don't know who his doctor was," he said, " you'd best inform the police. Let them take the rap. You see, if he wasn't under regular attention, it'll mean an inquest."

" The directors won't like it," Moxon muttered.

" Too bad," said Allen grimly.

" But—what was it ? " the porter insisted.

" I can't tell you without making a more detailed examination, but—well, you said yourself he was in a jam, and there's one way out on the table there." He indicated a bottle containing some tablets that was three-parts empty. It was a small round bottle with no chemist's label. Moxon didn't notice that detail, though the doctor did. " Let the police get on with it," he said again, and went away.

With a heavy heart Moxon telephoned to the local station.

" I don't know if he 'ad a family," he confided to Bertha. " Never got much in the way of letters, did he ? Never talked as if he had a soul belonging to him."

" You'll die of worry one of these days," said Bertha comfortably. " You didn't murder him, did you ? "

Moxon nearly shot out of his seat. " What a word to use. Who's talking about murder ? "

" No one. Heart, I expect."

" That doctor chap—Allen—said something about a

sleeping-draught. Not that he'd commit himself. All the same, I don't like it."

The police didn't like it, either. They asked Moxon a lot of questions he couldn't answer, and imported a doctor of their own.

" *I* don't know if he took sleeping-stuff," Moxon protested. " I wasn't his keeper. But if he did—well, I know he was in pretty deep."

" In what ? "

" I mean, he'd been acting queer for some days. Went off yesterday morning looking as pleased as Punch and saying he'd be away till further notice, and back he come, looking like a ghost, the same night. I'll tell you another thing, a police officer came in during the afternoon. Of course I said he was away, didn't know when he'd be back. He said he'd be round again . . ."

" Been round since ? "

" I 'aven't seen 'im. Nor 'e didn't say what his business was."

The policeman frowned. He didn't know anything about the call. (Nor, it turned out later, did anyone else in the district. That was one of the mysteries the police never solved.)

" Any relatives ? " they asked Moxon.

" If so I never saw them. Don't mean he hadn't got any," he added quickly, " but—well, you never know. They may have drifted. Happens sometimes. I've got a sister somewhere . . ."

But the police weren't interested in Moxon's sister and let him see it.

" I dare say there'll be something in his flat," they said, and started investigating. In the meantime, an ambulance had been sent for and the doctor whom the police had brought said Teddy had died of an overdose of one of the barbituric drugs. Seeing the bottle by the bed, the authorities imagined everything was going to be plain sailing. Another chap who couldn't take it making trouble.

They took the bottle of tablets as a routine measure ; it didn't occur to them then that the stuff Teddy had taken could have had any other source. Also as a matter of routine they searched the sitting-room. If Teddy had had letters he hadn't kept them. There was nothing in the black deed-box, which was unlocked, and no papers of any kind on the table.

Only in the waste-paper basket they found Julia's letter making the appointment for the previous night, and a man was detailed to call at her address to ask how much light she could throw on the situation.

"What am I supposed to do about the flat ? " inquired Moxon sulkily. " The furniture all belongs to the company, but . . ."

The police solved that by locking the flat and telling Moxon he'd get his instructions in due course. They had no notion at that stage that this was more than " another little job for the undertaker." The idea of murder never passed through their minds.

CHAPTER ELEVEN

OLD SINS HAVE LONG SHADOWS

On Fridays the House of Commons shuts up shop at half-past four and before five o'clock Charles was home. Julia looked much as usual to a casual eye, but he knew at once something was wrong, and the apprehension he had felt for her the previous day was intensified.

On guard, he reflected. It would be useless to try to press her further, it would only make her roll up like a hedgehog, exposing her prickles. So he made casual small-talk hoping she'd give him an opening, while Julia, never relaxing her vigilance for a moment, headed him off every time he came near a personal question. He had just brought her a glass of sherry at six o'clock when a maid came in, carrying a card that announced the arrival of the police.

Charles, who was nearest, took it off the salver.

"Inspector Pepper," he read. " Not more car trouble, Ju ? " But though he spoke lightly enough he knew it was nothing so simple.

As for Julia, she said nothing, just sat looking at the card as though she couldn't believe it. And yet it was what she had been anticipating all day. Every time a telephone rang or a bell pealed she had thought, " This is it." And now, at last, it was.

" Bring him in," said Charles, seeing that Julia was beyond speech. " Or—wait a minute—I'll come out."

A man in plain clothes was waiting in the hall. "It was Lady Silk I came to see," he insisted.

"Lady Silk's not very well," said Charles. "Is it essential . . . ?"

"I'm afraid it is, sir."

So Charles took him into the library and went to warn Julia.

"You know why he's here, don't you?"

"Did he tell you?"

"The original clam. And that's no answer to my question. All right," as Julia said nothing. "Any objection to my listening-in?"

Julia agreed hopelessly. It was too late for secrecy. Everything was bound to come out now. Because she hadn't the smallest doubt why the inspector was here. Nothing so simple as a car offence, you could be certain. No, it was Teddy Lane —Teddy Lane—Teddy Lane.

She said, "I'm sorry, Charles, I hoped you needn't be drawn in," and preceded him into the library. Inspector Pepper was standing looking at a picture of a horse.

"Lady Silk?" he said briskly, and, without the smallest preamble, plunged into his subject. "We're inquiring into the death of a man called Edward Lane, and we think you may be able to help us."

"Lane?" repeated Charles sharply, before Julia could speak. He had the photographic memory essential to a modern Member of Parliament, and as soon as he heard the name he saw himself standing by the window in Julia's bedroom watching her distorted face in the mirror.

Pepper swung round. "You knew him, sir?"

Charles shook his head. "There was someone of that name my wife worked with during the war—but that's a long time ago. Is it the same one?"

"This gentleman lived at No. 12 Ellison Mansions."

Julia's head came up; in an instant she seemed to have recovered her poise.

"That's the one. Did you say he was dead?"

"Yes, Lady Silk. When did you last see him?"

"He asked me to what he called a reunion party at his flat a week ago—exactly a week ago to-day. I haven't seen him since."

Pepper said quietly, "I think I should tell you, Lady

Silk, that we found a letter in his room, apparently written by yourself, making an appointment for last night."

Julia looked not at the inspector but at Charles. " It's perfectly true," she acknowledged unemotionally. " I did mean to go and see him. But I had a breakdown and didn't get back to London till nearly half-past eight." She turned suddenly. " What time did he—do they think he died ? "

" Probably last night," said the inspector uncompromisingly. " Any special reason for asking, Lady Silk ? "

" I tried to ring him up and explain I'd been delayed, but I couldn't get any reply. That might—must have been the reason."

" What time was this ? "

" Oh, about eight-fifteen, I should think."

" You rang up from here ? "

" No. A call-box."

Charles said, " My wife told me when she came in about the breakdown. What's the idea in dragging her into this ? How did this chap die, anyway ? "

" I'll ask the questions, Sir Charles," said Pepper. His manner was perfectly civil, but not encouraging. Charles drew back. He knew the inspector could insist on seeing Julia alone, and in his heart rang the words, Too late. It was too late. " Too late for what ? " he'd said. " Too late to prevent cook making the soufflé," she'd told him swiftly. But, of course, that wasn't what she meant. Too late to visit Teddy Lane. She must have meant that.

" There are some questions I'd like to put to you, Lady Silk," Pepper went on, " but you're not compelled to answer until you've seen a lawyer. You see," he added quickly, forestalling Charles's comment, " we have reason to believe this isn't a straightforward death. Now would you care to make any statement as to your reason for calling on Mr. Lane ? "

" I've told you, I didn't call. It was too late."

" For making the appointment, then."

" I—" she looked at Charles but Charles looked like something modelled from wood—" I had something to take him."

" And what was that, Lady Silk ? "

She burst out, " It's nothing that could conceivably have anything to do with his death. You still haven't told us how it happened."

" He died of an overdose of sleeping-mixture."

Before Charles could prevent her Julia burst out, "It must have been an accident. Teddy would never have committed suicide. He was—afraid of death."

Charles looked at her oddly but maintained a stony silence. "It doesn't look like suicide to us either," agreed the inspector. "You see, Lady Silk, though he had certain tablets in his possession at the time of his death, they weren't the cause of it. He died of an overdraught of a barbituric drug. Did you know he took drugs?"

Julia shook her head. "I've scarcely seen him in ten years. But—it's not fair to say you take drugs because you have sleeping-pills. I've had them myself and . . ."

"Ah! When was this, Lady Silk?"

"Oh, a long time ago. I don't remember exactly. I haven't taken any for ages."

"But you still have some, Lady Silk?"

"No, I don't think so. I'm sure I haven't. I came across the empty bottle only the other day. I don't need them any more."

Charles felt as though every word she spoke was a blow on his heart. Teddy Lane wasn't the only one to commit suicide (if he had, of course). Julia was simply rushing out to meet trouble, like some eagerly-awaited guest. "Come in, come in . . ." Oh God, thought Charles, what's the use of loving anyone if you're helpless when they're in a jam? But he said nothing. Just keeping quiet was all he could do for the time being.

The inspector was asking for details, and she told him the name of the doctor who had given her the prescription and the chemist who'd made it up. "Anyway," she said, "I've got the bottle if you want proof."

The inspector said, "Thank you, Lady Silk, and here's another queer thing. Mr. Lane didn't take the tablets in water as you might expect, he didn't even take them in whisky, though he'd been drinking it shortly before he died —we found the glass—he took them in a cup of coffee in his sitting-room."

"Well," said Julia obtusely, "I suppose there's no reason why he shouldn't. But how can you be sure?"

"Because we've found a residue of the drug in one of the coffee-cups."

"In *one* of them?"

"Oh yes, he had a visitor last night. We've established

that fact. Mr. Lane rang down to the porter shortly before eight to say he was engaged and didn't wish to be disturbed."

" I suppose he didn't happen to mention his visitor's sex," suggested Charles.

" Sir Charles," said the inspector in peremptory tones, " I must request you to keep silence. I am here to try to solve a death that isn't due to natural causes. Yes, Lady Silk, there were two people drinking coffee in Mr. Lane's flat last night. One cup contained milk and sugar, the other was black."

" Teddy's would be the one with milk and sugar," Julia agreed. " He couldn't bear black coffee."

" A great many people would agree with him," said Pepper smoothly. " I can't take it black myself."

" And I can't take it any other way. If you're going to ask me whether I know of any of his friends or acquaintances who drank their coffee black, the answer is No. I didn't know any of them, to start with."

" Oh Julia darling, why can't I knock you on the head with a hammer ? " wondered Charles in agony. " Can't you see you're simply playing into this fellow's hands ? "

But he remembered the inspector's warning and held his tongue.

" Moreover—and this really points to foul play—there was poison not only in the cup but also in the residue of milk in the bottle. Whoever wanted Mr. Lane out of the way was taking no chances." He let that sink in, then went on : " You told me just now, Lady Silk, that you didn't get back here until about eight-thirty. Was that according to plan ? "

" Of course not. I meant to see Mr. Lane at, say, half-past six and then come on home ; we dine at seven-thirty. But I had a breakdown," and at Pepper's request she repeated in detail the story she had told her husband the previous night.

Pepper seemed unimpressed. " Really, Lady Silk," he remarked, " that's a very strange story. You were going to see Mr. Lane last night—why, by the way, did you make the appointment for the evening ? Wouldn't the afternoon have been simpler ? It's not as though he could be detained at his work, since he had none."

" I didn't expect to be back from Rowlhampton till about six."

" Was it essential to go to Rowlhampton yesterday ? "
" Yes."

" You mean, there was some connection between your visit to Rowlhampton and your prospective call on Mr. Lane ? "

" Yes," repeated Julia.

" Lady Silk, you are not being very co-operative. I must ask you outright, why did you go to Rowlhampton ? Whom did you see there ? "

Julia turned in an agony. " It was a private matter. It can't possibly affect Mr. Lane's death, because I didn't see him yesterday."

" But you meant to. Why did you go to Rowlhampton ? Was it perhaps to get something from a chemist ? "

" No, no," cried Julia. " I've told you about six times already, I never saw Teddy last night. I didn't see him at all yesterday."

" I heard you, Lady Silk, but—someone called at about a quarter to eight, someone sufficiently important for Lane to ring down to the porter and say he didn't wish to be disturbed. Apart from the porter's evidence, we know someone was there, because of the two coffee-cups. I must ask you again, why were you proposing to see him ? " Then, as Julia remained obstinately silent, he said, " You were going to take him whatever it was you got at Rowlhampton. Isn't that so ? "

" Yes," said Julia desperately, " but it wasn't drugs. Charles, I promise you . . ."

" You're not being very wise," said Charles in a stranger's voice. " You'd do much better to tell the inspector what it was you went to get."

Pepper suggested, " Since you didn't see Mr. Lane, Lady Silk, this mysterious thing is still in your possession."

" Yes," said Julia, as though somehow that lightened the situation. " I've got it in my room. I can show it you. It's in my bag . . ."

" Is that your bag on the desk ? "

" Yes. I'd forgotten." She opened it and drew out a wad of bank notes. " I was going to take him this."

The Inspector took them and counted them. " Two hundred and fifty pounds. It's a good deal of money, Lady Silk."

" Only half what he asked for."

" I see. Was this at the little reunion party you spoke about ? "

" Yes." She looked at Charles with tragic eyes. " Do you remember saying, ' He probably wants to make a touch ' ? Well, you were right."

" Rather a heavy touch," murmured Charles non-committally. " Did he really think you were going to come across with five hundred pounds ? "

" I told him it was impossible, I didn't handle money on that scale."

" But—something happened, Lady Silk, to make you change your mind. At all events, you got the money for him ? "

" Yes. I sold some jewellery. Oh, nothing we cared for in particular. You've always given me so much, Charles." Her voice grew calmer. " I went to a man at Rowlhampton called Christmas. Isn't that a strange name for a jeweller ? "

" Presumably Lane had reason to suppose you would meet his demands ? " Pepper was quite unmoved.

" Oh yes," said Julia. " I suppose he knew."

" What was it, Julia ? " asked Charles.

She drew a deep breath. " It was a letter—a perfectly innocent letter as it happens, but I suppose that's what they all say."

" Worth five hundred pounds ? "

" If you think my life's worth as much."

" And—you got the letter without the money, Lady Silk ? "

She stared. " Of course not. I told you—I didn't see him last night. I've still got the money, I can show it you— I have showed it to you."

" I realise that, Lady Silk. Anyway, there was no money found in his flat. But—there was no compromising letter from you there, either."

" There must have been. In the deed-box in the corner. Perhaps you didn't notice . . ."

" The deed-box was empty. The key was in the lock, and there was nothing in it that could incriminate you or anyone else. There was no trace of it anywhere on the premises. Lady Silk, where is that letter ? "

" I've told you," cried Julia, " I don't know. I haven't seen it for ten years."

" Ten years ! " The exclamation burst simultaneously from both men.

" Yes. I wrote it to him when—when you came back, Charles."

" And he's been levying blackmail ever since, Lady Silk ? "

" Of course not."

Even Charles looked astounded. " You mean," continued Pepper, hardily, " he's kept it for ten years before taking any action ? "

" Yes."

" Doesn't that strike you as rather peculiar ? "

" I suppose he wasn't so hard up till now."

" And after ten years he thinks it's worth five hundred pounds ? " Charles at all events could see the thought moving through his mind. He didn't for an instant believe the letter was ten years old ; it was of recent date to his way of thinking. Or most likely there were several of them, beginning with one written ten years ago. It was hard to see how a woman who was married to Charles Silk could look twice at Teddy Lane, but one of the few points on which Arthur Crook, that unconventional lawyer—and at this stage nobody had any idea how soon he was going to be dragged in—agreed with the police was that where women were concerned there was no reliable yardstick. They were absolutely incalculable and upset anybody's rule of thumb.

" Well, it was," said Julia simply. " And please don't go on asking me where the letter is, because I haven't seen it for ten years."

" You mean, he didn't show it you when you went to visit him ? "

" No. I never thought of asking for it."

" But you knew he kept it in that deed-box ? " Pepper was on to that discrepancy like a hawk on a field-mouse.

" I don't know for certain. But he must have kept something in it."

" It was locked ? "

" Again, I don't know. It was shut."

" It was open when we found it. And empty. Lady Silk, can you suggest anyone else who might be interested in the contents of that box ? "

" No. Except that I don't suppose I was his only hope of income."

Pepper nodded. " When did Mr. Lane make his demand, Lady Silk ? " (Confound the fellow, thought Charles, must he drag her name in every time he opens his mouth ?)

" I told you—he asked me to a party last week."

" Oh yes. Were there many people there ? "

" Not many."

" I think you said a reunion party ? "

" That's what he called it."

" So that you'd recognise some at least of your fellow-guests ? "

" I didn't. There was no one else from the station there. I don't know why he called it that. Unless . . ."

" Yes, Lady Silk." Charles gritted his teeth.

" Unless he thought that would be an inducement to me to go."

" It was very important that you should go ? "

" Well, it was important to him," said Julia simply. " He wanted money, wanted it very badly, I gather."

" I meant—important to you ? Did you realise his reason for inviting you to visit him ? "

" He simply said it was a reunion party . . ."

" But you could have refused, pleaded a previous engagement."

" It wouldn't have been any good," said Julia desperately " He'd only have come round here or something."

" So from the outset you appreciated that the invitation covered a threat ? "

" I didn't think he simply wanted to see me again. I'd only seen him once in ten years and that was by chance."

Pepper left that and went on to the next point. " You say you didn't recognise any of the other guests ? "

" There weren't any introductions and nobody volunteered any information. I didn't tell anyone who I was . . ."

" That sounds rather strange, Lady Silk."

" It was a very strange sort of party. Oh, you must understand. Why do you try and keep me on tenterhooks ? We were all there for the same reason. Naturally, no names were mentioned."

" Here we go round the mulberry bush, the mulberry bush, the mulberry bush," thought Charles as desperate as Julia but better at playing poker. He could read the inspector's mind and indeed sympathise with his deductions. The chap didn't believe there had been anyone else there, just a *tête-à-tête* between this fellow Lane, and his wife—*his wife* in this beastly sordid mess.

" And he may be right," Charles had to acknowledge. It sounded more reasonable than inviting three or four victims simultaneously.

Pepper went on, like someone doing the household shopping, thought Charles, moving methodically from shop to shop.

" And you still stand by your original statement that that was the only time you saw Mr. Lane."

" Yes."

" You mean, that was the only visit you ever made to his flat ? "

" Yes. I've told you . . . What are you trying to do ? Break my nerve, make me contradict myself ? "

That was a mistake; Charles knew it if Julia didn't. The inspector stiffened. " I'm doing my duty, Lady Silk, which is to learn the truth about Mr. Lane's death."

" I've told you, I can't help you."

" You've also told me you didn't visit him at his flat last night. But you intended to offer him the two hundred and fifty pounds, so perhaps you called on him this morning."

" Where would be the sense ? He was dead."

Pepper jumped. " How did you know ? "

" You told me when you came in, you said . . ."

" I mean, how did you know *this morning* ? And if you didn't know, why didn't you ring him up or go round yourself ? You didn't go to all that trouble to get the money for nothing."

Julia was in a cleft stick and she knew it. " Very well then," she said, " I shall have to tell you. I did go round this morning and the police were there already. But it was this morning; this morning, not last night."

The situation was worsening momentarily. Charles was in an agony, though his face might have been made of wood for all the feeling he betrayed. Pepper seemed quite unmoved.

" So you went round this morning, Lady Silk. You didn't tell me that before."

" Since he was dead already what difference could it make ? "

" How did you know he was dead ? "

" I could hear them talking."

" Who was talking ? "

" Well—the porter, for one."

" So you knew the porter ? " This chap didn't miss much, thought Charles.

" No. I've never set eyes on him, but I heard him say something about being the porter. . . . I was going up the stairs and just before I got to the sixth floor I heard voices, so I stopped, and they were talking about someone being dead, and this man, the porter, I mean, I don't know his name, asked whoever he was talking to if the ambulance couldn't come to the back entrance."

" And you knew they were talking about Mr. Lane ? "
" Yes."
" Why ? "
" They—they . . ."
" They hadn't mentioned his name, had they ? But he's
not the only tenant on the sixth floor."
" They did say his name," said Julia. " I remember now.
Just as I was going downstairs . . ."
" Convinced that it was Mr. Lane they were talking about ? "
" Yes."
" I see. But how could you be so sure ? Other people die
suddenly. Or was it perhaps because you knew he was
dead ? "
" I didn't know. I didn't. But when a man has a number
of enemies . . ."
" I thought you hadn't seen him for ten years. How could
you know about his enemies ? "
" A man who lives as he did is bound to have enemies."
" As he did ? What do you mean by that, Lady Silk ? "
She said, " Blackmail . . ."
" So that was his living ? He told you so ? "
" He hadn't got a job. And he was asking us all for money.
What else could you call it ? "
Pepper nodded. (Quite a professional mandarin, thought
Charles, racked with fear.) " Now I want you to think very
carefully, Lady Silk. You're quite sure you can't help us with
regard to any of the other members of the party ? You see,
since you're certain you had nothing to do with his death,
it's reasonable to imagine that one of the others may be
responsible. There's nothing among his papers to indicate
who any of those others might be . . ."
" Well, it's no use looking at me like that," said Julia
wearily. " I've told you I can't help you. Nobody was
introduced. And I did go to the building this morning but
I didn't get inside the flat and I didn't see Teddy Lane. I did
go down to Rowlhampton yesterday and I did have a breakdown. You can prove about Rowlhampton by going to see
the jeweller, and you could prove about the breakdown by
finding the motor-cyclist. After all," she added with sudden
spirit, " if I'd put the stuff in Teddy's coffee would I have
been fool enough to leave the letter lying about for everyone to see ? The letter saying I was coming that night, I
mean ? "

" It had blown into the waste-paper basket," said Pepper slowly.

Julia uttered a harsh little laugh. " Don't forget I'm innocent till I'm proved guilty," she said. " You haven't got a thing against me yet. Nobody saw me there last night . . ."

" Did anyone see you there this morning ? "

A sudden light burned in Julia's eye. " Surely this, this releases me from my promise," she thought. " I'm not involving her by saying she was there ? But suppose"—the light died out like a cloud passing over the sun—" suppose she denies it ? Oh, but she can't," cried Julia to her distracted heart, " not when she knows what it means to me. She couldn't let me *hang*." For already she had visions of herself under arrest, being charged, being tried, perhaps even being found guilty. " No," she told herself, " she'd never let it come to that."

She didn't realise, as Crook was to realise from the start, that Mrs. Tempest would see all three of her allies dangling from lamp-posts before she would risk spoiling her beloved Henry's life.

Suddenly it was over. Pepper stood up. He seemed to have been asking questions for an eternity. Julia had almost lost count of her answers ; she felt as though a pitiless hammer had been beating for hours on her brain. Had she, she wondered in confusion, at last given him the answer he sought ? He said, " That will be all for the moment, Lady Silk," and Charles asked quickly if they'd want his wife at the inquest.

" If so you'll hear from us," said Pepper. " It's quite possible in the circumstances that the police will ask for an adjournment after evidence of identification has been given. You won't be leaving town, will you, Lady Silk ? We may want you at any moment."

After Pepper had gone Charles said thoughtfully, " Ju, why did you marry me in the first place ? "

Julia looked as if she couldn't believe her ears. " Because I loved you, darling. Oh Charles, it's true, it's just as true to-day as it was then."

" In that case," said Charles in the same voice, " why not give me the chance of showing it was—and is—reciprocal ? Why get yourself into this unsavoury mess with Lane ? "

" Because I was in it ten years ago. You don't understand."

" Suppose you put me in the picture," suggested Charles. And, five minutes later, " Honestly, Ju, you're fit to be tied.

Do you imagine any living person, seeing me and Johnny together, could believe he wasn't my son ? "

" Perhaps not, but—you didn't know Teddy. He wasn't always like this, but something's got warped. It would give him real pleasure to spoil things, not only for me . . ."

" Ah ! " said Charles. " The others come into this, too. I wonder why you should be selected by the police."

" Because I drew the Black Death," said Julia. " That's why the others are safe. Because *I* drew it."

Charles moved over to the telephone. " I think I'll have a word with Morsby," he said. " In any case if you have to attend the inquest you ought to be represented."

But when he got through to the solicitor's home address he learned that Mr. and Mrs. Morsby had gone away for the week-end, and wouldn't be back till Monday. Which was really why Arthur Crook came into the case, because by Monday the papers carried the news :

BARONET M.P.'s WIFE ACCUSED OF MURDER

" The police can't like grass much," Crook observed characteristically to Bill Parsons, his trusted partner and ally of a quarter of a century. " They don't let it grow under their feet. I see they've taken Lady Silk for the Lane murder. Well, these are the days of democracy. It's an age since a dame with a handle to her name was up for the Cemetery Stakes. But no reason why they shouldn't enjoy themselves the same as common chaps like you and me."

CHAPTER TWELVE

CROOKS IN COUNCIL

WHEN GERALD ROSS saw in the stop press news on Friday evening that a man called Edward Lane had been found dead in Ellison Mansions and that the police were inquiring into the circumstances of that death he thought, " What next ? On what the police unearth all our fortunes may depend," and for forty-eight hours he held himself rigid expecting momentarily a ring at the bell, the pealing of the telephone, an official voice saying, " Mr. Ross, I believe you were acquainted with the deceased." And yet—and yet . . . Was it probable that they could trace the link between them ? He'd written no letters, Teddy hadn't got that on him, he had no reason to believe that anyone except Julia had recognised him either on the Friday or the Saturday of their momentous meetings. But—that this should pass without himself being publicly involved, without his name being brought forward, that a verdict of accidental death or even of suicide (for by next day it seemed clear that the fellow had died of an overdose of a barbituric drug) should be recorded and the matter be allowed to pass into oblivion—that surely was too good to be true.

And he was right. It was.

He was not the only man in London to wait with nerves a-tingle for news of the inquest, and when it became known that the police had been satisfied with identification and the briefest of medical reports, it was obvious to anyone who understood the routine of such affairs that the authorities were on the trail.

The police have not ruled out the possibility of foul play !

That was their damned discreet way of putting it.

Harmsworth Ames read the paragraph over and over. He knew, better than any of them, what that implied. The police were pretty certain there had been foul play. Otherwise the case was perfectly plain sailing. A man, known to be in debt, to be living, no, existing, on the bare fringe of society, had been found dead in a building of dubious reputation. His affairs were in disorder. He had either no family or none prepared to shoulder any responsibility for him—because, argued Ames, if that had been the case, he wouldn't have been driven to summoning that fantastic sherry party and uttering his ultimatum. What more natural, then, that, seeing no hope ahead, he had quietly put an end to his life ?

Ames shrugged a huge shoulder. It sounded so simple, so obvious, but life was never quite so obvious as that. A single meeting with Teddy had assured him that his was never the type to take the quiet, the gentlemanly way out. He had sunk too far down for such consideration. " Not a doubt about it," said Ames gently, talking, it seemed, to his own shadow, " this is going to be a nasty business."

And nasty not only for whoever was responsible for Teddy's presence in the mortuary now and shortly in the burial-ground, but for anyone whom the police could prove had had any sort of association with him during the last week or so of his life. Without particular vanity, Ames was accustomed to think of himself as lifted slightly above the mass of the human race. Anything he did would assume a particular importance, though the action in itself might be insignificant, merely because it was Harmsworth Ames behind the activity. It did not, for instance, occur to him that his identity could remain unknown to any of his three accomplices and he would be more amazed than wounded to learn that Mrs. Tempest at least had no notion who he was. When, on Monday, he learned that Julia had been arrested his immediate reaction was : The weak link. That was clear from the outset. Ye gods, what a story the papers will make of this. A beautiful woman married to a man in a public position . . . Point is, will they break her ? That the police would get the story of the sherry party out of her he had no doubt at all. But—would she collapse and give them the information they wanted ? She had known young Ross before Black Friday. Ames supposed simply that she had also recognised himself. She had visited Mrs. Tempest at 10 Hunter Street. " We're all in the bag," reflected Harmsworth Ames, and even though all three of them might have unassailable alibis (and in his own case at least that wasn't the fact), they were none of them going to come out of this affair without considerable damage, if not absolute ruin.

Ames found himself wishing that any of them rather than Julia should have excited the suspicion of the police.

He was seated at his handsome writing-desk at the far end of a large expensively furnished room while these thoughts passed (passed ?—romped) through his mind. The door opened and closed with a crisp movement. He didn't raise his eyes. It was a trick of his to allow any visitor to come quite close to the desk before he lifted his head.

" And a pretty silly trick, too," thought the man who had just entered. " One day it'll catch him out." He said sharply, " Ames," and the Q.C. was so startled by the timbre of that voice that he jerked up his head and found Gerald Ross staring at him intently from the farther side of the desk.

" I wasn't expecting you," he observed.

" Don't you read the papers ? " inquired Gerald. " Perhaps this comes to you as a surprise, also." And he thrust a copy of the latest edition of the *Evening Record* under the Q.C.'s indomitable nose.

Ames pushed it away. " I'd seen it," he said. " Bad luck for Lady Silk. And I hope," he added reflectively, " it doesn't mean bad luck for the rest of us, too. One thing," he added as Gerald paused, aghast at such self-centredness, " it must bring relief to a good many people to know that Lane is where he can't talk any more."

" I don't give a damn for the people who're relieved to know he's dead," said Ross in a flat, angry voice. " What matters is—the thing's a mistake."

" Poisoning Lane ? I should have thought that was conferring a benefit on humanity."

" I don't mean that, and you know it. I mean—Julia didn't do it."

Ames's thick brows, black as thunderclouds, rose almost to meet the thick black hair.

" Any proof of that ? I mean, you didn't do it yourself by any chance ? This is off the record, naturally," he added.

" I didn't. Because someone else got in first."

" Able to prove that. Meaning, have you an alibi for Thursday night ? "

Ross frowned. " I was at the laboratory."

" Anyone with you ? "

" Not after six-thirty."

" And Lane's visitor came about 7.45. You'd have plenty of time to get to Ellison Mansions by then, and—meet anyone later that evening ? "

" I stayed at work till after ten."

" Any cleaners around ? Any night staff ? "

" There isn't a night staff. And the cleaners come in the morning. The telephone's switched off at six unless we ask for a special line, and I didn't."

" The police would make mincemeat of that," announced Ames juicily. " Still, if you were in the laboratory all the evening how can you be so sure Lady Silk is innocent ? "

" Because of this." Gerald put his hand in his pocket and drew out a small black disc. " I drew this in our lottery."

" Don't be proud," Ames warned him in a pleasant voice. " I can match you." And opening a drawer in his desk he produced his counter.

Gerald looked dazed. " You mean there were two ? "

" Since you ask me, I'd say there were four. The lady wasn't taking any chances. She couldn't be certain which of the four envelopes would fall to her lot, and she meant Lane to go where he couldn't do any more harm."

" You think Julia had one, too ? "

" And was the first to act on it. Yes, that's probably how it was."

Gerald shook his head. " I shall never believe it until she admits it herself. In the meantime, I'm going to the police."

Instantly he felt his arm held in a compelling grip. " Don't be a lunatic. How much good do you imagine that would do ? The police don't take a step like this without a reasonable amount of evidence. You tell me you're innocent, and I say I didn't do it. That leaves the issue between the two women. It's obvious that Lady Silk can't prove her innocence. More, there's a solid foundation for a case against her. Get this into your head, Ross. She may have done it. If she hasn't . . ."

" You're going to tell me that an innocent person never suffers. It isn't true and you know it. But even if they couldn't prove it, if the jury turned their case down, her life will be ruined. She's got a husband, a son . . ."

" It's too late to talk about them. They know, at all events the husband does. She's been accused. She can't simply fade out of the picture. Her one hope is to show she's innocent —if she can. You can tell me till you're blue in the face that she didn't poison Lane, but there's only one person who can say so with absolute assurance, and that's the man or woman who did. If you come forward what happens ? Your story will be told, your motives tested, your movements, so far as possible, traced. And you're an innocent man. You've just told me so. So how will it help Lady Silk for you to go grubbing in the mud ? The same applies to me. I was working late with the light burning, but that's no proof. I have an arrangement with the night staff that so long as my light's on they leave my room alone. If I work too late there's a second staff comes on in the morning and they tackle it. That night I was working till about ten o'clock, but I can't prove it. A clever counsel might suggest I'd slipped out leaving the lamp burning, done for Lane, and slipped back without being seen. And it's possible that that's how it happened, possible from the defence's point of view. As it happens, it wasn't that way but—I couldn't prove it. That other woman . . ."

" Do you know who she is ? " asked Gerald.

" Yes. *And* I know the nature of Lane's hold over her.

We don't know yet whether she has an alibi. But I'll tell you one thing. She's not going to come forward and throw in her hand as you want to. And she's got plenty of sense."

" If neither you nor I is guilty," said Ross slowly, " and if, as I'm convinced, Julia is also innocent, that only leaves this woman."

" Who may very well have done it. But if you imagine she's going to admit that, you're right out in your calculations. She'd see us all swing before she'd tell the truth. Now, tell me something. How well do you know the Silks ? "

Gerald considered. " I've been meeting them in this house and that for some years. I've dined with them and they with us."

" You're not intimate ? "

" No. We're on perfectly friendly terms . . ."

Ames drummed his fingers on the desk. " Any notion who their lawyer is ? "

" As a matter of fact, I do know. A fellow called Morsby, a connection of my wife's."

Ames made an impatient gesture. " He's no good. Regular old woman. The man you want is a chap called Crook. Name ring a bell ? " he asked, sharply.

Gerald shook his head. " Not that I've had much truck with the law since I came of age . . ."

" Quite. Well, Lady Silk's dilemma is that she can't tell her defence the truth without crashing the promise she gave to us, and landing us all in the cart, too ; and she won't give her defence a chance if she keeps her mouth buttoned up. Crook may get the story out of her, though not the names, but the difference between him and chaps of Morsby's kidney is that he's used to making bricks without straw and producing such an effective substitute you'd hardly know it from the genuine article. The other thing in his favour is his conscience. His professional conscience, he calls it."

" Which means ? "

" That he considers his job is to get his client acquitted, not to use his opportunities to set up as a judge, say, I don't believe this statement or that, therefore I can't undertake the case. If he saw a cat eating a canary he'd still undertake the defence and persuade a jury the cat had found the feathers in the dustbin—once he'd agreed to act for the cat, that is. Now you see why I asked how well you knew the Silks."

" Not precisely," Gerald admitted.

" At that you know them better than I do. Get hold of
Sir Charles and persuade him that Crook's his man. No,
don't shake your head like that, you can't afford to be
squeamish at this stage. You haven't any choice for all our
sakes. Or be selfish if you like and say for your wife's sake—
got any children ? Well, you don't want them to see their
father's name dragged in the gutter, paraded as a possible
murderer. And while you're about it," he added casually,
" you can tell Sir Charles that I'm prepared to act for the
defence, and he can pass that on to Crook."

" You can't do that." Gerald sounded horrified. " You're
in this with the rest of us."

" That's precisely why. Who else could watch our interests
so well ? I haven't got an alibi and nor have you. I know
the facts of the situation. I shall have more reason than any
Q.C. living for wanting to get Lady Silk acquitted."

Gerald looked at him sombrely. " That's one side of the
medal," he said.

" And the other ? Meaning that it might suit my book to
get her hanged ? My dear chap, you're off your feed. It
doesn't do any Q.C. good to lose a case. Besides which," he
added, " I can see you're cast in the Galahad mould. You'll
make the police a present of the facts if I don't get her off.
Isn't that so ? "

" Perhaps not the police, but her lawyer. And if fresh facts
are brought out that warrant an appeal, and . . ."

" Get it out of your head that Lady Silk is going to be
found guilty. It won't be the first tricky case I've swung."

His big ruthless face stared into Gerald's. The younger
man was torn with doubts. How far was it safe to trust the
fellow ? All this talk about it being essential to his own
reputation to secure an acquittal might be so much hot air.
On the other hand, how much good could *he* do Julia by
making the police a present of the position ?

" Forgetting your Hippocrene oath, aren't you ? " Ames's
voice cut coolly through his perplexity. " You're bound as
much as the rest of us to keep your mouth shut, and if you
were thinking of being that fictitious character, the parfit
gentil knight, let me tell you you wouldn't stand a chance
with the authorities. And I, for one, don't propose to have
my name chucked in the gutter because you have qualms.
Oh, be your age, man," he added more impatiently. " You
don't imagine the police are going to accept our bare words

that we had nothing to do with it. I don't even know," he added shrewdly, " whether you accept mine, and, as you've just pointed out, every medal has two sides. As for the fourth member of our party, you can take it from me she'd see all three of us in hell before she'd lift a finger to save us. Not because she's so madly attached to life *per se* as because something more valuable to her than her own life is at stake."

And so, reluctantly and with a feeling that they were both taking advantage of Julia, Gerald Ross agreed to sound Sir Charles.

Someone once said of Arthur Crook that the Judgment Day would find him as imperturbable and alert as always, probably offering to try and switch the evidence so as to sneak a sinner into Heaven. When the telephone rang and a voice said, " Mr. Crook ? My name is Silk. A friend of mine, Gerald Ross, has suggested that I should get in touch with you in connection with the accusation that has been brought against my wife for murder," he simply listened, said " O.K. I get you, yes, any time," and hung up.

" Things are moving," he told Bill placidly. " Who's Gerald Ross ? "

Bill, who knew all the answers, said at once, " Oh, one of the Government's tame team of chemists. Planning how to blow us all skyhigh one of these days."

" Since the sky's the limit and most people seem to want to spend eternity there they might be grateful to him," was Crook's characteristic retort. He was quite unlike any normal person's notion of a lawyer, being a big burly man, with fox-red hair and eyebrows and popping brown eyes as full of cunning intelligence as an egg of meat. " A bookie's tout," people generally thought, with as much conscience as the fox he resembled ; but Charles Silk didn't care if he looked like King Kong, so long as he got Julia out of the jam.

He came round immediately, apologising for his insistence. " The matter is so urgent," he said, " I feel there's no time for delay. You do know the facts of the case ? "

" If I knew the facts Lady Silk wouldn't be where she is now," returned Crook pleasantly. " My clients are always innocent. Didn't Ross mention that ? By the way, who put him on to me ? I haven't had the privilege of getting him out of jug yet not unless he's changed his name since then, of course."

Charles smiled faintly. " Oh, it was Harmsworth Ames. You know him, I expect ? "

" We have met. Thought of who you'll get to conduct the defence ? "

" Well, Ames has offered . . ."

" Has he indeed ? " Crook's mental eyebrows climbed. " Well, you couldn't get a better man. All the same—you won't take this amiss—but though the jury'll be told to keep their minds free from prejudice, that's a counsel of perfection, like the apostle saying it was every Christian's duty to keep himself unspotted from the world. You can only do that if you stay in out of the rain, which ain't much good to your fellow-men who're sweltering in the cloudburst. What I'm getting at is that if you pick a chap who's a personal friend . . ."

" But he's not," interrupted Charles. " I've never met him, and nor has my wife. The suggestion came from him, because he's interested in the case . . ."

" You're telling me," said Crook courteously. " Well, that helps us a lot. Now, tell me the story as Lady Silk told it to you. I'll be bound it's not the same story as the police are going to tell."

Charles complied with a brevity that Crook found impressive.

" Think she's giving you the gen when she says she didn't recognise any of the others ? "

" I can't answer that," said Charles carefully. " I'll only go so far as to say I'm certain she's holding out on us."

" Includin' you ? "

" She must know that anything she told me I should feel compelled to pass on to the police."

" Or maybe become an accessory ? Yes, I see her trouble. Still, I'm wearing quite a different pair of shoes." He looked at them complacently, huge brown brogues, big enough to float the three men of Gotham, thought Charles irrelevantly.

He left after answering a number of points raised by Crook with a candour that surprised himself, and on the way back was startled to discover that he felt convinced a definite step had been taken towards establishing Julia's innocence. It was the first time he had felt absolutely certain she wasn't involved, even indirectly, in Teddy Lane's death.

After Charles's departure Crook lay on his spine, doodling idly and doing arithmetic. " Interesting," he observed to Bill presently. " Wouldn't surprise me if this added up to something no one's thought of yet. Ever hear of Ames touting for a job before ? "

" No," agreed Bill, in a voice that suggested it was barely possible for something to happen without his having heard of it.

" Mostly he waits to be approached, and then there's as much palaver as if he were running for P.M. before things are settled. Wonder what his clerk makes of it. He won't like being passed over. They expect to have the say so when it comes to accepting briefs."

" Meaning he has a personal stake in the matter ? "

" Don't it look that way to you ? This fellow, Ross, too. He's a mutual friend, but I didn't gather he was a specially close one. But the minute the news breaks he gets in touch with Ames, and Ames sends him to Silk with a message to collar me, and a gratis suggestion that he'll act for the defence. Not even a mention of fees, you notice. How did Ames know that Silk hadn't got someone lined up for the job already ? "

" I don't suppose he did," said Bill sensibly.

" But they didn't have any hesitation about buttin' in. Besides, how comes Ross is so worked up about the case, unless it means something in particular to him. Wonder how well *he* knows Ames ? "

" About as well as chaps do who've met in casual circumstances—at a sherry party, say," suggested Bill.

" That's the way it looks to me, too. Oh, I dare say it's a bit of a high jump, but it's nothing to the one Lady Silk 'ull take unless we get cracking."

" Going to see her ? " asked Bill.

" One of these days. Always a good thing to have your quiver filled before you go out shooting. I'd say Sir Charles doesn't know the half. But then," he sighed gustily, " they tell me husbands never do."

Julia was fascinated by Arthur Crook, he was so huge, so brown, so altogether unexpected, after neat prim Mr. Morsby. Mr. Morsby had an immense respect for law and order ; Arthur Crook looked as if he were prepared to give those great twin brethren a kick in the pants any chance that offered. But if he didn't look the part he knew his onions, she had to admit that, and he got what he wanted from her as Charles, whom she loved, could never have done.

" Let's put first things first," he told her. " The first thing is that, bein' my client, you must be innocent. Get that into your head right away."

" I may have been crazy as my husband suggests, but I've never been crazy enough to doubt that," Julia told him.

" Well, that's good. Now—ever heard of Sherlock Holmes?" She stared. " Of course."

" Well." Crook smiled tolerantly. " He was before your time. He used to work on what he called a process of elimination, meaning that when you'd cancelled out all the impossible solutions the one that remained, however improbable it seemed, must be the answer. Mind you, we're working a bit in the dark. We don't know how many enemies this chap, Lane, had, but we do know of some of then. Let's start with a few facts. How many people were there at your murder party ? "

Julia started. " Do you mean the party at his flat ? "

" Were there any others ? "

" N-no."

" Sure ? Come on, Lady S., give me the gen. Or do you hanker after a martyr's crown ? Your husband won't be able to incorporate it in his coat of arms, you know."

Julia coloured up. " As a matter of fact—I think I can tell you this without breaking faith—we all met the following day to discuss the situation."

" All of you ? How many ? "

" Oh, just the few of us."

Crook sighed. " Not so hot on arithmetic ? " he suggested.

" I don't understand."

" Well, didn't they teach you at school to add up to double figures ? "

Julia capitulated. " There were five of us," she said.

" At which party ? "

" Teddy's. Including him, I mean."

" And four at the next one ? "

" Yes."

" One of the four bein' you ? "

" Yes."

" So there are three others with the same motive for wantin' him out of the way."

" I don't know what their motive was," countered Julia quickly.

" They didn't want to come toppling into the mud. Sure you don't know who any of them were ? "

" I can't tell you any of their names," Julia assured him.

He noticed her transposing of his question but for the moment he let it ride. " Still, you could identify one of them for me, couldn't you ? "

She shook her head. " I've told you—nobody was introduced."

" Have it your own way. Where did this second party take place ? "

" At—at a flat."

" Belonging to one of the victims. But you don't know who it was. And of course it never occurred to you to try and find out ? All right, don't answer that one. I can fill in two of the gaps anyway, and if I can't find out the name of the third party in a matter of eight and forty hours I'm ripe for the O.A.P. Still, tell me this. What happened ? How did you decide which of you was going to put out Teddy Lane's light ? "

" We drew lots."

" And it fell to you. Did the others know ? "

" None of us knew." She explained about drawing for the Black Death. " And we agreed that if the one who drew it got into trouble he or she would keep quiet and not involve the others."

" Seeing you don't know who any of them are how can you? " asked Crook smoothly. " Y'know, you never got past Grade I at school. In a minute you'll be letting on you believe the other three will really come forward. Well, they won't, not unless one of 'em's prepared to take your place, and you can take my word for it that sort of thing went out with Vincent de Paul."

" You don't have to put anyone in my place," protested Julia. " So long as the police can't prove me guilty I'm all right."

" I wonder if Sir Charles would say so. He won't want his wife pointed at for the rest of her days as one of the lucky ones who got away with murder. You've got a boy, too, haven't you ? "

Julia nodded, momentarily past speech.

" Well, then, we've got to put someone in your shoes. Now, this yarn of yours about going to Rowlhampton Yes, I know you went—the police have checked up with the jeweller,

123

but the important time is afterwards. Pity you can't find someone to confirm this alleged breakdown of yours."

" There's the motor-cyclist. I can't imagine why he hasn't come forward."

" Can't you ? " said Crook. " You'll never make a romantic novelist. Not enough imagination. There's half a dozen reasons why he hasn't come forward. He may not read the papers . . ."

" Oh, but surely . . ." began Julia.

" I know. You're going to say how could he miss it. But a chap like Lane being poisoned ain't news to the world in general. Even the arrest of a Member of Parliament's wife doesn't register as big as, say, the visit of a film star to a local village to shoot a few scenes. Well, there's one reason. Another is he may have come a cropper himself. Or maybe he'd ' borrowed ' the motor-cycle and don't want to advertise the fact. He was in the army, didn't you say ? "

" Well, he had been."

" Didn't he say something about his sergeant-major ? I've been shown a copy of the statement, you know. Well, he may have been out without leave or he might have been deserting. It's even possible he's not in the country any longer. He might have been scorching back to join his draft for overseas. That's routine. Bill 'ull look after that, find out if there was a draft leavin' the country that night and who they were."

" In that case you'll never find him till it's too late," said Julia in dismay.

" Too late for what ? If I've got a witness out of the country I can get the case held up till we have his statement, signed and witnessed. We can even get him repatriated, if necessary. You leave that part of it to your Uncle Arthur. Now—Friday morning. Sure you can't produce anyone who saw you at the Mansions ? "

" No," said Julia steadily, " I can't produce anyone." (Because even if she mentioned Mrs. Tempest what was there to prevent the woman denying the whole story ?)

" Of course," she offered, "it may not have been one of the four at all. I dare say he had other enemies."

" Why should one of the others remove the contents of the deed-box ? You tell me. No, I fancy we'll find one of the four visited Mr. Teddy Lane's flat that night.

" About this sleeping-stuff," Crook went on. " You had had some one time, your husband tells me."

" I hadn't used any for ages, for longer than I can remember."

" But you kept the empty bottle, because the police found it in the medicine chest. Any idea why ? "

" Well," said Julia lucidly, " one always does."

" Spoken like a true woman," nodded Crook. " There's something in a woman's make-up that makes it impossible for her to chuck anything away, anything worthless, I mean. I was acting for an old girl last month and we found four boxes of rubbish no one was interested in except moths, and they'd taken out 100 per cent of the shares, three feather boas—Bill tells me that's what they're called—and enough empty bottles to stock a shop."

" But I hadn't had the prescription made up for two years," Julia protested.

" There's no age limit for poisons. They ain't like milk that goes off in the hot weather. And you can't find anyone to back you up when you say the bottle was empty before Lane's death ? Too bad ! Still, if there weren't any mountains no one would ever get a view, would they ? "

" How is Charles ? " asked Julia in an agony as he rose.

" Your husband ? " He looked at her in genuine surprise. " If he's got any sense he'll sleep like a top now I've taken over. Why not ? Crook always gets his man has been true for a quarter of a century and you don't teach an old dog new tricks."

He put out a hand the size of a ham and nearly crushed hers. " Keep your pecker up, sugar, and don't forget your beauty sleep."

It might have been coincidence, but she slept that night for the first time since she heard of Teddy Lane's death.

125

CHAPTER THIRTEEN

FROM THE PRISON Crook went round to the Mansions to see Moxon, whom he found in a rather worse temper than usual, with one hand bandaged.

" One of the tenants started biting ? " asked Crook sunnily, " or is it just that you keep a parrot ? "

" Funny, aren't you ? " said Moxon in sullen tones. " What do you want anyway ? If you've come about the flat it's let as soon as we can get the stuff out of it."

" Teddy Lane's flat ? Well, in a sense I had, but not because I want to live there. I'm nicely suited, thanks."

" Who are you, then ? Another of the flicking police ? "

" The police have got their case all sewn up," Crook reminded him. ." No, I'm the chaps with scissors, come to unpick the stitches."

Moxon stared as sullenly as ever. " Aren't you going to ask me in ? " said Crook. " Or do you love the police so much—which reminds me, did he ever come back ? "

" Which one ? They've been all over the place, asking their silly questions. As if I can remember everyone who comes and goes. All I can tell you is Mr. Teddy Lane's no loss to the Mansions—even his rent's covered. Found forty pounds in his luggage."

" Who did ? "

" The police. They've been through his things like a rat through a cheese."

" Which police were they ? The one you told us about who came on the Thursday afternoon when Teddy was out ? "

" No," said Moxon. " We haven't seen him again. And that's a funny thing. There's no record of any copper calling here. It doesn't make sense."

" No ? " said Crook. " It makes a hell of a lot of sense to me."

" I don't get you," returned Moxon.

" Who told you he was the police ? "

" Well, he did of course."

" Offer you any proof ?   Draughty in this doorway, ain't
it ? "

Bertha Moxon called from within, " Who is it, Stan ?   If
it's the baker tell him to go round to the back."

" Lady Silk's defence," called Crook cheerfully, and in a
moment Mrs. Moxon flashed into sight.

" What are you thinking of, Stan, leaving the gentleman
on the step ?   Do you want everyone to hear what's going
on ?   Come in," she added.   " Not that we can help you
much . . ."

" You'd be surprised," said Crook genially, accepting the
invitation.   " Thanks a million."

Moxon said in surly tones, " Just missed tea," and Crook
said that was all right by him, he never touched the stuff.

" Offer the gentleman some of your kind, Stan," Bertha
advised.   And Moxon went to a cupboard and produced a
bottle.

" Make yourself at home," said Bertha.   " Tell us, did she
do it ? "

" Who ?   Lady Silk ?   Be your age, sugar.   What should
I be doing here, if she did ? "

" I'm glad of that," said Bertha.   " I know murder's
wrong, of course, but it seems just as wrong to me that someone's got to hang for poisoning that little rat, specially as he
probably did it himself."

" Well, I wouldn't go that far," murmured Crook cautiously.
" Now, I was just asking you—that policeman chap.   Did he
show you a badge or anything ? "

" He had something," Moxon admitted.   " I didn't take
much notice.   After all, who'd want to say he was a copper if
he wasn't ? "

" Never seen him before ? "

" Not flaming likely."

" Or since ? "

" No."

" And that don't strike you as odd ? "

" We've had plenty of the rozzers round here," said Moxon,
" you don't suppose I want to bring in an extra one, do you ? "

" Now listen," said Crook.   " Suppose I was to say I'm a
copper, and here's my card, and wave something at you, how
would you know it was the truth ? "

" Well, I wouldn't," the porter agreed.   " But why the heck
should you ? "

" Suppose I wanted to know where Mr. Lane was ? You'd tell a bobby, wouldn't you ? "

" I see what you're getting at. You mean he wasn't in the force at all ? "

" Could be," said Crook. " Think you'd know him again ? "

" Not blooming likely," said Crook.

" The police didn't mention they wanted him for anything, did they ? "

" Come to that, I did say something about a chap coming here . . ."

" And they didn't bite ? Well, that ties up with my information, too. I tried to make an inquiry through the usual channels "—he grinned—" and I came away with a flea in my ear. That's Point Number One. Point Two. The lady who called on Thursday afternoon. Ever see her before ? "

" Didn't see her properly then."

" Surprise you that Mr. Lane should be so much in demand all of a sudden ? "

" Well, he didn't go off like that without he had some reasons. Ants in his pants for days, he had, all of a jump, bolted the door when he heard me ringing, didn't want calls put through, didn't want visitors let up. . . . If you ask me he was expecting something of this kind."

" Did they ? Ask you ? The police, I mean."

" Not perishing likely."

" You didn't volunteer any information ? "

" I was never one for fleas myself. No, the less I had to do with our Mr. Lane the better. I never did like the fellow. Chaps that go cutting bits out of papers are up to no good."

" That a hobby of his ? " asked Crook casually.

" At it to the day of his death."

" Here we go," thought Crook exultantly. " How come ? " he asked aloud.

" Something—don't ask me what—in the *Evening Record* that night. Saw a chance to make a bit, I suppose."

" Got the paper by you ? " murmured Crook.

" What ? His ? I dunno."

" Maybe the police took it away with them."

Moxon stared. " Why should they ? "

" You're right," Crook acknowledged. " Nelson with his one blind eye was twice as well off as the average rozzer. They can see through a stone fence all right, but they can't see something lying at their feet."

It wasn't true, of course, but then Crook was never fair to the police. "My mother didn't christen me Galahad," he'd explain, though actually it had been a near thing.

"Mind you, Bertha may have got the paper pushed away somewhere," Moxon continued. "Seeing it was only Thursday."

Eventually the paper was found in the scullery, with a paragraph incised. There was nothing to show whom it had concerned, but it would be easy to learn that.

"No sign of a cutting among the dear departed's stuff, I take it ? "

"If there was the police got it."

"Could be just an advertisement for another flat," proposed Bertha, but Crook shook his head.

"Not on this page. This is Home News."

"An empty flat would be Home News," said Bertha.

"Anyhow, it's not the first time. Look at this." Moxon waved his injured hand at them as threateningly as though it held a weapon. "Pin," he announced. "Rusty pin used to hold papers together. 'Ow do I know ? Because there was a scrap of paper as red—as red as those eyebrows of yours stuck on the end of it. Found it in the waste-paper basket, where the rozzers overlooked it."

"Might have been there weeks," murmured Crook, but his pulses were racing.

"Not it. Only 'ad the basket a week. Always complaining about something, was Lane. The ones that are behind with the rent always do. So we got 'im a new one, and there wasn't any pin in that. I put it in 'is room myself. No, 'e'd just took it out of some papers . . ."

"And he'd just sliced another piece of the press ? Well, thanks a million. You've probably done more to establish justice than all the police in the country."

Popping back into the Scourge he made straight for the office of the *Record*. Cummings' secretary began to say the editor saw no one without an appointment but when she recognised Crook she sank back, defeated.

"Want a tip straight from the horse's mouth ? " demanded Crook. "Tell me, Cummings, are you ever off the premises ? Why the heck you bother to pay rent . . ."

"Who is it ? " asked Cummings.

"Lady Silk. Get one of your chaps to turn up a copy of the evening edition for the 17th."

" Women are always news," Cummings agreed, " and when they have husbands with a record, peace *and* war, they rate a headline. You acting for her ? "

" You've said it."

" Then of course she didn't do it. Any idea who did ? "

" Remember the Ancient Mariner ? " asked Crook. " He stoppeth one of three ? Well, I'm shortly going to do the same, only question being which of the three ? And I'm half-way there, chum, I'm half-way there."

A messenger came in with a copy of the evening edition for the 17th and Crook turned at once to Home News. Here he read :

MURDERER DIES AFTER ALMOST FORTY YEARS

" The Tempest Case," murmured Crook thoughtfully. " Can't say I remember it."

" Before your time," Cummings consoled him.

" If that's so, it was before Lane's time, too. Wonder how he stumbled on it. Come to that, it's surprising how these blackmailers do find their ammunition."

" You're slipping," said Cummings brutally. " Suppose you were a water diviner ? "

" Water ? Me ? " Crook looked shocked.

" Use your imagination," suggested Cummings. " Well, it 'ud be your job to find water. The same with blackmailers. It's their job to find victims. If the diviner doesn't find water he's out on his ear. And if chaps of Lane's kidney don't find compromising situations complete with the people concerned they end up in the workhouse. Anyway, if you want to know about Tempest consult the expert, in this case Snaith, our crime reporter. There isn't a case from the murder of Abel he doesn't know about."

Snaith, summoned, proved to be a mild-mannered little man who might have held down a job in the local bank, but he knew his onions all right. " Tempest ? " he said. " That's ancient history. Chap died the other day after forty years free board and lodging. A nasty case. Married man seduced a local tweeny and later killed her in a particularly unpleasant manner. He was lucky not to be lynched. They found him insane at the trial."

" Any family ? "

" There was a wife, much younger than he was, and a child

two or three years old. I did the case for the *Sun* some years ago when they were running a series of Crime Stories."

" Changed her name, I dare say ? " suggested Crook carelessly.

" No. It's not such a good idea really, because when the child grows up he's bound to ask why his father's name isn't the same as his own. And she's got to find some sort of explanation. After forty years he's not a bit likely to link up the death of a homicidal lunatic with his own father whom he's been told died when he was a kid."

" Meaning the odds are he never knew the truth ? "

" Well "—Snaith looked indignant—" would you let a kid of yours learn a story like that if you could prevent it ? "

" Not if I could prevent it," agreed Crook.

" What next ? " he reflected. It was a long shot that the new-made widow was one of the five at Teddy Lane's party, but if you want fresh water go to the fountain-head, was one of his axioms, so first thing next morning he set forth in the tireless Scourge on the long run to Clifftown, where the asylum was situated. He wasn't at all sure how forthcoming the governor would be ; he wondered if he could bribe a warder or entrap one into giving him the information he wanted, but Heaven helps those who help themselves, and as the little car took the long hill up to the Institution it overtook a clergyman toiling up on foot.

Crook stopped.

" Want a lift ? " he bawled.

" Very kind," said the clergyman, who was so used to things being out of the ordinary that the Scourge seemed a natural part of the landscape, and her driver, too, for that matter.

" Going far ? " he inquired, slamming the bright red door.

" Top of the hill," said Crook.

His passenger looked a little surprised. " It's not visiting day."

" Oh, I don't know any of the chaps behind the bars. Just making a small inquiry. You know the place ? "

" I'm the chaplain."

Crook beamed. " Whadayou know ? Very fellow I want to see. One of your congregation died the other day, man called Tempest, and I'm trying to locate the widow. Lawyer," he added quickly, hauling a card out of the pocket of his monstrous brown coat. " Matter of life and death."

" You've come a long way," said the chaplain glancing at the bit of pasteboard in his hand. " Mrs. Tempest lives in London in a flat somewhere near Knightsbridge. She came down for the funeral, first time I'd met her. She gave up visiting some years ago. The governor rang her up when Tempest had his fatal attack, but there was no time for her to see him alive, and, frankly, it would have made no difference to him. He was—beyond all that."

" Isn't there a son ? " asked Crook.

The chaplain sent him a sharp glance. " You don't know the family history ? "

" I know there was a boy. I'm new on this case," he added with a humility that didn't deceive his companion in the least.

" Thinks he's the cat's whiskers," reflected the clergyman. He thought it quite probable that Crook was.

" So far as I know he's still alive and quite unaware of the fact that he's had a father these forty years. Mrs. Tempest was—is—a very brave woman. There's nothing she wouldn't do for that son."

" Short of murder ? " suggested Crook.

The clergyman frowned. " One hopes she'd stop short of that," he said. " She's immensely proud of this fellow. He's a doctor somewhere in the West Country."

" Let's hope he returns the compliment," murmured Crook, politely, as they drew up by the prison. The chaplain descended and vanished. Crook waited a moment, then turned the head of the Scourge and raced her back the way she had come. He didn't stop to ask for the governor. He had learned what he wanted to know, and no nosy questions asked. All he had to do was track through the telephone book, and if there was any doubt ring up every Tempest within a radius of five miles.

It was a long day, but next morning saw him, as full of speculation and enterprise as an egg of meat, making for No. 10 Hunter Street. He had given his quarry no warning, and, her daily woman being ill, it was Mrs. Tempest herself who opened the door. She supposed he was trying to sell insurance or something of the kind, and would have shut it again immediately, but he put a big brown-shod foot over the threshold, and said, " Sorry you've been troubled, but I'd like a word with you about the late Edward Lane."

" Edward Lane ? " She didn't turn a hair. " I'm afraid you've come to the wrong address."

" I don't make that sort of mistake," Crook assured her, " Now, let's start going places right away. Incidentally, I don't know how nosy your neighbours are, but if you value privacy, well, it 'ud be a pity to blow the gaff after nearly forty years."

Mrs. Tempest stood back. " I don't know who you are or why you are here, but you had better come in."

Crook stepped over the threshold. " I'm representin' Lady Silk. You heard about her being taken for the murder ? Seeing she's my client, she can't be guilty, and seeing Harmsworth Ames is doing the defence she's pretty sure of an acquittal."

" In that case, it is difficult to see how I can assist you."

" I've come to explain," said Crook sunnily. " Ever met Ames ? "

" Not to my knowledge."

Crook pulled a newspaper out of his pocket. " I don't say this does him justice," he said, " but it appeared in the Royal Academy show last year. Now—still think you've never met him ? "

There was an instant's absolute silence ; then Mrs. Tempest handed the paper back. " As you say," she agreed, " an unforgettable face. And—he has agreed to undertake Lady Silk's defence ? "

" Agreed ? Came swimming up to ask for it, like a sea-lion at feeding-time. Memory still sluggish ? Well, let it ride. Now, can you suggest any reason why the late Teddy Lane should clip a cutting about your husband's death out of the paper ? "

" My husband ? " The treacherous colour mounted to her cheeks. " I am a widow, Mr.—er——"

" Crook's the name, Arthur Crook. And I know that. But seeing you're so new to the estate . . . Now, look," he added persuasively, " I was down at Clifftown yesterday. I know George Tempest was your husband, I know you attended the funeral . . ."

" May I ask what concern this is of yours ? " Sudden passion flamed in her voice.

" I told you. I'm interested in how Teddy Lane came by his death."

133

" And I have told you I've no information. I know nothing about Mr. Lane . . ."

" Your last word ? " insinuated Crook.

" My last word."

Her visitor looked round for his hideous brown bowler and crammed it on to his head. " I'm losing my grip," he admitted frankly. " Of course Lane wouldn't come to you. He didn't believe that if you look after the pence the pounds will look after themselves. It was the pounds he was after. And —no disrespect intended—he probably thought there was more to be had from a doctor with a flourishing practice and a family who didn't know about his connection with a murderer . . ."

He got no further. In an instant the quiet woman before him was transformed into a flashing fury.

" I forbid you to approach my son. He knows nothing— nothing . . ."

" It must be you or him," Crook pointed out reasonably. " I expect the doctor wouldn't tell you . . ."

" You had better sit down," said Mrs. Tempest in a voice like the silence that precedes the storm. " I can see I have no choice. Yes, that criminal, Lane, threatened to wreck my son's life unless I bought his silence . . ."

" Five hundred pounds, wasn't it ? " said Crook. " A tidy sum. By the way, don't get me wrong. I couldn't drag a word out of Lady Silk. She kept her bargain."

" How did you know there was a bargain unless she told you ? "

" Well, she wasn't holding her tongue for her health," Crook murmured, " and I wasn't born yesterday. I know she could say a lot if she liked, and she can't care for the prospect of bein' hanged for murder—they always hang poisoners, you know—so it stands to reason there was some sort of gentleman's agreement."

" And you think you will succeed with me where you failed with her ? "

" I know Teddy Lane didn't poison himself. I know he was blackmailin' all the people who went to his party, his reunion party, he called it. I know there were four guests, and I knew the name of three already. Teddy himself put me on to the fourth by slicing up his evening paper. Lady Silk says she didn't do it and, bein' my client, of course she didn't. That leaves three. Of course, if you have an alibi. . ."

134

" As a matter of fact, I have. I can prove it was impossible for me to have visited Mr. Lane on the night of his death. If I can satisfy you on that point, may I hope that you will keep the facts to yourself ? "

" If you didn't put out his light, you ain't—no offence intended—of any interest to me," said Crook kindly.

" Very well then. My income is not a large one and to augment it I do odd jobs from time to time. I can't type-write or drive a car, but I am an exceedingly good cook. Therefore I get a great many engagements. On Thursday night I was at a house in Exton Street—I arrived at six o'clock and I didn't leave until half-past nine. In fact, I have a letter here from the lady who engaged me thanking me for making her party so successful and hoping she didn't keep me too late."

" If I could see it—just for the record," Crook suggested.

Mrs. Tempest went to a desk and returned with an envelope bearing a Mayfair postmark. Crook glanced at the sheet it contained and handed it back.

" Well, that lets you out as the 8 o'clock visitor," he said. " By the way, this affair of the Black Death. Your suggestion ? "

" Yes," agreed Mrs. Tempest guardedly.

" Got your counter handy by any chance ? "

" After Mr. Lane's death I threw it away. It was of no further value."

" You don't leave much to chance, do you ? " Crook approved. " You threw it away because you drew the Black Death, same like Lady Silk and the others. But you mean to sit pretty and let her take the rap ? "

" I thought I had convinced you that I was elsewhere on Thursday evening, and so, putting two and two together . . ."

" Twice one are two and twice two are four, but twice two are ninety-six if you know the way to score," quoted Crook. " And, to be frank with you, I rather think I do."

And, leaving Mrs. Tempest suddenly uneasy, he beetled over to see Harmsworth Ames.

CHAPTER FOURTEEN

SHOT IN THE DARK

WHEN CROOK CALLED at Harmsworth Ames's chambers he found the Q.C. sitting behind his showy double desk, carefully reading a sheaf of letters. Crook came in at the double and looked about him. " Does himself well," he thought, but he wasn't envious. So much façade seemed to him obtrusive. If a chap was getting on he didn't have to boast about it even in this indirect fashion. Crook's income was probably as high as Ames's and most of *his* furniture looked as if it had been made out of orange-boxes. There was a second table against one wall supporting a typewriter and Crook remembered the story that Ames often stayed late typing his own most secret reports after working hours.

According to his rule, Ames didn't stop his work when Crook came in ; he was the very antithesis of his visitor, who would stop in the middl of a word if a client arrived. Ames finished his note, signed it with the spectacular black monogram that reproduced so well in the Famous Trials, and looked up.

" Interesting case, this," he observed, obviously referring to the Lane Murder. " Any fresh suspicions ? "

" Remember Foxy ? " inquired Crook. " When in doubt suspect everybody, except, of course, my client."

" I've been wondering," said Ames slowly, " if there's any chance of its turning out suicide, after all. Lane was a malicious little cur, he'd be delighted to think of someone standing trial for his life. He was being screwed in all directions, it's perfectly likely that he took his own way out, arranging it so that it would appear to be murder. No, hear me out. That stuff that was found in the milk, for instance ? Admittedly there was no sign in the flat of the particular sort of drug that was employed, but it would be part of his cunning plan to destroy it. In fact, that could explain the presence of the stuff in the milk. I doubt whether anyone else would have thought of that."

" No proof that he ever had those particular tablets," Crook reminded him.

"Not at present, but he had far more powerful ones. Naturally he wouldn't employ those, because it would be difficult, perhaps impossible, to show that anyone who had been in contact with him recently had access to that kind. I suppose," he added thoughtfully, doodling that characteristic monogram all over his blotting-paper, " it's too much to hope that we can trace the man who supplied him. He had no doctor, so far as we know, and nobody has come forward with any information."

" Chaps don't like being mixed up with a murder," explained Crook kindly.

" And then—that visitor. That might be camouflage, too. Is there any direct evidence that he did have anyone there that night, apart from the second coffee cup, I mean. I take it, by the way, that's been tested for finger-prints ? "

" No dice," said Crook laconically. " Whoever used it didn't mean to leave any traces."

" It could still have been Lane himself. I know he rang down to the porter about being engaged and having a visitor, but . . ."

" What the soldier said ain't evidence," Crook capped him.

" Precisely. And we know he was terrified of something or someone. Moxon's evidence about his bolting his door and baulking telephone calls is proof of that."

" He made the call all right," said Crook thoughtfully. " I've been doing a bit of snooping and, among others, I've had a word with the tenant of No. 11, that is, the flat across the passage. He was waiting for the lift that night . . ."

" Didn't see anyone going into 12 ? " interrupted Ames.

" If he did he don't want it put on record. His story is he heard the telephone ring and Teddy answer it. He couldn't hear everything that was said, but he did gather Teddy was in a hell of funk. ' You'll find the chain up,' he was saying. Don't ask me how the fellow could hear all that. There are ways . . ." He curved a large hand suggestively round his ear.

" Oh, not necessarily," Ames assured him. " Those front doors are made of plywood, and Lane's telephone's in the lobby he calls a hall."

" Well, that's helpful," said Crook sincerely. " Trouble is, Lady S. bounces into a cul-de-sac whichever way she turns. There's this motor-cyclist chap we haven't traced yet. And even if we do find him still she ain't in the clear. She says herself they parted before six ; she could have made it, you know, if she'd scorched."

" With a patched fan-belt ? "

" I didn't say it was likely. I said it was possible. Then there's the fact that she did once have sleeping-tablets that could have done the job."

" So, no doubt, had several hundred other people in London alone," Ames suggested.

" Unfortunately, from our point of view, they don't seem to have been tied up with Teddy Lane. Then there are the other three who were at the party. Lady S. ain't talking—and you can bet your sweet life they ain't talking, either."

Ames was frowning. " Pity about that note of hers to Lane," he said. " Just the sort of thing the police would drop on."

" Oh, I don't know." Crook was nothing if not pugnacious. " Not the bit about the police, I mean, but—well, say one of the others did come that night ? The other lady, by the way —yes, I've rumbled her—has an alibi even the police—even I—can't break, but that still leaves two. Say one of them was at Ellison Mansions on Thursday night. He empties the deed-box and—say he notices the letter on the table ? Here's a chance, he thinks. Leave that, and if questions are asked leave her to do the climbing out of the pit."

" Meaning that he counted on her keeping her mouth shut ? It was taking a long shot."

" Not if you know Lady Silk. I gather you don't."

Ames shook his head. " I know her husband's reputation, of course. This is hard on him, damned hard."

" It's not exactly a cream puff for her. Mind you, the police haven't been able to find any trace of the papers that must have been in the deed-box, and no proof that she destroyed any. They weren't burnt in the room—there was only a tiddling little gas-fire . . ."

" That brings us back to my first suggestion. That this may all be a put-up job on Lane's part."

" Even that don't solve the riddle of the papers. He came in just before six. Nobody saw him go out again. It was a stinking night. The papers weren't destroyed in the flat. Besides, why should he put out his own light when he was expectin' Lady Silk with the dough ? "

" It would explain his call to Moxon that he didn't want to be disturbed."

" That bein' so why didn't he bolt his door ? To give the

impression he had a visitor you think ? Could be." He
brooded. "A nice idea," he admitted, "but—anything to
bolster it up ? "
"Moxon told him the police were asking for him . . ."
"I noticed that, too. Funny thing is the police don't
know anything about it. Looks as if someone was having a
game with Teddy Lane. Besides, Lady Silk, who had known
the chap for years, says he was afraid of death."
"I dare say. But it's conceivable he was even more afraid
of what life had to offer. Y'see, I can't get round that doped
milk being left on the premises for the police to find. If X
had time to collect the papers, he had time to empty the milk
down the drain. And wash the second cup. But the milk was
left in the bottle, and the cup was left on the table. What
other solution could there be ? "
"There's just one that don't seem to have occurred to
you," said Crook, and he told Ames what it was.

They were still discussing the case when a tap sounded on
the door and a girl came in with a tray that would have
gladdened a spinster's heart.
"Very cosy," said Crook in appreciative tones.
"I put a cup for Mr. Crook," said the girl.
"You shouldn't have bothered, honey," Crook told her.
"I can't take coffee. Plays havoc with my stomach."
"This happens to be the best Orange Pekoe," said Ames,
smiling. "I don't take coffee myself. But you'll like this,
Crook."
Crook thought wistfully of Ananias. Striking down liars
where they stood seemed to have gone out of fashion ; or it
might be there were so many of them nowadays Providence
wouldn't have time for anything else.
"I suppose," he hinted, but without much hope, "you
haven't got such a thing as a bottle of beer in one of those
cupboards."
"Make a note to get in a supply against Mr. Crook's next
visit," Ames told the clerk cordially.
She looked demure and said, "Yes, Mr. Ames," and left
them and immediately forgot all about it ; but, as it happened,
that didn't matter, because Crook didn't go calling there any
more.
The murderer (call him Death for convenience' sake) saw
to that.

Death had been watching the development of the affair with growing unease. Death was as tough as Teddy had been, and knew you have to look after yourself. And so, when Julia was arrested, that was as good a solution as any.

" No hard feelings," Death told the pale face looking back at him from the glass. " But—someone's got to pay and I don't mean it to be me." A good lawyer would probably avoid the death penalty, pull out all the soft stops, and there was plenty of money where the Silks were concerned to buy the best legal aid. Not like some who had to go slow, being without natural advantages.

" No reason why they should pick on me," Death continued, speaking to that mute audience. " I left no clues, didn't try and fabricate an alibi. If you tell no lies you give the police no foundation on which to build a case."

But when Crook suddenly came shoving into the defence, everything changed overnight. Because Crook wasn't the polite lawyer playing by Queensberry Rules. Crook would gouge and kick and hit below the belt—his reputation was notorious. Crook might even deduce, in his shady way, the identity of the real criminal.

" Not he," scoffed Death. " I can look after myself."

But the dread remained. What if Crook *did* pick up some clue even Death didn't know existed ?

Crook always gets his man. Anyone with any knowledge of the criminal world knew that was his motto. And why should he fail here when he had so often succeeded before ? Death didn't care if Julia was acquitted, so long as suspicion continued to fall in the wrong direction.

Impossible as yet to know if Crook suspected. His method was to sneak round picking up a fact here and a rumour there and suddenly, when you were least expecting it, spring his mine. Well—Death looked grim. Before he had the chance he must be put out of the picture. And without delay, time being of the essence of the case. Death had no feeling where Crook was concerned. He could drop down dead with apoplexy this very night and Death would be *so* grateful ; but he wouldn't, of course. When did Crook ever go out of his way to oblige anyone who wasn't a client ? Or one of his other enemies (and a man in his shoes had as many as Teddy Lane) might pull a knife or flash a razor. But they wouldn't. Not likely. And there was no time left.

" I've taken chances before," Death reflected. " This is only one more."

It must be arranged, neatly, though, and this time, if possible, there must be a definite suggestion against another party. Goodness knew, there were plenty of people, not excluding the police themselves, who'd whoop with delight to know he was out of the way. Well, now was their chance.

" No time like the present," said Mr. Mell.

Death agreed with Mr. Mell.

Ames's secretary brought in a batch of letters for signature. " Will there be anything else to-night, Mr. Ames ? " she inquired.

" No," said Ames. " You can pack up. I have to meet a man at my club at six o'clock. Put out the Fenton file before you go and that's all I shall want."

Crook also left his office in good time that evening. A little black car that had been parked at the street corner moved unobtrusively away from the kerb as the Scourge began to thread her way back to Earl's Court, and parked again round the corner of Brandon Street. The driver went into the Lord Harry for a pint and left by the back entrance, via the Gents. A few minutes later he entered a telephone kiosk and rang a London number.

Crook heard his telephone ring and unhitched the receiver.

" Is that Mr. Crook ? " asked a polite voice.

" So I've always believed," returned Crook. " Who wants me ? "

" Mr. Ames to speak to you. Just a moment. You're through, sir."

The next moment the polite voice was replaced by a brusquer one, that said, " Look here, are you alone ? "

" That's right," said Crook.

" Now—think before you answer this one—are you being followed ? "

Crook roared with laughter. " Not something likely."

But the other man remained serious. " Well, I am. Mind you, I don't say I'm in any special danger. It's not the first time, but I'd like to ensure it's not the last. This chap's in a small black car fifty yards from my club. My car's parked in full view outside. My notion is the driver will stop where he is till she's been shifted."

" And that'll be ? " You couldn't rattle Crook. His enemies, including the police, had been trying for years.

" In about half an hour. Only—I shan't be in her. I've just given instructions to the garage people to move her as soon as I'm well out of the way. I'm speaking from the garage now. If this chap follows her he'll get a nasty shock."

" Meantime you're going to doss down in the garage ? " Crook sounded puzzled.

" Not at all. But I don't see any sense in taking unnecessary risks. There's been one sudden death already and you can't hang twice. I'd say X appreciated that as much as anyone. My plan is to go down to my house at Church Melton. I'm hiring a car and I shall drive myself. What I want you to do is come down and join me there. That's why I asked if you were being followed."

" I don't—quite," admitted Crook. " Follow, I mean. Why do you want me at Church Melton ? Or do you think X will come along and you want a witness nice and handy ? What d'you expect to happen anyhow ? "

" I think whoever really killed Lane has got the wind up. I'm a danger to him—but so are you. I don't propose to be a sitting target. Now when this chap realises what's happened the odds are he'll come to your place—may think I'm there, and I can't afford to have you out of the picture, not till this matter's cleared up. I've got my reputation to consider . . ."

" And, of course," murmured Crook, " there is Lady Silk's point of view." (Chap seemed to have lost sight of that.)

" Well, how about it ? Will you come ? You know where the house is ? "

Crook knew, of course. Everyone knew about Ames's fantastic country manor. The malicious said he must have pulled strings not to have had it requisitioned, seeing how little use he made of it. It wasn't above an hour and a half's run from London, though, and there were all kinds of speculations as to the purposes to which it was put. Some said he kept a harem there, others that he dabbled in black magic, was in with a gang—oh, there was no limit.

" What's he up to ? " Crook wondered. The sensible thing would be to notify the police, but no—Ames wouldn't do that, any more than Crook would himself. You could imagine the headlines—Well-known Q.C. seeks police protection. He'd get it, of course, but he'd never live the incident down. People expect clergymen to be saints, doctors to be infallible, lawyers invulnerable.

" If there's anything in the idea and this chap does come haring down it 'ud clear away a lot of dead wood," Crook reflected.

He finished his beer and took up the telephone, but he got no reply to his call, so, leaving a note on the table where it couldn't be overlooked, even by his slapdash char, he crammed a loud check cap on his head and went down to where the Scourge was parked in a ramshackle shed in an alley.

It was a poor sort of night and there wasn't much traffic on the roads. Once he was over Hammersmith Broadway he sailed along. He watched the little driving mirror for a time, but it was perfectly obvious no one was following *him*. Concentrating on Ames, perhaps, he thought. Maybe that's his idea, too, and he rather fancies the notion of reinforcements.

The telephone call had come at half-past eight. It was a little after ten when he halted the Scourge at the top of the hill leading to Church Melton to ask a policeman on a bicycle the precise whereabouts of The Refuge. Typical of Ames to give his pretentious house this suburban name, he reflected. The policeman, fascinated as strangers always were by the Scourge, gave him directions. In reply to Crook's further question as to whether anyone else had been inquiring the way he said no, no one had asked him, adding that he hadn't known Mr. Ames was in residence.

Crook pushed on, thinking, well, either he's thrown his pursuer off the scent or he hasn't arrived, but when he reached the house the first thing he saw was a large black car—a Daimler, nothing but the best for Harmsworth Ames, reflected Crook with a grin, standing in front of the wrought-iron gates. That looked as if Ames hadn't been there long, or the car would have been in the garage, unless, of course, he intended to drive back to-night.

" It's all according, I suppose," Crook told himself, putting the Scourge in the shadow of her expensive distant relative and hopping out. He wondered what Ames's servants would make of this sudden arrival, then remembered they didn't live on the premises. A couple in the village came in to keep the place aired and moved into the staff quarters when the owner was actually in residence.

" Got his head screwed on as fast as a coffin-nail," thought

Crook, pushing open the gate. " If they lived in, he'd have to pay 'em board wages."

The porch was festooned with some creeping plant—Crook was no botanist and they were all " creepers " to him—and there was a long old-fashioned bell-pull, that probably played " Onward, Christian Soldiers " for all its Victorian appearance; but he didn't get the opportunity of finding out if his suspicion was correct, because as he put out his hand, something—his boasted sixth sense, perhaps—froze him where he stood.

" Who's there ? " he called, swerving into the shadows. But he was too late. It had happened at last, the event all his detractors and some of his admirers had long foreseen ; he'd taken the one risk too many, chanced his arm once too often, and having dodged death a score of times walked at last, like any impulsive schoolboy, head first into the trap so neatly baited for him.

In that lonely place, with no other house nearby, and nobody likely to be coming out for a breath of air on such a night, the shot, though muffled by its environment, sounded appallingly loud. Crook went down like a falling rock, and as he fell a word was jerked from his consciousness.

" Ames ! " he choked, but there was no one to hear him, no one, that is, likely to pay any heed to what he said, and there was no time for more. The darkness that came down on him was as complete as the grave.

The man in the shadows grinned, not with amusement but with a fierce satisfaction. Not much sense even Arthur Crook showing wisdom after the event, that grin declared. Then he stole out of his hiding-place, flashing on a minute pencil torch. There was a horrifying amount of blood to be seen and he didn't want to take unnecessary chances—not like Crook who took 'em all in his stride and now had misjudged his capacities. Blood on his own clothes, blood on the hired car might sign his own death-warrant. He was debating the wisdom of a second shot to make assurance doubly certain when he heard a sound that chilled his blood. Someone had paused at the gate ; he saw the gleam of a bicycle lamp.

" Got there all right, sir ? " called a voice. He had to make up his mind in a split second. He knew who was there—a policeman. He knew too much about them not to know.

" O.K.," he called back, wondering if his voice would pass muster, and then he pulled the bell and (as Crook had surmised) it played a tune. It seemed an age before the constable remounted his machine and rode on. Death drew a deep breath and waited ; he wasn't out of the wood yet. But the chap didn't come back. After all, why should he ? All the same, he didn't risk a second shot. Someone else might pass and hear it. But the house stood away from the main road and the shadows and shrubs veiled it in impenetrable shadow. It was likely to be daylight before anyone noticed a body sprawled on the step and by daylight he'd be miles away. Pocketing the torch he came softly to the gate. He looked up and down the road. The constable was out of sight already, gone round the corner presumably. The only lights to be seen were those of the black Daimler and the cocky insolent little Scourge. He looked derisively at the latter standing like some unpedigreed cur beside a thoroughbred. He'd have liked to kick its teeth in but there was no sense in that. The Daimler started without a sound and then silence came down to be broken only by the occasional cry of a bird and a steady sticky drip-drip as blood flowed from the stricken man to the step below.

CHAPTER FIFTEEN

DEATH AT THE DOOR

P.C. ALBERT WHISTLER was an ambitious young man whose secret dream included a vision of the Superintendent (or possibly even the Chief Constable) saying, " Smart work, man. We'll have to see about getting some stripes sewn on that sleeve of yours." An hour later he passed the house once more, this time minus his bicycle, and he noticed that the little red car (assuming in your charity that you'd dignify the contraption by that name) was still in front of the gate with her lights on, but the black Daimler had disappeared. And for some reason that seemed odd. Of course, Mr. Ames might have garaged his car, but in that case why not put the red biscuit-box away as well ? She was wasting her battery with her lights full on, and everybody knew the garage would take a chauffeur and his family, as well as the car. He proceeded on his way still brooding on this discrepancy. It was about twenty minutes before the obvious solution occurred to him. Someone had stolen the black Daimler. Obviously nobody in his senses would want the Scourge. What should he do now ? Report his suspicions to his sergeant ? Ah, but he'd look a proper fool if it turned out the car was in the garage all the time. Maybe the chap in the red contraption meant to go home to-night. All the same, what a scoop if his first suspicion proved correct. Ames was a big man and not only in the neighbourhood of Church Melton. Couldn't be any harm, he thought, in ringing the bell and putting a question. He turned back. When he once more stood opposite the house other considerations struck him. There wasn't a light to be seen anywhere. But, if the owner of the red car was still inside, surely the windows of one of the ground-floor rooms would be unshuttered ? He moved round to the back entrance, that also led to the garage. And here his suspicions returned to him fourfold, for not only was the back gate locked, it was also padlocked. Of course, Mr. Ames might have gone back to town, but if so what had happened to the chap in the red car ? Resolved to take a chance, Albert pushed open the front gate and walked a few steps up the drive. He turned on his bull's-eye lantern just in time to prevent his falling over something that lay horribly still and glistened suggestively in the lantern's light. He knew the man at once ; he was the owner of the red car and it seemed pretty obvious he had never got inside the house at all.

Regardless of blood on his uniform he went down at the fellow's side ; he must have bled like a pig, it was a wonder really that he was still breathing. But he was, and P.C. Whistler walked round the house to see how he could break in. There were shutters everywhere on the ground floor but he was an athletic young man, and Ames' predilection for creeping plants and violent growths of all sorts proved his salvation. He managed to swarm up to the first floor windows, one of which he broke, so entering the house. He seemed to be in the main bedroom ; anyway there was a telephone extension here and within a minute he was in touch with his sergeant. Then he returned the way he had come, trying to remember all he had ever learnt about first aid. Luckily none of it seemed applicable to the present case, which probably saved Crook's life ; afraid to try and move the body, Whistler contented himself by covering it with a tatterdemalion rug he found in the little red car. Anyway they didn't have to wait long before reinforcements arrived.

" Ambulance will be here any minute," said the sergeant, briefly. " What is this ? "

" It looks like attempted murder, sir. I mean, I've taken a look round and there doesn't seem any sign of a weapon."

The doctor, who had accompanied the sergeant, pushed Whistler unceremoniously out of the way and went down on his knees beside the body.

" I'll tell you one thing," he said after a minute. " This is no suicide attempt. A chap doesn't shoot himself through the right breast when he wants to take a quick road out. You don't keep your heart that side."

Whistler said quickly, " I heard a sort of noise, as if someone had stepped on a branch and it went off like—like a shot." Then he flushed dully. After the heavy rain all twigs and boughs would be sodden ; you could tread on them without a sound. He should have realised that before he spoke.

" When was this ? " inquired his superior rather grimly.

" Round about ten o'clock. The gentleman stopped me at the top of Heartbreak Hill and asked me the way. I came past the house on my bicycle a bit later and saw the car there —both the cars."

" Both ? "

" Yes, sir. Mr. Ames was here to-night. This gentleman had come down to see him."

" Is that what he told you ? "

" He said he'd come to meet Mr. Ames, and asked if anyone else had wanted to know the way, and when I came along there were two cars at the gate, and a light in the porch. I just called out——"

" What made you do that ? "

Albert reflected. " Come to think of it, it was that noise I heard. I thought it was queer without knowing I thought it, but when he said he was O.K. I went on, not bothering any more till I came past again and noticed there was only one car."

" Did you happen to notice the number of the other car ? " asked the sergeant.

But alas ! Albert had not. " It was a big black car," he said. " Daimler by the look of it." But he wasn't absolutely certain. He had only heard the one voice, so of course he couldn't *swear* it was the gentleman in the red car who had stopped him and asked the way a little earlier, but he had assumed it was.

" Didn't see anything ? " asked the sergeant, in what Albert thought was rather a hectoring tone.

" Well, no. You don't go turning your lamp on a gentleman visiting, not without you've some reason to suspect he's up to no good," said Albert, regaining some of his former spirit.

The sergeant nodded sharply, and turned to the doctor who had been examining the fallen man.

" How much chance has he got ? " he inquired.

" Precious little," said the doctor grimly, " and if your chap hadn't found him when he did he'd have had a label marked ' Mortuary ' round his neck. And if that ambulance of yours doesn't get a move on," he added with sudden ferocity, " that's where he'll end up anyway. Any idea who he is ? "

The sergeant began to examine the contents of the un-conscious man's pocket.

" Name seems to be Crook. That's an odd name to go through life with. Comes from London, S.W.5 district. We ought to get a message through to his family. They ought to be sent for, even if he hasn't a chance."

" I didn't say he hadn't," said the doctor, who sounded vague, as though his thoughts were engaged elsewhere. An instant later in a quickened tone he asked, " What did you say his name was ? "

" Crook. Arthur Crook, 2 Brandon Street . . ." He stopped because a sort of minor convulsion was taking place at his side.

" Arthur Crook ! Of course. The numbskulls that we are ! So that's what the chap looks like. And this is Ames's house ? Why, it all adds up. Good Heavens, haven't you got there yet ? " he added with a lack of respect that secretly enchanted Albert Whistler, who felt he had been treated in a rather cavalier fashion. " *Arthur Crook*," he repeated.

" That's the name on the card," the sergeant agreed. " But . . ."

" Heaven help the police ! " ejaculated the doctor, whose name was French, " and even more the unfortunate public. Harmsworth Ames is acting for the defence in the Silk case. Don't you ever read the papers ? And Crook's the lawyer associated with him. And then in a crucial moment Crook's found shot on Ames's doorstep. I didn't," he went on with a viciousness that startled the sergeant half out of his wits, " I didn't realise there were any horse-drawn ambulances left in this country. I take it that's what we're waiting for. I warn you," his voice became yet more pungent, " if this chap dies I shall sue the police for culpable homicide."

" It would be a waste of time," said the sergeant angrily, " and the ambulance is coming as fast as it can."

" They ought to commandeer an extra chap to push it," said French. " And when you've got another minute or two to spare you might put through a line to find out if Ames is lying in another jungle waiting for another ambulance. Can't you see, this is a put-up job ? Chap said he was coming down to see Mr. Ames. But nobody here was expecting him. Henderson, the caretaker chap, was in my surgery this evening. He'd talk the leg off a brass monkey but he never said a word about Ames coming down, and if you think he'd come on the q.t. you don't know Harmsworth Ames. He expects the red carpet put down for every visit, and why not, if he pays for the carpet ? "

" You seem to know a lot about it," said the sergeant. " Mr. Ames . . ."

" To hell with Mr. Ames. It's Crook I'm concerned with. I've never met him before," he went on thoughtfully, " but he once did a considerable service to the lady who's now Mrs. French. And by the same token I'd say he was half-way to doing likewise for Lady Silk, and the real murderer knows it, and got the idea of spiking his guns."

At this moment (" and about time, too," said French, pugnaciously) the ambulance arrived and Crook was hoisted on board. The sergeant departed to the station to get in touch with the appropriate London office.

It was a young constable who took the message, who knew no more about Crook than the sergeant had done. His superior, however, lifted his eyebrows till he almost raised his helmet, and whistled softly. " Hoist on his own petard at last," he said. " Arthur Crook, the man even death can't catch. We'll go round right away. There must be someone we can notify, though the chap's a bachelor by all accounts."

And that was how they came to find the message Crook had left conspicuously on his writing-table.

" Gone down to Church Melton at Ames's request," he had scribbled. " Whoever finds this ring MAR 1890."

" Looks as though he suspected something fishy," murmured the sergeant, and he dialled MAR 1890.

" This is the police speaking from Arthur Crook's flat," he said as soon as he was connected. " Who are you ? "

" Parsons. Crook's partner. What's happened ? "

The police told him.

" Accident ? What sort of accident ? "

" He's been shot."

" That was no accident," said Bill at once. " Who in thunder sent him down there ? "

" We have no statement beyond the message he left in his room," said the sergeant rather icily, not approving, perhaps, of Bill's cavalier treatment of the news.

" Where's he been taken ? "

" I told you . . ."

" Where's he been taken ? "

" The Cottage Hospital. He's still unconscious."

" Meaning he hasn't made a statement yet."

" He's on the danger list." The officer sounded restive.

" So's X, the chap who shot him. I'll see to that. What's Ames got to say about it ? What ? Well, what are you waiting for ? Yes, I should like to hear, too. Send me a message to Church Melton."

" You're not going down there ? " expostulated the policeman.

" I'm on my way."

" They won't let you in," the sergeant warned him.

" Let 'em try keeping me out," said Bill. " Lord, to think of Crook being caught like that. Must have been off his feed."

" If you've any information," the sergeant began, and once again Bill Parsons interrupted him.

" I haven't seen Crook since morning. If he left a note that shows he thought there was some funny business going on. Probably tried to get me," he added. " Pity I was out last night. Just one more example of what happens when the police arrest the wrong person."

" I don't get you," said the sergeant sharply.

" Crook don't agree with the official conclusion about the death of this fellow, Lane, and he's out to find an alternative. From what you've just told me I'd say he was getting pretty warm and the chap, whoever he is, knew it. And if I don't get down there in time the odds are nobody else ever will."

When Bill reached Church Melton the village clocks had just tolled two o'clock. He made his way to the Cottage Hospital, where he was stopped at the gate by the porter.

150

"Relation?" said Bill impatiently. "Next-of-kin. Yes, the chap that sticks closer than a brother. It's like those Dunmow Flitch couples—twenty-five years and never a cross word. How is he?"

"His condition's very serious." He rang through to some-one and reluctantly told Bill to go through to the ward. Here he was informed by the house surgeons whom he met in the corridor that Crook hadn't recovered consciousness and possibly never would.

"If you knew Crook as I know Crook," retorted Bill grimly, "you'd know he doesn't retire in the middle of a case. He's probably Lady Silk's last hope. I'll wait . . ."

"He won't be able to see visitors if he does come round," the doctor warned him.

"I've got all the time there is," offered Bill.

"It's scarcely worth your while at the moment," the doctor insisted. "If you'll give us a telephone number . . ."

"Crook wouldn't like it if I wasn't on the spot when he came round," Bill explained, quite unmoved. "If he's as low as you make out you don't want him to waste any of his precious strength crossing t's and dotting i's for *their* benefit. I know all the previous instalments. Where's the night sister?"

The doctor grinned faintly. St. George tilting against the dragon had a soft job compared with any poor fool who thought he could get past her, said that grin.

"It's Lady Silk I'm thinking of," Bill explained to the determined woman when at last he had cut through all the nonsensical red tape and found himself face to face with her. "Crook's her last chance."

"If you wish to wait, Mr. Parsons," said the matron, " seeing that you've come down from London without making any arrangements for the night, you're at liberty to do so. But—the doctors are very apprehensive."

"So am I," said Bill grimly, "and so I should say was Harmsworth Ames."

"He's not likely to regain consciousness for some time," the night sister continued.

"I'll take a chance," said Bill, "and any chair that's convenient. And if all your chairs are occupied, I'll prop the porch. It looks as though it could do with a bit more support."

They made him as comfortable as they could, and brought him a cup of tea. And, as unruffled, on the surface, as if

he were making a night journey by Pullman, Bill settled
down to wait.

CHAPTER SIXTEEN

THIS MAN IS DANGEROUS

In London the police had been in touch with Harmsworth
Ames.

"Church Melton?" the Q.C. exclaimed. "I haven't been
there for the past month. I was being followed, certainly,
though not very expertly, and I spent the evening in my club.
I looked out some time after dinner and I saw that the small
black car that had been on my track was still parked by the
kerb, though I didn't notice the driver. But, then, he could
have been any one of the people strolling up and down the
pavement, or he could have been in the park."

"Hardly the sort of evening a man would choose to sit
about in a London park?" suggested the police official.

"Of course," continued Ames, "it's fairly simple to see
what must have occurred. He kept watch to see where I was
going, may even have telephoned the Club, you could find
that out from the porter. I had a fancy to make a monkey
out of him, so I slipped out by the back entrance—I'm pretty
well known there and I only had to pass the word—and I took
a bus from the next corner. There's a blessed anonymity
about a bus. If you're trying to get quit of an unwelcome
follower I'd always recommend it."

"You really did believe that this man meant some sort of
danger to you?"

"Well, I hardly imagined he was following me for his own
amusement. But as you'll readily understand this isn't the
first time it's happened."

"Did you associate it with the case of Lady Silk?"

Ames passed a powerful hand over his clean-shaven jaw.
"Not in particular. I'm involved in a number of cases—to
tell you the truth I was far more concerned about a malicious
wounding case in which I'm prosecuting. There's not much
secret about it. Black Andy—ah, you recognise the name, of
course. He'll get fourteen years if he's found guilty, and

152

I had a rumour that the rest of the gang meant to see I never got as far as the court."

" You could ask for police protection," said the policeman unguardedly.

Ames tipped back his great head and shouted with laughter. " I'd never be able to show myself in the courts again if I did. Well, how would it seem to you ? I'm asked to take off the gloves with fellows like Black Andy, and I can't do it without a tame policeman in my pocket. Besides, I didn't think they'd go to the lengths of attempted murder. It certainly wouldn't help Andy if they did. All the same," and he grinned as frankly as Crook could have done, " your would-be murderer has done Lady Silk a service. If X thinks it worth while trying to exterminate Crook . . . the Silk case is the only one in which we're jointly involved—well, it does look as though X really exists, and isn't just a figment of the defence's imagination."

Then he sobered and asked how Crook was. His dark brows drew together. " What defeats me is how he could let himself be caught in a trap like that. He could have put a call through to my club to know if I'd left."

" X, as you call him, may have told Mr. Crook that you were officially on the premises," he suggested. " If someone could ring Mr. Crook and pretend to be you, the same person could equally have rung your club pretending to be Crook."

" Well, let's hope it's not too late to mend matters now," said Ames. " What's the latest news about Crook ? "

" He hasn't come round yet. The doctors seem to think there's a chance he may not recover consciousness."

" If he does," said Ames, thinking aloud, " the odds are he won't know who attacked him. Once he was inside the gate the place is as dark as a tomb."

But under his surface brusquerie he was secretly alarmed. He hadn't anticipated this and, inevitably, the thought went through his mind that the next funeral might be his own.

And in this he was right.

There was no striking development throughout the day to confirm or rebut his fears. He telephoned twice to know how Crook was progressing. The first time he was told rather curtly, " No change." The second time they said there were now some hopes of his recovery.

" Put me through to the matron or someone in authority," Ames commanded, announcing his identity. But even when he was transferred there was little they could tell him. Crook's friend, Mr. Parsons, was on the spot. Crook was still very weak and there could be no assurance that he was out of the wood, but yes, he had a chance. The will to live was very strong.

" Did he see who attacked him ? " insisted Ames. But the voice at the other end of the line repeated that Crook was not yet conscious, and the doctors would certainly not allow him to be badgered.

Ames rang off, but most uncharacteristically he couldn't settle to his work. He was on tenterhooks to know how much Crook had been able to glean before the shot sent him down into the dark. He had a pretty clear picture of the police in attendance, with Crook, as always, refusing to oblige them. All the same, it seemed improbable that he would be able to tell them much if and when he did come round. If he was taken unawares, as was obviously the case, he couldn't hazard any guess as to his attacker's identity. But was it likely the police could trace a car hired from a London garage, without adequate details ? Why, how could they even be sure it came from London ?

Up and down, like soldiers parading, went his thoughts, but they were bad soldiers, for they didn't keep in step, sometimes even broke ranks.

It was a positive relief when the telephone rang and there was Charles Silk on the line. Charles's first reaction to the news of the attack on Crook was, " How's this going to affect Ju's chances ? " and his second : " Ah, but surely this lets her out. It must be obvious even to the bone-headed police that she can't have been concerned in this."

He said as much to Ames, but the Q.C. was disappointedly cautious.

" There's no actual proof that the attack was on Lady Silk's behalf. It's true it took place at my house, but my name may have been dragged in as a bait. Crook's got his finger in half a dozen pies. Till they have more proof the police won't lift a finger."

" How much more do they want ? " demanded Charles.

" And be your age," counselled Ames. " The Force works by rule of thumb. You might have shot the chap up to create just this impression. All the same," he added in more human tones, "it ought to give us a lead. If Crook can tell us anything when he comes round . . ."

" If he comes round," said Charles rather bitterly, ringing off. It seemed to him the case was as tatty as a moth-eaten shawl, rough ends at every turn. They hadn't found the motor-cyclist, and, though the outrage against Crook was twelve hours' old, they hadn't traced the black car. The whole machinery of the defence seemed to him at a standstill. Like the majority of his compatriots, he had never heard of Bill Parsons.

Crook came round for a short period during the following afternoon. The police were all round the bed but Crook said, " Where's Bill ? "

" Mr. Crook," said Authority, " we don't want to waste your strength, but if you could make a brief statement. . ."

But Crook only said again, " Where's Bill ? " and because they didn't dare risk his relapsing into a coma, Bill was sent for. He leaned over the bed so that Crook should make the least possible effort.

" Ames says he don't know anything," he confided. " Any idea who called you down here ? "

" Chap who said he was Ames. Bill—this is the last lap. Tell Ames . . ." the words were coming slowly now, " know who killed Teddy Lane. Tell him—look out, Bill, he's dangerous. You can't hang twice . . ." His next few words were incoherent and he sank back into the pillow. The doctor turned them all out. There'd been enough death already, without his losing his patient in addition.

" Pity he couldn't say more," murmured the police, leaving the ward.

" Oh, he said a mouthful," Bill reassured them coolly. " Enough to choke the chap who did it, with any luck. I'll be back to-morrow," he added, and off he went. You'd never have guessed how anxiety gnawed at his vitals.

The doctor came as far as the door. " Look out for yourself," he said uneasily. " The chap who did that won't hesitate at trying again. This time it might be you."

" Compliment to me really," said Bill. " Don't take it too much to heart. Crook's been up against it before."

" This time," said the doctor, " it'll be a miracle if he pulls through."

Bill laughed shortly. " Miracles are Crook's bread and

butter," he said. " Didn't you know that ? " And he was gone.

It was half-past six when he reached London and made straight for Ames's office. Ames, as usual, was the only man still at work and for once he forgot his affectation of busy-ness.

" You've got news," he said, and it was a statement rather than a question. " How's Crook ? "

" Sent you a warning," said Bill.

Ames looked staggered. " You mean, he's conscious ? "

" Was. I couldn't catch it all. But here it is for what it's worth."

Ames listened with an almost painful intensity. " This man is dangerous," he repeated. " But—no hint who the chap might be ? "

Bill's face, white and rigid, reminded him of something, something unpleasant. A bird of some sort. A hooded crow ? Ames's knowledge of ornithology was slight. Were hooded crows a dangerous species ? Crows do not pick out crows' eyes. Who had said that ? At all events Ames could experience a pang of sympathy for whoever incurred Bill's wrath. He looked as intolerant as the vulture that ate Prometheus' liver.

" Why me ? Does he think I'm in danger ? "

" I'm giving you his message. But—it could be he does, and it could be he's right. Got a gun ? "

Ames's hand flashed to the left-hand drawer of his desk. " I didn't say use it," said Bill sharply, " and it'll do very well where it is."

Ames glanced up in amazement at the change in his companion's voice to discover himself staring into the mouth of a small automatic.

" What the hell ? " he began furiously.

" Save it," said Bill. " Just remember someone's done his best to put out Crook's light. I want to be sure no one puts out mine." He came round the side of the massive desk and glanced at the half-open drawer.

" Mawson-Moberley," he said. " They're good guns. All right. You can shut it if you like."

" What did that bit of play-acting mean ? " demanded Ames.

" Just wanted to be sure what kind of a gun you carried. Crook," he added casually, " was shot by a Webster .38."

" You mean you thought—have you taken leave of your

senses ? Do you imagine I should want to put you out of the picture ? You're Crook's man, aren't you ? "

" That could be why," said Bill.

" Let's get this straight." Ames's voice was as deadly as the gun he had just revealed. " The only person who could want to get rid of Crook would be X, the real killer of Lane."

" That's the way it seems to Crook and me."

" And does Crook still think X was Lane's visitor on the Thursday night or has he changed his views ? "

" No," said Bill in the same flat, deadly voice, " he's still of the same way of thinking."

" Has he any notion yet who the fellow might be ? Has he mentioned any names ? " The Q.C. was sitting hunched at his desk ; with his immense shoulders and dark powerful features he resembled some piece of modern sculpture. Bill would hardly have been surprised if he had suddenly developed a third eye, in the middle of his forehead, say.

" As a matter of fact, he did," acknowledged Bill. " Some days ago. He mentioned yours."

There was nothing phony about the incredulity with which Ames received this announcement.

" You mean Crook entertains the preposterous idea that *I* was Lane's nocturnal visitor ? What in thunder put such a notion into his head ? "

" I fancy you did," returned Bill coolly. " At all events, you made it clear you'd visited the premises on at least one occasion. How, otherwise, could you know the telephone was in the hall and that the doors were made of plywood ? "

" And so Crook has decided that I'm the man he wants ? Perhaps he also thinks . . ."

" I'll tell you what he thinks. He thinks you were one of the original four at Lane's sherry party. He knows about the draw for the Black Death and there's no reason to suppose you had less to lose than Lady Silk."

" Perhaps," suggested Ames, showing his handsome teeth in a wide grin, " he also told you the nature of Lane's hold over me ? "

" Crook don't give a button for that," Bill assured him, " and since the deed-box has been emptied the odds are there's no record any longer. At all events he knows it wasn't Lady Silk, because she's his client, it wasn't Mrs. T., because she has an alibi, so it rests between you and Ross."

ANTHONY GILBERT

" What gave Crook the idea that Ross is involved ? "

" He had to have some reason for intervening in the case at
all. It was he who suggested Crook's name to Silk, and he
let on that it was you who put him up to it. Crook can add
two and two with anyone," he pointed out drily. He stood
up. " I won't keep you any longer. I can see you're busy.
But I thought I better hand you Crook's message, that you're
in a hot spot and should know it."

He went away, a cool arrogant figure, so assured that he
didn't look back to see Ames standing in the window, watching
him vanish. The street was almost empty ; a man went by
carrying a despatch-case, a couple passed arguing with the
nervous intensity of youth, a middle-aged woman turned the
corner riding a bicycle and was almost thrown by a small
questing dog that appeared from nowhere. A man on the
other side of the road crossed and apparently asked her if she
were all right. A green car came sailing down the street, a
girl hurried by as if late for some eagerly-awaited appointment. Ames thought in an odd inconsequent way that there
was a situation there a modern crime writer would turn into
a book. He'd sometimes thought of writing one himself.
The woman was rich and eccentric ; the man on the other
side of the road was an assassin ; the dog had been sent out
to throw her from her machine ; the girl—oh, the girl would
be a heroine, he supposed . . . He shrugged at his own
fancifulness. The room behind him seemed unusually cold,
and a sense of being suddenly alone overwhelmed him.

" And leave the world to darkness and to me," he thought.
He came back to his desk and sat down, thinking over what
Bill had just told him, and doodling his arrogant monogram
furiously all over the blotting-paper.

The street emptied like water pouring out of a jug. Bill
had disappeared round the corner in the direction of the
underground ; the cycling woman, having successfully
avoided being thrown by the dog, sailed away into space ;
the young couple had gone into a snack bar at the end of the
road and the man had gone into one of the buildings. The
hurrying girl turned into a side-street and the green car,
of course, had long been out of sight.

A clock somewhere chimed the half-hour and some pigeons
who had been chattering softly on a nearby window-sill rose
suddenly in the air in a soft coloured cloud and flew away as
if in sudden alarm. But Ames stayed in his office, though he

had stopped doodling, and a little later the sound of frantic typewriting could be heard.

"Don't go into Ames's room, dear," said one of the cleaners to her neighbour about half an hour after Bill's departure. "Working late again as usual."

"Goes fast, don't he?" said the other, listening to the rapid tap-tap of the typewriter keys. "I tell my girl, 'You should hear Mr. Ames, that's what I call work.' But these young ones—they don't know. Life's been made easy for them."

"Seems queer all the same," said the first cleaner as they went past the closed door. "I never trust men who do more than they need. I mean, it seems against nature. It's different for women."

"Oh well," said the second, opening a door farther along the corridor and preparing to start work, "'e's a foreigner reely, ain't 'e, and of course that makes all the difference."

Crook was conscious again when Bill returned to Church Melton. "Give Ames my message?" he asked. He was very pale and pretty weak, though his powers of recuperation must have startled the Recording Angel. "How'd he take it?"

"It was a shock to him," said Bill. "Of course he said he didn't send the message . . ."

Crook nodded. "Naturally." It was what he had expected.

"Considerably shaken to realise how he'd given himself away," Bill continued.

"How did he take the gipsy's warning?" whispered Crook. "Grateful?"

"If looks are anything to go on he was about as grateful as a charging rhinoceros. I felt lucky to get away intact. He carries a gun," he added. "At least, there was one in his drawer, the twin of mine, ready for emergencies."

Crook lay back against the pillow as a nurse bustled in to turn Bill out.

"Bully for him," he murmured. "Only hope he knows when to use it."

"Well, he's gone at last, thank goodness," said the first cleaner to her companion, as she returned to the floor an hour later. "Light's out." She squinted under the door. "Nice to get them finished the same day," she added rather obscurely. "All right, dear, I'll do 'is Lordship to-night. You get on back to Bert. If 'e's feeling queer . . ."

She opened the door and switched on the light.

The scream she gave could be heard almost as far as Piccadilly Circus.

CHAPTER SEVENTEEN

LAST WILL AND TESTAMENT

CHARLES HAD SPENT a miserable night and was grateful to the strained situation in Parliament that made it imperative for him to attend the House that day. You never knew what might not come up, and Governments have fallen by a single vote before now. He dressed and shaved and came downstairs, poured out his coffee and shook open the *Record*.

And then he saw it—sprawled right across the front page.

FAMOUS Q.C. FOUND SHOT

Mr. Harmsworth Ames, the well-known Q.C., was found last night shot dead in his chambers. A revolver was found near the body. The discovery was made by Mrs. Jane Hunt, a cleaner, who gave the alarm.

On another page there was an interview with Mrs. Hunt.

We could hear him typewriting when we came in, she said. He often worked late.

Editorial comment was that Ames's most prominent case at the moment was the defence of Lady Silk for the murder of Edward Lane ; the solicitor in the case, Mr. Arthur Crook, had been shot in the porch of the dead man's house at Church Melton the night before. It was understood that Mr. Crook's condition, though still serious, gave good ground for hope.

" And now let 'em do a bit of arithmetic," said Cummings, who didn't give a button for Ames's death but had experienced a pang of personal loss when he heard about Crook's predicament.

As for Mrs. Jane Hunt, once the first appalling shock was passed, she found herself the recipient of more offers of cuppas and half-pints of stout at the local than she had had for years. The police had warned her against irresponsible

talk, but with the independence of her kind she consigned the
police to what she considered their right place.

"Talk about being irresponsible," she told her cronies over
a glass of black velvet (by no means the first of the evening).
"I was always told it was the police's job to prevent crime."

"Don't be silly, ducks," said her neighbour. "If there
wasn't no crime there wouldn't be no police. They ought to
be grateful to criminals really." Irresponsibility could hardly
go further.

"Well, we could hear 'im typewriting away when we come
in and I said to Mrs. Black, 'That means he'll be there half
the night, I suppose.' Well, we passed a few remarks about
him, and then we got on with the work. As we come back
I noticed the light was out under his door so I said to Mrs.
Black, 'I'll do his Lordship to-night,' and I opened the door.
Of course, I didn't see nothing right away because the light
was out, and when I put it on and sor 'im I thought I was
going to pass right out. Lying right over his table he was,
and the blood ? All over everything. I screamed—I couldn't
help it—and Mrs. Black come along, and she went down and
got a policeman and . . ." and so on and so forth. In plain
fact, Mrs. Hunt was having the time of her life.

"Shouldn't be surprised if the Sunday papers was after
you," her friends encouraged her. "You'll be able to have
that suite for your lounge, after all."

The document that had been so feverishly typed in Ames's
room on the last night of his life ran :

"This is the last will and testament of me, Harmsworth
Ames, Q.C., set down in my right mind. That is important.
I want no coroner's jury to bring in a verdict of suicide
while of unsound mind. I was never more sane. I take
this path as an invalid in obedience to doctor's orders
goes to the seaside for a change of air. I bequeath to Lady
Silk her freedom and an acknowledgment of her complete
innocence in the death of Teddy Lane. I bequeath to the
police my confession that I killed him and have no regrets
about it at all. In any sane civilisation he would have died
by popular acclamation. He was no good, a twister, a drug
addict, and a cheat. Also, of course, he was a blackmailer.
He was blackmailing me as well as Lady Silk and I dare say
there were others. He was in debt and he couldn't be

161

trusted as far as you could see him. In a way, you could say he committed suicide. He asked for what he got, and I never had a qualm about destroying him.

It was almost too easy. I called on Thursday night and insisted on coming in. He knew I was coming, though he pretended to look surprised. I had brought the stuff with me, an ordinary kind of sleeping-mixture that I knew how to lay hands on without any dr's certificate, and when he left me alone when he went into the lobby to answer the phone I put the stuff into his coffee. He helped me by being half-drunk ; he didn't offer me any whisky but when he went into his room on some flimsy excuse he came back reeking of the stuff. That and the drug, which I watched him take, soon made him unconscious, and it was easy to help myself to the documents I had come to get.

When the police arrested Lady Silk I was in a quandary, but my luck held again. I was asked to undertake the defence. It is only now that I realise Crook's cunning. Under the pretence of working with me he has been building up a case against me. So clearly Crook had to go. I rang up his flat and told him I was being followed, but that I had hired a car and was going down to Church Melton where I asked him to join me. I was waiting in the porch when he came through the gate and I shot him before he could ring the bell. I would have given him a second shot for luck but some interfering policeman bobbed up and I didn't dare risk firing again. In any case I didn't think it neces-sary. I came back to London and returned the car to the garage and waited to hear the news of his death. His partner, a man called Parsons, has just been to see me and deliver the last warning. I can see that the game is up and there is no other way out."

At the foot of the typewritten page was the immense scrawl—" H. A.," looking rather more extravagant than usual.

Crook heard the news in hospital. He lay still so long that even the imperturbable Bill became alarmed.

" This is what you expected, isn't it ? " he asked.

" It's what I thought might happen. That's why I sent you. For Pete's sake, look after yourself, Bill. You'll be the next. This chap's not going to stop at one more murder if he can pull it off. You can't hang twice and well he knows it."

He said as much to the police. "Don't you chaps ever add two and two?" he demanded. "After this fellow had taken a pot shot at me what else did you expect? Once the three of us are out for the count, me and Ames and Bill, that is—he hasn't got much to fear, not on your life."

"Only the police force," said the sergeant icily, and Crook said: "Yes, that was what he'd meant. Next thing you know he'll be after Bill," he insisted.

And then the police played their trump card. Ames's death was nothing whatever to do with X. It was suicide.

"Who says so?"

"The deceased left a confession that will be put in at the inquest to show that he took his own life."

"Don't make me laugh," Crook begged. "If I burst these stitches I'll be *hors de combat* for weeks, and then you'll find yourselves sweltering in a sea of corpses, like Billy-be-damned. Or was he before your time?" he added, noticing a look of perplexity pass over his companion's face. "Oh well, let it ride. There's no time to be lost. Where's that alleged confession?"

"In London, of course."

"Any chance of getting a peep at it?"

The sergeant said grudgingly that probably it would be made public in due course. Readers of newspapers were avid for details no matter how melodramatic . . .

"Good for them," said Crook unsympathetically. "Nice to know someone takes an interest in justice being done. I'll tell you this for what it's worth which might even be the reputation of the chap who's looking after the Ames side of the affair—this isn't just another little job for the undertaker, it's a second murder, and the proper headlines should be:

MURDER CALLS AGAIN WHILE POLICE ARE NAPPING

Get hold of a copy of that document for me, and I'll guarantee to make so many holes in it it'll look like a game of cat's cradle."

The Inspector said drily, "You seem to know a lot about it," and Crook said:

"Well, use your loaf. If you were going to leave a nice

signed confession and then put a bullet through your head, *would you take the trouble to switch the light off first?* Of course not. But if you'd just committed a murder then automatically you'd turn off the light, probably thinking that 'ud give you time to cover your tracks. If this chap, whoever he is, had known more about Ames, he'd have known that when the light went out the cleaners came in, and the time of death 'ud be pretty roughly established. And here's another point," he went on. " These cleaning women heard the sound of the typewriter even when they were working, *but none of them heard the sound of a gun.* What was he shot with ? "

" A Webster. It was found by the body. What's more, it's the same weapon as was used on yourself. Our ballistic experts . . ."

" Save that for the witness box," said Crook fretfully. " I'm a sick man. I don't want to be bothered with un-necessary details. Of course, it's the same. But—you make inquiries and see if Ames ever took out a licence for a Webster. His gun was a Mawson-Moberley. Bill saw it that evening, in a drawer in his desk."

" There was no sign of any such weapon in the room when we found him," said the sergeant. " Is your man prepared to swear to that ? "

" Ames was a lawyer," said Crook with an awful air of patience, the air men use when dealing with imbeciles. " He knew even a Q.C. can't keep a lethal weapon without a licence. Of course, Bill's sure. Now get hold of a copy of that document. And I'll run rings round it for you. Well, what are we waiting for ? Your job's to catch criminals, ain't it ? "

A copy of the supposed confession was shown to him not many hours later, and he read it as rapidly as if it were some casual paragraph in the newspaper. But those prominent brown eyes missed nothing.

" I told you it would be a fake," he said, throwing it down on the hospital blanket. " The chap who typed that knew a lot about Teddy Lane but precious little about Harmsworth Ames. It's been established that whoever poisoned Lane was drinking coffee with him on the night of his death, *but Ames never drank coffee.* He told me so himself. You don't have to take my word for that. You'll find a dozen people who'll bear me out."

The inspector was watching him carefully, as a Londoner watches a cow in a field, anticipating a mad charge at any moment or a sudden transformation of the harmless creature into a wild bull.

" I tried to warn him," Crook went on. " Bill went up on purpose, but X must have been keeping tabs on him. He'd know Bill had been down here, and he followed him and saw him go to Ames's office. He knew then, of course, he hadn't any time to lose. Probably marched in as soon as Bill marched out (as clearly as though he had been there he visualised the casual passer-by who had nipped into the office doorway the instant Bill was out of sight, chancing his luck that no one would see him at such an hour), and made straight for Ames's room. You know his habit of never looking up when anyone comes in ? Probably thought it was Bill coming back for something. It wouldn't surprise me to know he never knew what hit him. Bill left at 7.30, the cleaners were in at 8, and the typewriter was going hell-for-leather by then."

"'Are you suggesting that he actually typed a spurious confession with the man he'd murdered at his elbow ? "

" Why not ? Ames ain't the only man who knows how to type. Besides," he slapped the copy with a scornful hand, " Ames was a lawyer. He'd know you need a proper signature to a document if it's to hold water in court, but that paper's only signed with a monogram. I noticed when I went to visit Ames his habit of doodling his monogram all over the blotting-paper. X only had to practice for a minute or two—why, he could even trace the outlines, knowing that it was all Lombard Street to a china orange that anyone would suspect the confession was a phony. If Ames had really written that he'd have told you the whole story—the sherry party at Lane's flat for one thing. And then—' he was blackmailing me as well as Lady Silk and I dare say there were others.' Power and glory, man, he knew there were others. Then—there's no mention of the deed-box or the papers it contained. Why ? Because he didn't empty the deed-box. All of which goes to show we've been barking up the wrong tree from the start. Any one of our four would have gone for the papers right away. I tell you, Inspector, this chap had nothing to do with the party on Black Friday. He didn't even know it had happened. And there's no mention of a second party that took place the following afternoon. Or a little mascot called the Black Death. No, Inspector, the fellow you want had nothing to do with Lady Silk or any of her friends. It was a private vendetta."

"That's pure guess-work," objected the police officer. "It might quite as easily have been one of the others."

"Well, not my client, because she was drivin' back to London. And not one of the other members of the sherry party because I've tested her alibi. It was between Ames and the fourth guest."

"He wasn't to know that Lane would be drugged into insensibility. He was taking a chance . . ."

"Not much of one. You're forgetting the fifty pounds, ain't you? How many people do you suppose loved Teddy Lane enough to send him fifty pounds? I'll tell you." He held up his big thumb and first finger in a large derisive O. "But someone wanted his flat empty that night, and he knew the one way to ensure Teddy going out of London was to supply him with funds. He nearly succeeded, too. But something happened that drove Teddy back. Ames couldn't know that, of course . . . He was expecting to find an empty flat, and in point of fact that's probably what he did find. Teddy was on his bed, the communicating door had probably blown shut, the lights were off, and X would have too much sense to switch them on, seeing Teddy might have told someone he was going away. It wouldn't take him long to open the deed-box—as a matter of fact it was open because Teddy had been checking up on one of his victims—he simply had to grab the lot and scram. We'll never be able to prove it now, but I'd say Teddy was drifting into his last sleep while his belongings were being rifled. The real murderer may have seen Ames come in; I fancy he knew the identity of the visitor which made him fix on Ames. Well, all you have to do now is to go out and take your man. He's practically told you in his confession who he is. Anyway, there ain't much choice. Teddy don't seem to have many friends, and this one stands out a mile." He put a great pudgy finger on the manuscript in front of him. " ' He was a drug addict . . .' Now who knew he was a drug addict? Not Ames, or he'd have told me. Not Lady Silk or she'd have told me. She told me a lot, but not that. The person who put Teddy Lane where he belonged knew him a hell of a lot better than any of our four, three of whom were meeting him for the first time. It's perfectly simple." Crook lay back feeling a bit tired.

" Hard work knocking sense into the heads of the police," he told Bill later.

Pepper repressed his natural choler at what he regarded as insufferable conceit, and said, " So your theory is that Ames was Lane's second visitor that night? Any proof, Mr. Crook?"

Crook sat up suddenly like a cobra striking after a long period of swaying back and forth.

" That's your job. You wouldn't like it if I was to—what's the expression?—usurp your prerogative, come home with all the bacon. Mind you," he added more temperately, " I don't say you can get proof of that, now Ames is out of the way. I don't take it he'd confide in anyone. But I'll tell you. X knew who that second visitor was. That's why he's trying to fix the blame on Ames. Now take it all away and sew it up into a nice pattern," he added, suddenly exhausted. " It's time I had forty winks, while you put a man on Ames's bank, and see if he didn't draw fifty pounds in one pound notes round about that date. If this hospital had any humanity at all," he wound up, glowering at the nurse who came in to put an end to the session, " they'd bring me a drop of the real stuff, but here if I say I'm parched they offer me barley-water. Barley-water."

" You mustn't get excited, Mr. Crook," said the nurse skittishly.

" It's enough to give me a temperature of 104, lying here and watching the police muck up my case," asserted Crook. He turned back to the inspector. " Why, this fellow's practically told you who he is, given you a hint as broad as the seat of my trousers. Only act fast and ask questions afterwards. Otherwise he'll slip through your fingers yet."

" You don't suggest, Mr. Crook, that it was Mr. Ames who made the murderous attack on yourself?"

" If Ames had been at the other end of the gun I wouldn't be talking to you now. I'd be lyin' in state and Bill would be refusing fantastic offers from the Sunday press for my life story. Well," he lay down with his back to the inspector, " there you are. Your job is to get him with the evidence on him. If you don't, he'll probably live to draw the Old Age Pension for twenty years."

" The evidence?" repeated the inspector.

" Yes," said Crook and kindly explained his meaning.

CHAPTER EIGHTEEN

HOUNDS OF DEATH

DURING HIS WORKING week Gerald Ross lived as austerely as any monk. On alternate week-ends he could join his family ; for the rest he lived, breathed, thought and ate his work. There were momentary diversions, like the cocktail party where he had had his astonished glimpse of Teddy Lane, but these were so few they were to be counted on the fingers of one hand over a period of months. He lived very simply in a furnished room and ate at a restaurant. Sometimes Mrs. Penny, his landlady, thought he forgot to eat at all. Since the Lane affair his lean distinction had turned into something more haggard. " Looks as if he was waiting to catch someone," Mrs. Penny told a neighbour, but what she should have said was, as if he expects someone to catch him. He had been horrified by Julia's arrest, convinced, even after he knew the facts about the Black Death, that she was innocent. The attack on Crook had shocked him to a lesser degree. In a sense it came as a relief because it showed that the enemy was still at large. It never occurred to him that Crook could have been attacked on anyone else's behalf. Then came the staggering news of Ames's suicide, and he was still pinching himself to make sure he was awake when a fresh sensation swept down upon him. He was working late in the evening when his landlady informed him that a gentleman was in the hall.

" Who on earth is it ? "

Mrs. Penny genteelly didn't know.

" He'd better come up, I suppose." Gerald supposed it was someone from the laboratory, but he had never seen the tall man who came in walking with a slight limp, and carrying a portfolio under his arm.

" Mr. Ross ? " said Bill Parsons briskly, without offering any signs of identity. " Very fortunate to have caught you at home. I'm in the market for second-hand typewriters. No, just a minute, IF you please. You're going to tell me you're perfectly satisfied with the one you operate already.

If that's the case, I can assure you you haven't seen our new model. Now available on hire-purchase terms. You won't find more generous terms anywhere. We . . ."

Here Gerald contrived to get a word in edgeways. "I'm afraid you've been misinformed. I'm not interested."

"Not interested?" His visitor's expression was comical in its incredulity.

"That's what I said. I don't operate a typewriter myself, as you put it. I'm a scientist, not a journalist or a clerk. And most of my work is done better with pen and ink. If I do want a typewriter I can send for a stenographer and it's nothing to me what sort of machine she uses. I don't pay for it and I'm not responsible for its upkeep."

"But surely you have considered the value of a typewriter for your personal correspondence?"

"The little correspondence I have is achieved with a fountain-pen. And don't tell me that you also travel in fountain-pens. The one I have is perfectly satisfactory. Also it was given me by my wife."

"As a piece of logic that would delight Crook's heart," said his visitor with a complete change of tone and manner. "Now, having cleared up that point, let's get down to brass tacks."

"May I inquire who the devil you are?" demanded Ross with commendable self-control.

"My name's Parsons. I'm Crook's A.D.C. He's not going to die, which I am sure must be a relief to you . . ."

"Why do you say that?" demanded Gerald.

"Well, you got him into this case, didn't you? You recommended him to Sir Charles Silk. I doubt if he'd even heard his name before."

"I hadn't myself, until Ames mentioned it. Ever since I heard the staggering news I've wondered why."

"The news of Ames's death, you mean?"

"Yes. According to the Press, Crook has the reputation of always nailing the real criminal, even if his methods are on the unconventional side, so, seeing Ames had murdered Lane himself, you'd have expected Crook to be the last man he would suggest. Or am I being remarkably dense?"

"I dare say if he had poisoned Lane that would be common sense, but we've no proof that he did."

Gerald stared. "The confession . . ."

"We've no proof he wrote that."

" In that case, why did he commit suicide ? " Gerald was all at sea.

" Crook's case is that he didn't," explained Bill patiently. " That's why I'm here, to help to clear away the dead wood. Now perhaps you see the point of my original patter ? "

" I get you," said Gerald after a moment. " You wanted to know if I could typewrite."

" Precisely. Whoever shot Ames could type and type fast. The cleaners who heard him, and hadn't the faintest idea that only the width of a door separated them from a particularly cold-blooded murderer, imagined it was Ames himself, as you'd expect."

" I suppose," hazarded Gerald politely, " Crook has some grounds for his contentions."

Bill nodded. " I believe you when you say you'd never heard of Crook till Ames mentioned him."

" And—why do you imagine I can help you ? "

" You were one of the original four at Lane's party. Otherwise you'd hardly have gone hell-for-leather round to Ames's chambers as soon as you heard about Lady Silk. So it stands to reason you drew the Black Death the same as the others."

" Well ? " Gerald still looked puzzled.

" Well—" countered Bill, " we still have to find Lane's murderer, who is incidentally Ames's murderer, too, though his death isn't our job."

Gerald sat up, suddenly rigid. " Are you suggesting *I* had a hand in it ? "

" You drew the Black Death," Bill repeated. " You must have had some plan, like all the rest. Lady Silk meant to buy Lane off, Ames intended to draw his fangs. Mrs. T. doesn't matter, because she couldn't have been Lane's visitor on Thursday night. But you—you had some plan, surely."

" Yes," agreed Gerald slowly, " but I didn't propose either to put my neck in the noose or see my life wrecked. As for the third alternative, paying his price, that was out of the question. I hadn't got the money. Besides, it would only have been a first instalment. My case was rather different from the others in that it wasn't simply a matter of buying back a single document, an indiscreet letter or a forged cheque ; the hold he had over me would have been equally strong five years hence as it is to-day. It seemed to me the only way I could shut his mouth would be by a kind of— counter-blackmail. I was convinced that he had some pretty unsavoury passages in his record, some possibly criminal, so I set myself to dig into the past. The trouble was I had so little time."

" What did you find ? " asked Bill, obviously because he wanted to know and not because he was testing his companion.

" I found that he was involved, or rather, I had every reason to believe he was involved in the black market in drugs. That's pretty serious, just murder in another and more lingering form. There's a chap who works at the laboratory with me, a chemist who did some research into the subject a few years ago and what he's told me is horrifying and almost incredible. Of course, there's any amount of money to be made in it, and the drug pedlars, who're generally addicts themselves, are astonishingly hard to identify. The stuff's passed so neatly at parties or in buses, or even in crowds on tube stations. It's much more profitable than black market butter or nylons, though they were a good enough racket for a time."

" You got definite information, then ? "

" If you mean, had I a case I could put to the police, the answer's No. But I believed I had enough data to put the fear of the law into his mind. They give pretty severe sentences for that sort of offence, and if they hanged them," he added with a lack of emphasis more striking than any explosion of rage could have been, " it would be no more than they deserved. My plan, then, was to visit Lane and let him know what I suspected, underlining it a bit, perhaps, to strengthen my hand. I was convinced he wouldn't dare risk a police investigation."

" You mean it was a case of bluff cut bluff."

" Yes. And on the whole I thought I held the stronger hand. He had nothing on me that would have landed me in a police court, simply a record of the type of indiscretion most damaging to a man engaged in government service, and particularly the branch in which I'm employed. If he had challenged me to go to the police I should have accepted the challenge, but I knew I was taking remarkably little risk. I was convinced he would agree to my terms."

" And that," continued Bill, neatly picking up his cue, " explains the anonymous police officer who called at Ellison Mansions that Thursday afternoon. The authorities have been puzzled about him ; they had no knowledge of any such person. Did you wear a disguise, or, if not, how did you hope to escape detection ? "

" I never thought of escaping detection. I went as myself, but when that insolent porter employed at the Mansions said vulgarly, ' You're too late, chum, he's hopped it,' I rapped out, ' If he should ring up for any reason tell him the police are anxious to interview him in connection with a private matter,' and went out. I thought that would shake him a bit. You see, I didn't believe Moxon when he told me Lane had left London. Why should he, on the eve of what he had reason to suppose would be a day of reckoning for him ? I thought he had tipped the fellow to say he was away."

" Any proof of that ? " Bill inquired.

" I telephoned that night and Lane himself took the call. He was obviously in a state of jitters, said he was engaged and warned me I'd find the chain up if I came round. I pulled my line about being the police, and you could almost hear his teeth chatter over the telephone. I promised to call in next morning."

" And did you ? "

" I didn't have the opportunity. I had unexpected instructions from headquarters to go to one of our midland stations and when I got back late that evening his name was the first I saw in the paper. I could scarcely believe he was dead—by his own hand it was originally reported. It seemed to me too good to be true. And, of course, I was right. It was."

He stopped and for a moment neither man spoke. Then Gerald said decisively, " All the same, I never for a moment believed Lady Silk was guilty. Of course, at that time I didn't know the trick Mrs. T., as you call her, had played on us. I went round to see Ames and discovered he, too, had drawn the Black Death."

" And he put you on to Crook ? "

" Yes. It didn't go through my mind he might have been responsible though in the circumstances I suppose it would have been a logical deduction."

" Why ? " asked Bill colourlessly. " Did he tell you anything you didn't know before ? Anything to give you the impression he might have paid a second visit to the flat ? "

" Nothing I recall." He brooded an instant, remembering that conversation. Suddenly his face changed.

" Yes ? " prompted Bill who, like his partner, didn't miss much.

" He said one thing. I didn't pay any attention to it at the time. He said he knew the identity of Mrs. T., and he also knew the nature of the hold Lane had over her. Now, he had met her for the first time in Lane's flat, I think there's no doubt of that. And he met her again the next day with Lady Silk and myself but we left simultaneously, and she certainly told us nothing then."

" So it rather looks as though he was the nigger in the woodpile, so far as the looted deed-box was concerned. They never traced any of the contents to Lady Silk, the papers haven't been found anywhere, her servants have told the police there was no evidence of her having destroyed them, and she herself swears she never went inside the flat that night, or indeed at any time after the first party. Well, that supports Crook's view. He's always maintained that Lane had two visitors on Black Friday, one who killed him and one who took the papers. The choice for the latter lay between you and Ames, and it looks pretty certain it was Ames."

" And X—the murderer—knew that ? "

" Say he was disturbed by Ames's arrival and had to hide somewhere. It's possible, you know. It seems quite likely that Lane was in his room and Ames never realised he was on the premises. X may have been hiding there, too. That's bound to be speculation until we have some evidence of X's identity. Now, tell me just how much you learned of Lane's activities in the drug field. You see, whoever gave Ames his quietus knew that Lane was an addict, so it's conceivable and even probable that they were in the racket together."

He remained some time further with Gerald, sifting every scrap of evidence or conjecture, and it was pretty late when he left the house.

When Death learned that the police had asked for an adjournment for the inquest on Harmsworth Ames, he sweated with terror, because it was obvious they smelt a rat and intended to trace it to its hole. He might tell himself over and over again, " They've nothing on me, they'll never come looking in my direction," but he was a guilty man and guilty men know no peace of mind. A steady series—not of mistakes, he wouldn't call them that—but of misfortunes had dogged him from the start. He had expected the verdict in Teddy's case to be suicide while of unsound mind, and he had employed a drug not difficult of access to insomniacs, thinking that would make him safe, but he had been wrong. When Julia was arrested he had breathed again, but Crook had been called in and he knew then his chances of detection had increased a hundredfold. For if Charles hadn't heard of Crook, Death had. Crook always gets his man, and why break his record now? It was too big a risk to take, so Crook must go, and he had played his elaborate charade. But for his enemy's sudden swerve at the critical moment, that would have been successful. Even then he had imagined that after a night's exposure and steady loss of blood his end would have been gained, but once more Fate in the guise of an interfering young constable had upset all his calculations.

Desperate now, he had played his last card. His vigil on the staircase at Ellison Mansions had shown him that Ames was involved in Teddy's affairs, and he had no doubt that it was the Q.C. who had removed the incriminating papers. So, he thought, if he could persuade the authorities that Ames had also been responsible for Teddy's death, the case would be closed. Even Crook could not move in the case of a definite confession. All Crook cared for was the acquittal of his client, and this should let her out. He had left his business in the charge of an assistant and travelled down to Church Melton. It had been easy to ring up the hospital and learn that Bill was in constant attendance on the injured man. He had returned to London by the same train and shadowed Bill to Ames's office. He had been hanging about on the opposite side of the street when Bill took his leave and had plunged forward to the assistance of the plump lady on the bicycle when she was intimidated by the little brown dog. It had been simple to march up the stairs to Ames's office, push open the door and put a bullet through Ames's head before the barrister realised his danger. Then he left the confession, folded the dead man's hands round the butt of the revolver and sat down to the typewriter. No one, he was convinced, had seen him enter, no one saw him leave. He had spent a frantic night sponging the blood stains from his clothes, constantly reminding himself that, since he had never been in the picture, no one would ask him inconvenient questions. The next morning he had seen the news in the paper, and felt as though a crushing burden had been lifted from his shoulders.

And then Fate played her last trump. The police asked for a postponement of the inquest, and at once he was hag-ridden with doubts. What could such a course imply but that the authorities believed there had been some hanky-panky? Then—had he made some blunder? left some clue? But he had gone round the office removing his fingerprints, making sure that a verdict of suicide was a foregone conclusion. Even if he had been seen in the street, and he was convinced there had been no peeping Toms when he took his departure, why should his presence be associated with the death of Harmsworth Ames? Over and over again he repeated to himself the vain assurance that he was safe—safe—safe. Teddy was out of the way, Teddy who might, in his malevolence, have turned King's Evidence, and betrayed him. Ames was gone, leaving behind him a signed solution to the mystery. But it was no good. He shook like a leaf whenever anyone pushed open his door, suspected every creature who went into the telephone booth on the opposite side of the road. If, by some process of reasoning he could not foresee, the suspicion of the authorities turned in his direction, he was lost. A search of his premises would pin the crime to him. He thought of packing up the suit and depositing it at a railway parcels office, but memories of other men who had taken a similar course and had not thereby escaped the gallows deterred him. He couldn't give it away for fear of arousing comment—for when had he ever given anyone anything? He dared not leave London in case a search of his premises was made during his absence. He knew, of course, that the police have no right of entry without a warrant, but suppose they could obtain one? And there was other evidence, too. He'd been too much alarmed (and elated) on the night of Ames's death to finish the job outright. And now he never walked to the post office to buy a stamp or heard the door open or the telephone ring without the instant dread, " This is it."

He was thinking this for the fiftieth time when his door opened and a policeman came in. He wasn't in uniform, but there was no mistaking the plain-clothesman, not to anyone who knew as much about the police as Death. But he controlled himself and said easily, " What can I do for you? " and the policeman told him.

He gasped. Why, it was nothing to do with Ames at all.

That showed, surely, how absurd it was to let things prey on your mind. All the same, he would get rid of that evidence somehow, and so that same evening, he locked his door, and came out wrapped in a camelhair coat and got into a little black car and shot off in a westerly direction. And two fellows who'd been hanging about round the telephone kiosk, one talking to an anonymous correspondent while the other loitered on the pavement, exchanged a sharp glance, and went round the corner to where a small blue car was waiting.

" This is it," said one, and " Let's hope so," said the other. " This is no night for a pleasant drive into the country." For the weather had been getting steadily colder and that morning the Meteorological Office had said sharp frosts were on the way, more suited to January than early April. But everything was haywire that year.

Their quarry drove carefully, his eye on the driving mirror. He told himself it was all right, he was becoming an old woman, his name had never even been mentioned in police circles, but conscience doth make cowards of us all, etc., and when he'd been going about half an hour it seemed to him that a blue car was persistently in his wake. He tried one or two ruses, taking sharp side-turns but when he came back to the main road the car was always there. He thought of stopping and faking a breakdown, but the blue car would probably draw up alongside, offering assistance, so he let that plan go down the wind and held steadily on.

Suddenly it had disappeared. He couldn't believe his luck. Then abruptly he pulled himself together. He was losing his nerve. No one had been after him. Why should they be ? He drove on in better heart.

The blue car, meanwhile, had turned off at a corner where a light grey car was waiting, and the two men transferred into that.

" Think he rumbled you ? " asked the driver of this second car.

" Getting windy," said one of the men. " Wonder where he's heading for ? "

" These chaps are all the same," grumbled the other. " Always make things as difficult for us as they can. Why couldn't he have stopped on Hammersmith Bridge and chanced his arm there ? No soap trying to dredge things up from the river and we couldn't have touched him without some proof, which seems to be just what we haven't got as yet."

"It won't help him anyway," chimed in the first. "He can't change the number of his car without being seen, or drive into a hollow and repaint it like they do in some of these flicking detective stories; and there's a general warning out for it."

The hunted man meanwhile had been able to reassure himself that all his inner turmoil had been for nothing. The blue car didn't reappear and he paid no special heed to a grey car that ran past him and went into a side-turning. When it stole out again he was topping the rise of a hill, about as conspicuous as an exposed lighted window during a black-out. The question put by the grey car's driver —where's he making for ?—was one that exercised him also. The cold seemed to increase steadily, and the surface of the roads was treacherous with frost. He couldn't make the pace he'd have liked for fear of a skid, but he kept reminding himself he'd got all night, all night, and so contrived to quiet his thumping heart.

At last in a long stretch of dark country road he found a place that seemed suited to his purpose. If anyone did pass and see the lighted car at the roadside it wouldn't seem odd that the driver had found it necessary to slip away among the trees for a minute. He knew where he was now ; not far in the woods was an ornamental lake with a bridge over it, leading to a dilapidated old house that had been a manor once but had taken a beating from a German bomber during the war and was now a ruin. No fear of interruption from anyone there, because no one inhabited it but bats and possibly an owl. He pulled up and opened the door of the car.

The pond was farther than he remembered, but he sighted it at last and ran quickly forward to the little rustic bridge. As he reached it the moon sailed triumphantly out from a sheath of cloud, covering the earth with silver light. He shrank instinctively from that brilliance, casting his eyes to the ground, and what he saw chilled his blood. For the surface of the water was frozen over by a sheet of ice, and his plans were wrecked.

Terror held him for a moment, then he drove it off. There was no time to lose, any instant they might be on his track. He turned once again into the woods ; beneath his feet twigs and boughs, sharp with frost, crackled disconcertingly ; the world seemed very still, not a hedgehog rustled the leaves, not a bird called. Surely, surely this darkness offered some hiding-place, some cranny among thick-grown roots where a man could hide something that now seemed to him the image of death ? Quickly he moved forward ; then his heart seemed to suffocate him. Was it imagination or—had one of those black trees moved a little nearer than a minute ago ? Once again he battled with fear, compelled himself to pass a second tree, blown into a fantastic shape by years of exposure ; a stray branch touched him and he suppressed a cry, paused once more, tense and prickling : all round him the trees waited, black and motionless. The silence seemed complete till the slow cracking of a twig, when he himself had not stirred, drove him to sudden frenzy.

" Who's there ? " he whispered sharply, and once again one of the dark trees moved a little nearer. He flung up a protesting hand and immediately the blackness was pierced by a sharp sword of light. Turning blindly he started to run, anywhere that might promise obscurity. But in his haste he caught his foot in an exposed root and an instant later his enemies were upon him ; they had him fast and now one had drawn from his pocket that object whose possession was to sign his death warrant.

" What's this ? " said one of the men. " A Mawson-Moberley ? Funny thing, we're looking for a gun like that. Have you a licence for this, Mr. Morell ? "

CHAPTER NINETEE N

THE SHROUD IS DONE

" WELL, OF COURSE he hadn't," said Crook, " and though he tried to make out he'd had it for a long time, that cock didn't fight. It was Ames's gun and it had Ames's fingerprints on it. Ames's and not Morell's, because he'd been careful to handle it in gloves or in a handkerchief."

" But what led you to Morell at all ? " asked Charles. Crook was poodle-faking, as he called it. Julia was home again, cleared of any responsibility for Teddy Lane's death, and people were saying all's well that ends well and how delighted Charles must be. But Charles knew, if they didn't, that Omar Khayyam was right, and you can't blot out what has once been written. Julia was free to come and go as she pleased, no one was going to be able to point a finger at her and say she was one of the lucky ones. But nothing could change the facts. The appalling thing had happened. Charles could say that the past was over and done with and that by brooding over it you were simply losing the present. He didn't say that what he knew did not affect his love for his wife, because that wasn't necessary. But to the end of her life Julia would feel the stain. And Charles would be aware of it. That was the price exacted from them.

Crook, who saw a great deal more than he allowed most people to guess, was answering Charles's question.

" It was Ross who blazed the trail," he acknowledged. " He's not figured much in the case, less than any of the others come to that. But his was the best solution of the four. Paying Danegeld, with all due respects to you," and he bowed to Julia, " is always risky. Breaking and entering, as Ames did, puts you in danger of jug. Your best chance is to play your enemy's game, and go one better, and that was what Ross was going to do. I've heard his story, in camera. He knew Teddy was in the drug racket, and the man who killed him knew he was an addict. Matter of fact, Ross was putting himself in a very nasty position, only, luckily for him, he don't know how to type."

" Meaning he was the only one of the four who knew he had any connection with drugs ? " put in Charles.

" That's right. I don't say he'd actually tracked Morell down, but there were a number of bottles in the flat—oh, quite harmless, hairwash, cough mixture and so forth, with Morell's label on them. Which gave us a line to work on. It's always the same with these amateurs," he went on. " They will try and play safe. It's like those pestilential robins in the kids' story who went on heaping leaves on the children till even a rozzer must have realised there was something cooking. If he'd been content to shoot Ames and get out, he might still be at his dirty game this very minute. But a guilty man's a nervous man. Once the police started tickling up Morell the game was practically over."

" What puzzles me," confessed Charles, " is why he ever burdened himself with the Mawson-Moberley."

" Well, even the police would have started asking questions if they'd found a second weapon on the premises. And you don't know Ames very well if you think he'd have taken a pot-shot at me and kept the fatal gun in his possession for more than five minutes. Why should he ? He only had to chuck it away on his road home, though it's a fact," he added, " that it's harder to lose something you want to get rid of than anyone who hasn't tried has any notion. Y'see, you're sure somebody's watching you, and you keep thinking ' Round the next corner ' or ' Wait till I get to the river.' That was Morell's trouble. He spotted the Mawson-Moberley when he was taking a final look round. Bill had seen it half an hour earlier and I dare say Ames hadn't quite closed the drawer. Or else Morell had an inquisitive temperament. At all events, he found it and took it off with him."

" He may have thought it was safer on his premises than anywhere else," suggested Charles. " He'd no reason to believe suspicion would ever turn against him. By the way, what was his motive for poisoning Lane ? "

" Oh, he was like St. Paul," said Crook confidently. " Stood in jeopardy every hour. We know Teddy's line. Your money or . . . and there's no reason to suppose he didn't let Morell realise that he could get him ten years any time he cared to turn King's Evidence. Morell didn't know anything about the rest of you, not till he saw Ames enter the flat that night. Oh yes, he's made a clean breast of it now. If ·only he'd waited twenty-four hours one of you would have done the job for him."

Julia spoke for the first time. "None of us meant to murder him," she said slowly. "Not Gerald or Mr. Ames or me. As for Mrs. Tempest, do you suppose she drew the Black Death herself?"

Crook regarded her with an expression of comical dismay. "Why, honey," he said softly, "she's the real McCoy. She wasn't taking any chances; she was the only one of the four who would have sent Teddy Lane into another world and never lost a night's sleep. The quiet ones are always the most dangerous."

"But she didn't do anything," protested Julia.

"No? Think again, sugar. Get Handsome Harry here to help you. I'll give you one tip. If Morell had never gone near the flats that evening we should still be singin' ' Now the labourer's task is o'er ' for Teddy Lane."

He couldn't resist stopping at 10 Hunter Street on his way home for a final word with Mrs. Tempest.

"Not keeping you from an engagement?" he said earnestly, stepping into the hall. "Just come to offer my congratulations. If ever I need a lady to lend me a hand I'll think of you, if you're in the market. More payin' than cooking somebody's dinner," he promised her. "And how you managed to turn out such a dainty feast that Thursday night is beyond me. You must have been all of a tremble."

"I don't think I understand, Mr. Crook." Mrs. Tempest appeared quite unmoved.

"You don't do yourself justice," Crook assured her. "Or me, either, come to that. Did you really think I was taken in about the dope in the bottle, or believed Morell, who had the chance of poisoning the coffee in the cup, would do such a blame silly thing as put an extra dollop in the milk and leave it for any interferin' rozzer to find? Of course he didn't. Such an idea never went through his crawlin' crooked mind. That was an outside job. I got that from the start, as soon as I heard about Teddy's lady visitor. You must have had a nasty shock when Moxon told you Teddy had gone away for the week-end. Y'see, you couldn't be sure he wouldn't beetle up and collect the bottle and then Mrs. M. might have given a tea party and if people had started dyin' left, right and centre, even the police would have started askin' questions.

You couldn't go back and smash the bottle or poke it into your reticule, because you'd just called Moxon's attention to the fact that it was there. And you couldn't hang around till he went off duty, because you had this dinner date. What did you really believe when you heard Teddy had been poisoned ? "

Mrs. Tempest smiled. " I haven't the faintest idea what you're talking about, Mr. Crook."

Crook grinned. " Of course you haven't. You're a daisy, Mrs. T. and don't let anyone tell you different. But, for your information, Teddy Lane 'ud have died without the stuff you put in the milk. Morell wasn't taking any chances. In a way, y'know, you might be grateful to him for takin' the rap."

" Do you suggest that anyone would imagine that *I* . . ."

" Come off it, sugar," Crook besought her. " Of course I don't mean the police would ever have rumbled you, but you'd have found yourself up against Arthur Crook, and all the Queen's horses and all the Queen's men couldn't have saved you. So, just as a favour, and seeing you're the kind of lady I'm proud to know, next time you want a little help, just ring this number."

And, like a conjuror pulling a rabbit out of a hat, he whisked a card out of his pocket, and laid it on the table.

Mrs. Tempest watched the little car out of sight. Then she sat down and after a moment she put her head in the crook of her arm. The slow unaccustomed tears came into her eyes until the sleeve of her dress was soaked. They were tears of relief and thankfulness. Until now she had not been certain that she hadn't, in fact, murdered Teddy Lane.

≫ If you've enjoyed this book and would like to discover more great vintage crime and thriller titles, as well as the most exciting crime and thriller authors writing today, visit: ≫

The Murder Room
Where Criminal Minds Meet

themurderroom.com